DANGEROUS INTENT

A NICHELLE CLARKE CRIME THRILLER

LYNDEE WALKER

LAURA MUSE

SEVERN RIVER
PUBLISHING

Severn River Publishing
www.SevernRiverBooks.com

ISBN: 978-1-64875-519-4 (Paperback)

ALSO BY LYNDEE WALKER

The Nichelle Clarke Series

Front Page Fatality

Buried Leads

Small Town Spin

Devil in the Deadline

Cover Shot

Lethal Lifestyles

Deadly Politics

Hidden Victims

Dangerous Intent

The Faith McClellan Series

Fear No Truth

Leave No Stone

No Sin Unpunished

Nowhere to Hide

No Love Lost

Tell No Lies

To find out more about LynDee Walker and her books, visit

severnriverbooks.com/authors/lyndee-walker

To the queer kids: may you find a safe place to land.

1

The news never sleeps—it's a fundamental fact of my job I've never minded.

The problem these days is that the life cycle of the average crime story is about five blinks: if all goes well, a suspect is usually apprehended in twenty-four to forty-eight hours. That's enough time for a daily news source to do a teaser, a full story, and a follow-up, back-to-back-to-back. For a weekly? Not so much.

I never thought I would miss the days of getting phone calls in the middle of the night with tips on a story, racing competitors to the scene to ask all the right questions, and surviving on too much coffee and not enough food or sleep while dashing from interview to interview. But after the third major crime story in a row was done and dusted before I could do much more than tease my upcoming piece on Twitter? I was about ready to throw my favorite pair of sapphire Jimmy Choos through the wall.

Slouching into the morning staff meeting with nothing to show for myself has always been the worst feeling. If only the familiar orange chair and Bob's usual greeting were enough to conjure a story from the big bucket of nothing I had to offer. At least I had coffee, which I set precariously on the edge of my editor's desk to free my hands.

"Morning, kiddo," Bob said. He leaned forward, bracing his forearms on the leather blotter. I could tell by the firm set of his mouth that he was disappointed and trying not to show it. "Did you see the headline in the *Telegraph* this morning?"

Nope. But I had a feeling I was about to see it and hear about it, too.

I picked up the paper resting on his inbox. The new crime reporter at the *Richmond Telegraph*, a "rising star"—or so Rick Andrews proclaimed when he brought him to Richmond from Tampa, anyway—named Mark Lowell, led the daily paper's front with the headline: "Subway Slasher arrested."

"Subway Slasher? Really?" I shook my head. "It was a stabbing in the parking lot outside of a Subway restaurant. There was no slashing. Ergo, no need for a catchy serial killer nickname."

"Catchy serial killer nicknames sell newspapers," Bob said.

"Lucky for us our paper is free?" I tested a smile, which he met with a scowl. "Come on, Bob—even Charlie Lewis had more tact than this in her coverage last night. And me admitting Charlie did something right is cause to pinch yourself and make sure you're not dreaming. Charlie dug far enough to find the reason for this mess, which was a feud over a woman, who is the victim's current girlfriend and the suspect's ex-wife; and a child, who is the suspect's son."

"So what else can you find out about it to get us more than they had?"

"I'm not sure there's anything else here to get. There's certainly no cause for this kind of fear-mongering language. It was an isolated incident, and they arrested the guy."

Mark had only been on the *Telegraph*'s staff for a few months, but he was already dancing on my last nerve. To totally dehumanize the situation like that and remove all of the motivating emotion went against my personal reporting philosophy: the center of every story is a person, and putting the human element first is the key difference between muckraking nonsense and good journalism. But Mark was exactly Rick Andrews's kind of man: a snappy writer with a great grasp of what sells papers.

"You have to give the guy some credit," Bob said. "He knows how to keep you reading."

I had to stop myself from rolling my eyes, burying my nose in my coffee cup and taking a sip of sugar-free white mocha. Hearing Bob praise Mark Lowell brought out a petulant side that had me feeling more like a cub reporter fresh out of school than the professional journalist with more than a decade of experience that I was.

"He did get the scoop on three big cases before I could even draft a feature." Three long swallows of my latte later, my voice sounded smaller than usual. "Seriously, Bob. Am I losing my touch?"

"Still got weekly jet lag?"

It had been almost a year since up-and-coming *RVA Week* plucked me, Bob, sports reporter and local baseball legend Grant Parker, and veteran photo editor Larry McCoy from the *Richmond Telegraph*, and I was more than a little ashamed to admit that I was still struggling to get my feet under me.

"I don't know whether to be mad at Aaron for doing his job too well or at myself for not keeping up." I sighed, dropping my head into my hands. Aaron White was the public information officer at the Richmond PD, long a favorite and trusted source. But he had to give Mark and Charlie the same information he gave me, no matter how much of a deadline advantage they had. I let the wallowing go on for thirty more seconds before straightening my spine and looking back at Bob. "What I need is something they don't know to look for."

"Unless you plan on committing the crime of the century yourself, you can't exactly force it." Bob's face softened into a smile. "You couldn't lose your touch, kiddo. You just need to find your new groove. You've had a few big hits along the way here—the only thing left now is making that consistent."

I swallowed the "And how long is that going to take?" when the rest of the staff started trickling in. Grant Parker dropped into the chair beside mine. "Morning, Lois."

As in Lois Lane, intrepid investigative reporter. The nickname had never felt more off-base.

"Hey, Parker. How's Mel feeling?"

His face lit up with the thousand-watt grin that made women all over

Virginia call for smelling salts even now that he was a self-described "old married dude."

"She's gorgeous. And starving all the time. Like she's making up for the months of misery and puking all at once."

"Morning, everyone," Bob said, picking up his notes and launching the meeting by asking Larry about possible cover art before moving on to the food section.

"I stumbled on something yesterday you might want to check out." Parker spoke softly out of the side of his mouth as Bob got a rundown of this week's music news.

Interest officially piqued, I was about to whisper-ask what when Bob turned to me.

"Sounds like the big crime cases have been slipping right through our timeline." Bob's searching gaze didn't let up even when I started squirming in my seat. "Which means you need to look elsewhere. Try out a feature; you've done them before." He snapped his fingers a few times, lost in thought.

I knew better than to interrupt him when he was digging through his internal filing system. I may have a relatively reliable photographic memory, but my editor unfortunately did not. Then again, he had a Pulitzer and I did not—yet, anyway.

"The drug dealer's brother." Bob pointed a finger at me, the details finally surfacing. "Even Eunice said your feature on him was solid way back when."

He was talking about Troy Wright—and Eunice, the features editor from our *Telegraph* days. When Troy's older brother was killed and then framed as part of an elaborate coverup, I found the truth...and got myself kidnapped and almost murdered for the trouble. In the aftermath, Troy and I had become friends. Bob was right about that feature: a star student, Troy fostered dreams of becoming a TV sportscaster, even doing a ride-along with Parker for some sports reporting experience before he went off to college, and with the tragic death of his brother for a backdrop, it made for a fantastic human-interest piece.

"You want the story that people won't stop talking about, even if they don't know anything about it right now," Bob said. "What this newspaper—hell, this whole city—needs are big-picture discussions, and you, kid, can write a story that paves the road to them."

It sounded strangely less daunting when he put it that way. There was so much going on in Richmond and the world around it, I couldn't spit without hitting "big picture."

"Larry, we'll keep you in the loop if Nichelle comes up with something that will require different cover art." Bob clapped his hands. "My office isn't newsworthy, so get out and find me something to print."

"Thanks, Chief." I drained the last of my coffee and stood up.

Parker's eyes were shining, a hint of that superstar smile already teasing up the corners of his lips. His artfully tousled blond hair caught even the unflattering fluorescents in the office to complete the picture of gorgeous male specimen. It was funny to think about how off-putting I once found his good looks and self-confidence, given how I almost didn't notice anymore after so many years of calling him one of my closest friends and standing up as a bridesmaid at his wedding.

"Okay, tell me what you've got," I said, "but you have to walk with me to the kitchen for my coffee refill first."

"Deal." Parker fell into step beside me.

The coffeepot was almost empty, so I topped my mug off to the brim and quickly started another brew for the next person. I'd been on the receiving end of an empty pot way too many times to count, and I needed all the good karma I could get. Besides, it was just common shared-coffeepot courtesy.

As soon as the coffeemaker was gurgling, I turned to Parker. "Now, what was it you wanted me to check out earlier?"

Parker swept an arm toward the door, shepherding me to his desk. "You know your old pal Troy Wright?"

Two mentions of Troy in one morning? "Yeah, what about him?"

"He wrote a killer article this week for his campus newspaper."

"Campus newspaper? Has he crossed over to the print side?"

Parker laughed. "Not even I could convince that kid to abandon his TV dreams." And that was saying something, considering how Troy had looked at me like I was offering him a Golden Ticket to the Willy Wonka factory the first time I introduced him to Parker.

"This was an op-ed," Parker continued. "One-off piece, not a staff job or anything."

"Now you're just teasing me. What was the topic?"

"Their first-string quarterback was benched." Parker raised his eyebrows, as if waiting for me to guess why.

I was raised in a house where Dallas Cowboys football was as much a part of fall Sundays as church and baked chicken—and I can quote player stats and scream at the TV during games with the most diehard fans—but I didn't know quite enough about behind-the-scenes locker room detail to guess what he was getting at. Fraternity hazing, underage drinking, allegations of sexual assault...a quick scan through any newspaper's sports section would provide way too many possibilities to make guessing practical.

"He's gay," Parker said. "And when he decided he was tired of being closeted, he lost his starting spot."

Not even in my top ten.

"Why would that get him benched? Pretty sure the NCAA doesn't have a 'heterosexuals only' rule for football or any other sport." I took a long sip of my coffee.

"That's just it," Parker said. "They don't—and your boy Troy wasn't afraid to say so." He steered me to his computer, where the article was already up.

Two weeks ago, Holden Peters decided he was tired of living a lie. In an environment, on a campus, that likes pretty words about equality and acceptance, a top collegiate athlete decided to trust those pretty words and tell the world he's a gay man.

His trust was met with shattered dreams when Coach Don Farrelly benched him three days after his coming-out Instagram post.

Picture it: first-string quarterback at a division one school, second-year All-American, a Heisman contender, a potential draft pick for the NFL, his name regularly brought up on ESPN. All of it gone with the flick of Farrelly's pen.

I paused after the first paragraph, glancing over my shoulder at Parker.

"He's good, right?" he said. "It's a little heavy on the commas for my taste, but kid's got heart. You can feel it."

"No kidding." I kept reading.

While I can't say Peters's absence is the sole cause, the "winning team" Farrelly promised lost last weekend with fewer yards passing in the entire game than Peters posted in his average first quarter last season. I don't have a crystal ball, but if this is the team culture—if this is our school culture—it would be no surprise if we had a losing season this year.

Peters has done nothing wrong, nothing that needs defending. His sexuality does not make him a bad football player or a bad teammate. What it does, though, is show us as a school, as football fans, where we still have room to grow.

The official line is that Peters was benched for failing a drug test. Peters, who is notorious for not drinking at his fraternity's parties even though he's of age, failed a drug test? I, for one, would like verification, or at the very least a public statement from Peters himself. Coach Farrelly has been in every local paper about this issue, but Peters hasn't had a single statement printed in his defense. I've talked to him myself, and he says he would gladly retake the test publicly, in front of cameras if that's what it takes. Farrelly shot down that idea, saying that Peters will spend the mandated six games on the bench, thus killing his shot at the Heisman before the season even really gets rolling.

Coach is on year four of a very expensive ten-year contract to turn the Crimson football program around. The hopes—and wallets—of countless donors, shareholders, and alumni are riding on Coach's success. He clearly wants to win.

So how much notoriety, how much in revenue does the team and the school stand to lose by knocking Peters out of the running? Millions in ticket sales and free press. Perhaps that's a language that even Coach Farrelly can understand.

Dear Coach Farrelly: let Holden Peters retake the drug test. Apologize for this heinous display of homophobia. Grow up and do better.

And to the rest of the Crimson community: hold Coach Farrelly accountable and don't let a star player be punished for something he can't change and shouldn't have to hide or apologize for. Demand evidence in support of Farrelly's claims. Do not stand by and let a young man's dreams crumble beneath him.

As a member of the Crimson LGBTQIA+ community myself, I refuse to sit silently and let this continue. Do better, y'all.

I leaned back from the computer with a few hard blinks. I needed to get a hold of Troy. Now.

"Here's what scares me about this," Parker said. "Troy's specifically called out the money side of college football—and it's true, the Crimson athletics department and alumni association have invested big bucks in the football program and Coach Don Farrelly," Parker said. "Farrelly is essentially a hero to their fans right now, and Troy could be harassed or even hurt for saying things like this, even if they are true."

"Give him a little credit," I said. "I'm sure if Troy was willing to put this in the paper, he's thought that through, and I'd bet my favorite red Manolos that if he says there's something off about the coach, there is. I mean, what's this about the QB not getting quoted anywhere? That's a pretty glaring red flag."

"Beats me." Parker shrugged. "But it sounds to me like you might have something new here to chase."

"Indeed. Thanks, Parker." I pulled out my phone and fired off a text. *Hey, Troy, it's Nichelle. I was wondering if you wanted to grab coffee next time you're in town? Catch up?*

Back at my own desk, I flipped open my laptop and clicked into the browser. A search for "Holden Peters + Crimson football" returned more than a dozen hits. ESPN clips from the end of last season as well as talking heads going through Holden's stats and signature plays. The bombshell had landed two weeks ago at the local TV station, quickly followed by ESPN and CNN. Every outlet used the same headline: *Gay college football star benched after failed drug screen.*

The school newspaper had it the next day, followed by at least some coverage in every issue since.

The elephant on every page was, as Troy pointed out, that no one had interviewed Holden Peters. On my screen were interviews with teammates, members of the coaching staff, players on other sports teams, even the sportscasting students, but not a single person got Holden on the record. It was easy enough to dismiss as the kid just dropping out of the public eye and refusing to talk about something he didn't want to discuss, except for one thing that had me skimming the articles one more time. Nope—I hadn't missed it, it just wasn't there. In nearly two dozen articles in two weeks, no one mentioned that Holden Peters declined to comment.

Could the journalism program up there be so lousy that the student staff on the paper wouldn't do their due diligence? Doubtful. They had one of the top-ranked programs in Virginia. And I knew damn well the staff writers at national cable networks knew better. There was definitely some kind of story here, and nobody in Richmond had a word of it. But would our readers, more than an hour south of the campus and—according to demographic research—not exactly a football-loving group as a whole, give a single damn?

Back to Google. I found pages and pages chronicling kids getting their dreams crushed because of something as inconsequential to their chosen sport as their sexuality.

That would probably interest our target audience. And—maybe more importantly right then—it wouldn't interest Charlie or Mark in the slightest.

I went back to Troy's op-ed, scrolling to the bottom and watching the comments stack up faster than I could read through them, vitriol practically pouring out of my laptop. Dozens upon dozens of people flinging slurs of every kind from behind their keyboards, and more than a few making bald-faced threats to Troy's safety.

I scooted my chair back so I could see around the cubicle wall and found Parker leaned back in his chair, feet crossed at the ankles, phone cradled between his ear and shoulder, pen twirling absently between his fingers. Occasionally, he would reach to jot a note down on the yellow legal pad in front of him, but most of the time, he was just laughing. Must have been an old buddy.

Investigative journalism 101: who you know is sometimes more important in the moment than what you know. And right then I was damned glad I knew Grant Parker, because he knew everybody who was anybody in Virginia sports. High school, college, professional, football, basketball, water polo—Parker had friends everywhere.

Amid all that, he probably knew a number of kids with crushed dreams, especially considering he'd been one once. Fresh into the grueling world of minor-league baseball, on the verge of being traded home to pitch for the Richmond Generals, a devastating shoulder injury left him hanging up his glove for good. Lucky for him, he had a winning smile, a hometown hero's star power, and a stunning way with words to fall back on.

When he hung up, I jumped to my feet and grabbed my coffee, stepping closer to his desk.

"You can't possibly need another refill already." Parker's grin was back at full wattage after the morning's pep talk, but his eyes were on the mug in my hand.

"No, I just worry if I put it down, I'll forget to drink it, and it'll go cold." I laughed. "Nothing more criminal than a cold cup of coffee that isn't made that way. Actually, I have a sports question for you."

Parker swiveled around in his chair, steepling his fingers in front of his lips. "Is this about Holden Peters?"

"Not just Holden Peters." I dragged my own chair over to sit across from him, smiling when he tapped the tan Manolo sandal on my left foot with his own bland, scuffed loafer. "You've been at this for a while; you must have seen..." I didn't want to try to put a number to it. "Too many kids in Holden's situation."

Parker nodded, his face folding into a look of contemplation. "Holden is not my first."

"Is this...I don't want to say 'normal,' but from a quick Google search, it's looking that way."

"Relatively?" he said. "Especially in football. Most of the successful coming-out stories I've seen have been after they're done with the sport for good."

I plucked at a lock of hair, twisting and looping it around my fingers. "So people just pretend that whole time?"

"I can't speak for someone in a situation I've never faced, but I can tell you I gave up a whole lot for baseball. This seems like a farther bridge, though. We're talking about a choice between the sport you love, that you've worked so hard for and sacrificed so much to play at this level, and a piece of your identity...that's an impossible ask, Nicey."

"And yet we ask it over and over again." I buried my nose in my coffee mug. "So, is there a story here?"

"You're asking me?" Parker glanced toward Bob's open office door.

I winked. "You're the sports expert."

Parker let out a long sigh. "I think this one could lead to trouble, Nichelle. That's why I'm worried about Troy."

"That's a yes." I stood up and guided my chair back to my desk.

~

Troy texted me back at 10:33: *Hey Nichelle! So good to hear from you! I guess you read the article?*

I sure did. Grant Parker showed it to me. I'd love to get more info from you. Got time for coffee sometime this week?

I can do you one better. Come to campus and I'll give you the full rundown and a tour. I also have another story I think you'll love.

Sounds perfect! I texted back. *Getting in my car now.*

Sweating from the thirty-second walk between the door and my car, I slid into the driver's seat of my little red SUV, the steering wheel radiating enough heat to warm my whole house in the winter. Late summer in Virginia carries a double whammy of heat and humidity that even my Texas-bred system has trouble handling.

My phone buzzed in my purse. I dug it out, cranking up the air conditioning and smiling when I saw the text from Joey: *Going to the store on my way home tonight. Any special requests?*

So very domestic—and I loved every second of it. It was nice to always have someone to go home to at the end of a long, shitty day of chasing dead-end leads or, worse still, lacking anything at all to show for a day's work. Equally nice were evenings snuggling on the sofa and long baths together and having a partner to celebrate the good days with. Plus, he remembered things like groceries—which I had a tendency to forget when I was tangled up in a story. Joey says I rarely ate a decent meal before I met him.

Pop-Tarts are a meal, right?

I typed: *I think we need more coffee.*

Buzz. *Got it.* Buzz. *You eat lunch yet?*

Damn. How did he always know when I forgot to eat lunch? He had some kind of Nichelle radar that told him whenever I wasn't drinking enough water or eating square meals. *Not yet. May have found a new story worth chasing. Finally.*

Buzz. *Can't wait to hear all about it.*

I put the car in gear and pointed it toward the highway. Even if I didn't get a single story out of this trip, Parker wasn't wrong about the danger Troy had stirred up by getting in the middle of a situation like this—and with threats already flying online, laying eyes on my young friend and seeing the campus atmosphere for myself was the only way I'd manage to sleep tonight. Troy's momma wasn't losing her only remaining son on my watch.

2

I parked in the lot beside the student center, where Troy suggested we meet. It was one of only a few places that had free parking—a tiny lot sandwiched between a loading dock and a parking garage with a central location on the suburban campus.

When I walked in, he was sprawled across an overstuffed couch, shoes dangling off one arm and head propped on the other. He was reading a floppy paperback whose title I couldn't make out from my vantage point, brow scrunched and eyes flicking quickly over pages. I cleared my throat and drew his eyes up, his face breaking into a grin as he shot to his feet, wrapping his arms around me, book entirely forgotten. "Nichelle!"

I hugged him back. "It's been too long, Troy."

He gave me a final squeeze before he stepped back, his eyes going to his shoes like they had the first time I met him, a skinny teenager lurking in hospital hallways, worried about his mom and grieving his dead older brother. "Thank you," he murmured to black-and-white Nikes.

"For what?"

"I never would have had the courage to write something like that guest column if I hadn't met you." He laughed. "Honestly, I never would have thought to express myself in writing if it weren't for you—and Grant Parker, of course."

"I'll be sure to let Parker know he's a footnote in your story—and I'm honored to join him there." I bent my knees until I caught his gaze. "But you're wrong. That courage was always inside you. And it's been a great privilege to watch you grow into it."

He scratched at the back of his neck, bending to retrieve his book and flipping page edges with his thumb. Troy was lithe: all long limbs and focused energy. His smile could be blinding, and his dark eyes glittered with mischief. When we first met, he tried to make himself small, like so many Black men in America who don't want to be viewed as threatening. But across from me now stood a beacon of confidence. His spine was straight, his lips predisposed to quirking upward. It was hard to look at him and imagine that right at that moment, strangers on the internet were threatening his life.

He stuffed the book into his khaki backpack and slung the bag over his shoulder, leading me back out into the August sunshine. "I hope you don't mind walking and talking. You really have to see what all this means to get it."

Walking and talking meant no notes, but my memory was good enough to get me through until I could stop to jot things down. Plus, we could always do a serious sit-down interview later.

"As long as no one melts. Let's start with what inspired you to write that article, and don't say me, because that's cheating—a piece like that came from your heart."

Troy led me down a path shaded by trees green enough to change the color of the light filtering through. "I know I said it in the article, but...I'm gay." He laughed, a short, breathy sound. "It's still weird to say. It's not something..." He swallowed, glancing over at a stream of students coming out of a nearby building. "My brother would never have accepted it. He would have spewed some bullshit about being raised by a single mom making me soft." He shook his head. "But it's not about being soft; it has nothing to do with softness. I don't even know where that idea comes from. Growing up poor...growing up Black and poor, there's so much pressure on the 'man of the house' and all kinds of toxic masculinity and these ideas of what a man should be or do."

"And did Darryl fill this role?" Troy brought up his brother first, so I felt it was fair game.

"Hell no." His voice was a little sharp; there was definitely still unresolved tension there. "He was hardly ever around. It's so typical too. It's a vicious cycle. He was so unwilling to admit when he was hurting or overwhelmed that he just got himself in deeper."

Troy and I had met when he was in high school. His brother had been killed, and he knew, deep down, that no one wanted to tell a poor Black drug dealer's story—not when it ended with him dead instead of a Lifetime movie special of redemption packaged up for guilt-free entertainment, anyway. But I've built a career on telling stories no one else wants to.

"So, after your brother's death..." I prodded.

"It was just me and my mom, and you know my mom, she'd love and support me into her own grave if I let her, no matter who I love or what I do." That was true. His momma was a force of nature. "But she sees everything from a different perspective: she doesn't have time for Facebook or Instagram or Tumblr or Twitter or TikTok. She doesn't have the avenues to look for queer excellence, and so she doesn't know it's there." He shook his head again.

"Parker is worried about you, you know." It was easier to use Parker than to tell him the whole truth, provide some distance between me the journalist and him my interview subject.

"Worried about me? Why?"

I stared hard at a statue we were rapidly approaching, all a mottled gray-brown except for the shimmering gold of the man's shoe. "Because of the threats."

Troy laughed. He actually laughed. About people threatening his life. "You mean the comments on my article? You know what they say."

We said it together: "Don't read the comments."

I picked up the thread. "But in this case, you need to make sure you're safe." I pulled up the article on my phone and started scrolling. When I reached the bottom, my finger froze over the screen. Four hundred and twenty-seven is an unheard-of number for a college newspaper piece, especially one that was just published the day before. Before taking the dive into the comments themselves, I clicked to a few other articles from the school paper for comparison. Thirty comments, 71 comments, 23 comments. Nothing anywhere close to the 427 (now 431) on Troy's column.

Since I'd checked last, they had devolved into doxxing Troy, revealing personal and identifying information about him—which dorm he lived in, his major, that he was from Richmond. People piled on with every detail the internet could give them.

"Damn," I whispered, pressing my fingers to my lips to keep from scrolling even more. I touched his arm and held the phone between us. "This is serious, Troy."

He leaned forward just enough to see what site was up on my phone and then shrugged. "That's nothing. Someone figured out my school email address and spammed it so much I had to request a new one." He winked. "Total anonymity now."

To give my own brain time to process, I spun around to take in the campus. Plenty of green space and a mixture of buildings old and new, chalk art on the sidewalks and posters in windows, flags hanging from the sides of dorm buildings. Then the trees opened up ahead of us, revealing the massive new football stadium like the crowning jewel of the campus.

"But," there went that made-for-TV smile again, "I didn't say a single thing about Holden."

"No, you didn't, but I wasn't about to say so."

"Of course you would have, but you wanted to keep me talking to see if I let anything interesting slip."

"Every good reporter knows when to ask questions and when to shut up and let people talk." I winked.

"Let's take a walk around the brand-new forty-million-dollar stadium and sports center, shall we?" Troy pulled open the door and gestured me in ahead of him. "A little backstory: this monstrosity was funded by the state, and the university president had to pull more than a few strings to make it happen, according to word on the street."

"So what did he have to promise as return on their investment?" I mused.

"Exactly." Troy waved an arm in the general direction of the campus behind us. "I'm sure you noticed how mismatched the academic buildings are—the president is trying to rewrite history by turning this run-of-the-mill state school into a Place to Be." I could hear the capital letters in this last phrase. "But think about it—where does most of the school budget come from at big-name universities?"

"Not the state," I said, taking in the wide corridors, recessed lighting, and large works of art surrounding us. Talk about sparing no expense.

"Nope. The real money comes from sports ticket sales, advertising sales, and alumni donations—particularly wealthy alumni. For an up-and-coming school like ours, with money being poured like water into new buildings, those become very attractive funding sources when the state grows tired of emptying its pockets and tuition hikes are maxed out. They can't price prospective students out of being able to come here."

"Totally rewriting the funding and admissions culture here wouldn't necessarily be a bad thing, would it?" I asked as he pointed to a set of wide double doors.

"That's what you would think."

We emerged from the covered portion of the complex into the open-top stadium between clusters of seats that were so new I could still smell the paint. Banners along the edge of the field and LED screens between the lower tier and the mezzanine seats provided countless advertisement and sponsor space. I pointed them out to Troy. "Looks like there's plenty of room for ads here, which will be all over TV screens when the games are aired."

"Oh yeah." Troy dropped into a seat at the forty-yard line, gazing down the solid white stripe to the far side of the empty stadium. "Apparently the president's goal was big money and Coach Farrelly's very expensive salary in exchange for school spirit and national attention—which should lead to increased alumni donations and interest from upcoming athletes who want to have the resources and support they need to go pro."

"So why Farrelly?" I pulled a notepad out of my purse, jotting a few quick details from our walk while I waited for his answer.

"Word in the athletic department is that Coach promised a ten-year payback on the investment between ticket sales and alumni donations. We're four years in and not even a quarter of the way there."

"You'd think a Heisman contender would be a huge point of pride to help nudge donors toward that goal." I followed Troy's gaze out into the wide expanse of green.

The field was pristine with a freshly painted logo on the fifty-yard line and brilliant crimson and gold in either end zone. I could already picture the stands filled with screaming fans; hell, I'd been to a few college ball games in my day and seen more than a few on TV. The stadium was gorgeous—tailor-made for a capacity crowd that would bring in big money.

"Listen," Troy said, swiveling in his seat to face me. "Would you be willing to interview Holden for the *Week*?"

"Of course, but wouldn't such an interview get more traction coming from a local paper?"

Troy slumped back into the seat. He spoke so much with his body and movement. It was bigger than just using his hands: there was language in the postures of his shoulders and his head and his torso. "That's the thing. Farrelly is a local hero, the man who is *single-handedly* taking the school to the next level. I think this whole failed drug test thing is fake. You don't know Holden—he's as straight and narrow as they come."

I arched one eyebrow, and he laughed.

"Without being straight, of course." Troy scrubbed his hands down his face. "And that's the problem. I swear Coach is doing this for all the wrong reasons. He has all the local media under his thumb and is keeping Holden's side of this out of the news."

"So what you really need is someone totally on the outside to shine a light on all of this."

"A real spotlight, though, not the fly-bys the national news did, basically just running the press release the athletic department folks wrote. Farrelly thinks he's in total control." He put a hand on my knee. "So will you do it, Nichelle? Will you talk to Holden on the record to get his story out there?"

"Of course I'll talk to him, if I can. I don't have any connections here besides you, though." My mind was already spinning through how to pitch this to Bob, with the campus so far outside of our normal coverage area.

"I can get you in with him. Holden's been following every letter of the press coverage, so when my piece came out defending him, he came looking for me."

"You weren't friends before?"

"We'd never even spoken before. He's a hotshot athlete, and I haven't even been on the campus station's football coverage team yet. Next year, though. If I'm lucky. I just made it to field hockey and softball—and let me tell you, field hockey is way more badass than I ever gave it credit for."

"Truth. My freshman roommate at Syracuse was on the field hockey team," I said. "I never really understood all of the rules, but I definitely remember watching her ice some wicked-looking bruises. She was tough as nails—and could've given any football player a run for his money any day of the week." I tapped the pen on my notebook.

Troy nodded to the Lion in the center of the field. "So he just...shows up at my dorm one day, Holden Peters, knocking on my door in the middle of the afternoon. Thanking me, like he didn't expect anyone to take his side." Troy shook his head, then laid his hands flat on the armrests. Watching his fingers, I noted he was pressing down, like he was resisting the urge to curl both hands into fists. "I never thought I'd feel sorry for a guy like Holden Peters."

His hands told me he felt more than sorry for the benched quarterback —Troy was a mellow guy. The kind of mellow that required an especially righteous brand of anger to push him to curled fists and blowing off vile threats. I couldn't pinpoint the cause, but right then I was way more worried about the possible effect.

"You've seen the backlash from just speaking out." I set my pen down deliberately to make sure Troy was watching me. "As someone who's been threatened—and, admittedly much worse—for digging for the truth, I'm telling you: you have to be careful."

Troy frowned and opened his mouth, but I cut him off.

"Look, if you want this to blow up, I can run with it. I can shout this from the rooftops with links to your article and many others in the same vein. I need to talk to Holden and Farrelly too, of course, but if you want me to, I can help. I just want you to stay safe."

"Pinky swear." He flashed the grin again and stuck out his hand, last finger extended. I hooked mine around it and shook, laughing.

"It means a lot to me," Troy said, catching my gaze, "that you care about people some other folks don't."

"I care about telling stories that deserve to be told." I waved a hand at the notebook in front of me. "Do you think I take notes during purely social visits?"

"I figured you were just drinking in my every word. Sometimes my kids take notes."

The non sequitur threw me. "Kids?"

"At the youth center near my neighborhood."

Um. As far as I knew, Troy lived in a dorm on campus. While the school had a significant percentage of commuters from the north and south, he had a scholarship that covered housing and a car that wouldn't take the miles of the daily drive back and forth to Richmond. Campus was also fairly insulated from the surrounding town. There was no way that Troy had a neighborhood here.

"You mean in Richmond?"

"Yeah, I used to spend time there after school when my mom wasn't home. The sense of community there seemed to me like the perfect place to create a safe space for queer kids."

"You mean like a support group of sorts?"

"Exactly. I've been going home once a week and hosting meetings for queer and questioning teens. I started volunteering during the summer, and I couldn't give it up, even with school starting. I want to give these kids a place to learn about themselves, to experiment with labels, with pronouns—without the fear of being hurt or judged."

"When you say kids, you mean..."

"The youngest is thirteen, and the oldest is seventeen. It's important to create a support network—but also to have fun. We've been planning to go to the Richmond Pride Parade in a couple of weeks: T-shirts, banners, face paint, the works."

I picked my pen back up, flipping to a new page in my notebook and flashing a grin. "That's amazing, Troy."

He winked. "I know that look. Do you want to come to a meeting? Talk to some kids?"

"My boss's lawyers might want me to get parental permission to interview minors on the record."

Troy's expression shuttered like I'd flipped a switch.

"I can't promise that. I'm not sure everyone is out to their parents."

I sighed. "That has to be so hard on a young person."

"My situation is so much better." He shook his head. "Not everyone is as lucky as I am, though. There are hundreds of young people who'd be out on the streets if they came out to their families."

"If I live a thousand years, I'll never understand a person who could turn their own child out of their home because of something they don't understand." My thoughts strayed to my own grandfather, who'd done just that when my mother, sixteen and pregnant, had refused to marry my father. While my grandmother and I talked often lately and she'd even spent last Thanksgiving with Mom and me, my grandfather was always conveniently busy with work. And I was coming up on thirty years old. "If your young people are willing to talk with me, I can keep their names out of it in the interest of privacy and safety."

"You can use my name all you want." Troy grinned. "And I'm sure I can connect you with some experts who will go on the record if you need that, too."

"When's your next meeting?"

"Tuesday at four."

Tuesday was deadline day for *RVA Week*, so the kids would have to wait for next week's feature. I could swing the Holden Peters story if I could talk to Holden and Farrelly by Monday. Troy had turned into a regular fount of good stories. Maybe even the kind of stories I needed to get *RVA Week* back on track.

I stood. "Thanks, Troy. When you talk to Holden, give him my contact info. I'd love to talk to him."

"You know I will." Troy plucked my pen from my fingers and tucked it into his pocket, pointing to the seat I'd just vacated. "But catching up with old friends is a two-way street. And you haven't said anything about you."

My investigative reporter shoes had turned our casual chat into a full-blown interview. It was impossible not to laugh at the realization—and Troy's quick assessment of it. "Well. I bet you can tell I'm desperate for a good story."

"The great Nichelle Clarke?" Troy raised one hand. "A reporter as rare as the designer heels she manages to kick ass and take names in every day —desperate?"

"Most days lately, I'm not sure I'd pass as a mediocre street-sale knockoff Nichelle Clarke." I sighed, settling back into the seat. "I haven't had a big story in months. Part of that is the new schedule—so far, every time I think I have the weekly versus daily reporting thing down, something else bites me in the ass. I worked the daily news thing for a decade. I was damned good at it. And then I just...changed the scene completely. You'd think after a year, I'd be all right, but it's like something just isn't clicking." I buried the urge to shrug by tucking my notebook back into my bag. "You can't force a great story out of nothing. It's like unraveling a whole sweater by picking at a single loose thread—it usually only happens by accident. Trying to make there be something where there's nothing just leaves me holding a tangled wreck that belongs in the trash."

Troy laced his fingers behind his head, looking past my shoulder to the digital scoreboard. "Think about it this way," he said. "What percentage of the total number of stories you reported for the *Telegraph* were those explosive knock-outs? Maybe one in a hundred? Two hundred? I think you need to zoom out, here, because you're writing six hundred percent fewer stories in a year." He tapped his fingers on his knee as I pondered the truth in his words. "That's about as much math as I've got in me today. Don't tell my stats professor."

"I hadn't thought about it that way—and I'm pretty sure nobody else has, either. Thanks." I smiled. "I suppose when you get right down to it, it's probably a good thing that there's no serial killer or corruption to uncover at the moment. Bonus: if I'm not chasing one of those things, I'm not getting shot at. The problem is that without that, I'm hunting the kind of stories people don't know they need but that they'll want to talk to their spouse about over dinner or share with their coworkers in the break room."

"Well, you're more than welcome to write about my kids if you can do it without using their names. Every one of them has a story that needs to be heard—maybe especially the ones whose families wouldn't want to hear it."

"Let me see what Bob will agree to." I stood, picking up my bag and pointing to the fading daylight. "It's been a joy to see you, but I better head back south."

We parted ways with another hug. "Give your mom my love," I said. "I hope she's doing well."

Back in my car, I turned over twenty different ways to pitch the story—or stories—to Bob. Finally, I had a couple of at least mostly accidental stray threads to pull, and my gut said they might just unravel neatly into the kind of brilliant cover features we'd been searching for.

3

Human remains discovered, partial decay evident.

I didn't even make it halfway home before my scanner app bleated the alert and waylaid my attention. Habit had me adjusting my GPS route on the fly—I couldn't shake the urge to chase the next big crime story, even when I was up to the top of my favorite Jimmy Choo motorcycle boots in homophobia and college athletics, which I knew was probably a better candidate for a cover story.

Weekly newsmagazine reporting 101: a corpse has to be way more interesting than average to be worth writing about. Run-of-the-mill body dumps are off-limits because by the time we can get the story out, the TV and the *Telegraph* have already reported everything there is to know about them.

I almost dropped my phone when "Second Star to the Right" started blaring. Caller ID said it was Detective Aaron White with the Richmond PD. Maybe this dead person was indeed more interesting than average?

"Hey, Aaron." I put my phone in its cradle on the dashboard and pulled up the map, hoping he was about to give me a reason to change my route.

"Nichelle." Aaron's voice was gruffer than usual. "I haven't heard from you in a while, but I'll try not to take it personally."

"I miss the daily story hunt more than you can possibly imagine, so I'm taking it personally enough for the both of us, don't worry. Please tell me you've got something for me."

"Better you than that new guy at the *Telegraph*—but don't tell him I said that."

"Not much danger of me telling him anything."

"Human remains discovered out by Broad Rock Creek, in the woods off Terminal Avenue."

"It just came up on my scanner. Something weird about it?"

"Could be. It's a hasty body dump, no attempt at burial, animals have been at it already. From what we can see, it looks like an execution."

"Bullet to the brain?" I knew from recent experience that execution-style murders are often the more complex sort. A beloved professor and recovering addict found in similar condition in a southside motel room last spring had led to my last big cover win.

"Single shot, they think."

"You said off Terminal?"

"Yep. You coming out to take a look?"

"You know I can never say no to you, Aaron. I'll be there as fast as traffic will allow."

"Good." He sounded relieved. "I know Mark and Charlie will be running me down about this soon, but something tells me there's more here than the quick-and-dirty daily guys are going to take the time to figure out. My gut says this one has Nichelle written all over it, though I have been wrong occasionally. See you when you get here."

Aaron hung up, and I couldn't help but think that his gut had never steered me wrong yet.

I pulled off onto the embankment at the address Aaron provided, my tires sinking into soft almost-mud as the sun disappeared behind a deep tangle of old-growth trees, standing where they had for centuries despite the city that had sprung up all around them. Red and blue flickered through the branches and around the next bend in the road. No Channel 4 van yet.

Mark hadn't been on the cops beat long enough for me to recognize his car on sight, but there were no civilian vehicles apart from mine.

Balanced carefully on my toes so my sandals wouldn't get sucked into the mud, I rounded the bend and approached the uniformed officer guarding the edge of the crime scene. I offered him a winning smile and my press badge.

The officer leaned in, pretending to examine my proffered credentials. "It feels like I haven't seen you in a long time, Miss Clarke."

"Don't I know it? Detective White thinks this one is interesting enough to catch my boss's attention." I winked. "Speaking of, he should be expecting me?"

The officer grinned and lifted the yellow tape. "He's about fifty yards that way, near the base of a thick oak." He pointed. "You know the drill."

Camera flashes popping and glimpses of a lab coat between branches marked the scene as I picked my way down the path, careful to avoid disturbing anything. A ring of technicians facing every which way in their black uniforms, latex gloves, and shoe covers were crouched all around an area the size of my living room, some taking pictures, some bagging evidence, some laying tags next to points of interest. In the center was the figure in white I'd spotted from a distance.

"Nichelle Clarke, if you come any closer to my crime scene in those sandals, I'll kill you—and not even because I want the shoes for myself." Jacque Morgan, my favorite medical examiner and fellow shoe enthusiast, looked up from where she was kneeling next to the victim. I caught the barest glint of shiny exposed viscera before one of the techs circled around for more photos and blocked my view.

"You know I'm always careful." I stopped walking anyway as she stood and approached me, glad she didn't offer a still-gloved hand to shake.

A voice from behind me interrupted before I could get my mouth open.

"If it isn't Nichelle Clarke." Mark Lowell, the *Richmond Telegraph*'s new cops and courts reporter, swaggered toward us. Mark had the look of a roadside tent-sale knockoff Grant Parker: he wore gray slacks under an untucked, short-sleeved collared shirt (to be fair, the only sensible choice on a humid Virginia summer evening) and had a head full of thick, ash-blond hair that he tried to artfully tousle (he didn't succeed at anything other than making it look like he didn't own a comb). He was what most folks with a pulse would call attractive, sporting a shadow of stubble on a strong jaw—but his deep-set eyes and heavy brow made him look almost menacing, even when he smiled. The fake smile he offered me didn't help him look one bit less sinister.

I rolled my eyes and signaled to Jacque to talk later before turning to face my latest nemesis. I knew I was a touch dramatic in the way I viewed this guy, but some people were just assholes, and Mark was one of them. Even Charlie—though she used to run me ragged in our daily races to the next big scoop—couldn't make my blood boil the way Mark could.

As if the thought conjured her from the ether, I spied Charlie Lewis coming in on Mark's heels, ignoring us both and heading right for Aaron.

"Shall we?" Mark swept a hand in Aaron's direction in some pantomime of a gallant gentleman. I barely took one step past him before he started asking questions. "Did Detective White give you anything yet? We all know you're his favorite."

"Come on, Mark, I heard it on the scanner just like everyone else." Which was true, of course. He didn't need to know Aaron called me before I could finish reading the dispatch information.

"What gives with you, anyway, Clarke? It's like you're not even trying to follow the crime beat anymore." He was right at my elbow, taking long, slouching strides, his hands buried in his pockets. "You tweeted about the Subway Slasher but never followed through." The comment was Mark Lowell in a nutshell: using his ridiculous, made-up moniker for a sad reality to try to rub a missed headline in my face. I stayed quiet.

"I mean, it's got 'human interest' all over it," he rambled on. "The guy's kid goes missing and he takes it out violently on the man his wife left him for? How did Jeffers keep you off that?"

Missing kid? My brow furrowed. I must not have read the police report —or Mark's article—as carefully as I thought I had, because I didn't know that tidbit. Crap. His smug silence told me he knew I didn't know. Crap, crap, crap.

"Well, you'd already given him a serial killer name and everything." I went for a breezy tone to cover my irritation. Hopefully it worked. "Figured I'd let you have that one. Consider it a 'Welcome to Richmond' present."

"Or maybe..." Mark turned so suddenly in front of me that I had to choose between stopping short and running him down. It was a close call —but shoving him over would make Charlie's whole week, and she had a cameraman panning the scene. Bob would be annoyed if I went viral for tackling my replacement. "Maybe you're losing your touch."

Years of body combat classes meant I could take care of myself, but the ability to throw a perfect kick requires knowing when to use it: so, to keep myself from sending a stiletto-tipped *ap chagi* into Mark's sternum, I shouldered past him and greeted Charlie and her cameraman of the week instead. The cameraman—I gave up learning names years ago because no one can stand to have Charlie snapping her fingers and barking orders at them for long—gave me a brisk nod, but Charlie turned her TV smile on me, which was more than a little disconcerting. She wanted something. Before she could pounce, Aaron waved us closer.

"At about two thirty this afternoon, two hikers found human remains about twenty yards off the main trail. There was no apparent attempt at burial or concealment, but also no spatter evidence indicating that this was the scene of the murder. Cause of death appears to be a single gunshot wound to the head. Victim is an adult Caucasian male."

Mark asked the first question without waiting for Aaron to give a go-ahead. "Any hints on the victim's identity?" Because as soon as a reporter has a name, they have the ability to dig into the victim's life.

"No ID yet, though the medical examiner has not had a chance to fully examine the remains at this time." Aaron stood in his element, comfortable with this familiar dynamic of fielding questions from nosy reporters.

"And were there any defensive wounds or signs of a struggle?" Charlie this time.

"Jacque can't determine that yet. Time of death based on visible indicators is tentatively estimated at ten to fourteen days ago, and between last night's rain and the local wildlife..." Aaron let that one hang in the air unfinished, all three reporters shuddering a bit.

My glimpse of the victim's insides on the outside earlier was enough for me—it wasn't anywhere close to the most gruesome scene I'd walked in a decade covering homicides, assaults, and burglaries. I wouldn't still be here if the more nauseating aspects of the job were enough to turn me away. But you still never truly get used to seeing someone's entrails—if I ever had, it'd be my cue to change career paths.

Charlie asked a few more questions before Mark wandered off—like he couldn't be bothered to get all the facts—and Aaron started feeding a microphone through his shirt for a quick statement for Charlie's evening timeslot while Charlie herself retreated to huddle with her cameraman.

Aaron stepped closer to me, checking the mic's transmitter to make sure it was off.

"You're awfully quiet today." He clipped the little microphone in place and straightened his collar.

"Frustration often shuts me up." I smiled to soften the edge in my words. "I know it's not your fault. Just having a little pity party with myself because you didn't have much to give us, and Charlie has all the bases covered. Story of my life lately when it comes to the kind of stories I used to clobber everyone else on."

"You've been at the weekly awhile now," Aaron said. "You know Andrews would take you back in a hot minute, his page count is down twenty percent since you left, which means they're hemorrhaging ad revenue."

I raised an eyebrow, and he flashed a grin that made his blue eyes brighten. "Does it surprise you to know I pay attention to the business of newspapers in this town?"

"I'd rather lose every headline to Charlie and wear Ugg boots for the rest of my life than go back to Rick Andrews, crawling or otherwise."

"Fair enough." Aaron nodded when Charlie signaled she was ready for him.

"The new boss is a big believer in mantras, and his favorite is 'work smarter, not harder.'" I lowered my voice and tipped my head toward Jacque and the crime scene techs to my left. "I'm going to talk to Jacque while you're distracting Charlie."

"There's the Nichelle I wanted on this scene." Aaron grinned and stepped toward Charlie for soundcheck.

Still stepping gingerly (I could already feel the mud sticking to my left heel), I flagged Jacque down. "Tell me something no one else here will find interesting."

"The Real Housewives of River Road are all Marie Kondo-ing their closets again, because our favorite thrift store just got a new stock of last season's styles." Jacque winked, peeling off her gloves. Behind her, the technicians were loading the victim, now hidden in a black body bag, onto a stretcher to carry back through the woods to the medical examiner's van. "But that's not the kind of interesting you meant."

"No, but I'm definitely writing it down." I dug a pen and notebook from my bag.

"The victim was in bad shape. You know it rained most of the week, and being out in the woods uncovered in this heat does weird things to decomp. Some things speed up, others slow down, but on the whole it's just a big, gross mess. Not much left of either clothes or flesh, but I did see a few old silver fillings, so I have high hopes that dental records will hit an ID. There's also what looks like a tattoo—or at least a piece of one the scavengers didn't make off with—on his left forearm. I can get you a picture of that when I get him cleaned up back at the morgue."

"What kind of tattoo?" I almost-whispered, glancing at Charlie. She took her mic back from Aaron, checking her watch before she looked my way and frowned when she saw me talking to Jacque. I knew she had to get back to the station and put her story together for the six o'clock or risk Mark—who had apparently actually left—getting it on the web first, and I watched until she turned for her van. Aaron waved as he walked toward his unmarked cruiser, cell phone to his ear and a rush in his step.

"Hard to tell based on what's left, but I saw something that could be an arrow or a triangle, maybe, and what looks like part of a wreath or plant." Jacque waved me to one side with the dead-guy-infused gloves she was still holding as her team returned. "I'll try for a good image and get it to you tomorrow."

"Thanks, Jacque." I was so focused on her mention of the tattoo, I almost didn't notice the dismissal. When I looked up, she was already several yards away, huddled up with the technicians. "Wait!" I called after her, staying put. This was about my two hundred and thirty-seventh rodeo, so I wasn't about to compromise the scene—or get myself yelled at by the tech who was already giving me the stink eye.

Jacque grinned and shook her head. "A picture tomorrow isn't good enough," she called from a few yards away. "Am I right?"

"As the perfect pair of black slingbacks."

"Meet me over by the van. I'll tell Mitch to take a smoke break so he doesn't try to talk you out of looking."

The back of a medical examiner's van is tight. It's not like an ambulance where the ability to move and access medical equipment is essential. Jacque put a hand out to help me squeeze inside with her and handed me a jar of menthol rub as she smeared a liberal fingertip-full under her nose. I followed suit before she opened up the body bag, reaching in to draw out a mangled forearm.

The coffee from that morning swirled in my stomach with only a protein bar to settle it. The guy's skin was grayish, and I could see patches of bone through the rusty burgundy of decaying muscle. I steadied my phone and snapped a picture, getting as close in on the remaining bits of the tattoo as I could without actually touching anything.

"You're a lifesaver," I said as soon as Jacque and I were both standing on solid ground and there was a closed door between us and the victim.

"Not quite my line." She waved a hand at the van with a small smile. "I'll see if I can get a better shot when he's cleaned up."

"Thanks, Jacque, I owe you one."

Jacque laughed. "I will take a pair of those coral Manolo sandals if you can find them in a ten."

"You doubt my shoe-hunting skills? Challenge accepted."

She disappeared around the van, still laughing as she slid into her car, parked in front of the body wagon. Mitch didn't mind riding with the recently deceased, waving as he climbed behind the wheel of the van. I heard the engines start, the crunch of tires on gravel, and then nothing but the keening song of cicadas from the trees.

When I made it back to my car, I pulled a few tissues out of the glove compartment to clean the mud off my shoes. A few dozen cops and coroners have advised me to throw some rain boots into the back of my SUV—I see the practicality, but I just flat can't do it. Traipsing through the mud in heels looking at things other folks run from used to be part of my job. Somewhere among the dead people and deadlines, the races with Charlie and nearly getting myself killed, it became part of who I am. And it felt damned good to be back in my grimy, Virginia-clay-caked crime scene Manolos, even if it was only for a little while.

4

Joey's car was in the driveway when I got home, the front window lit up from within. The new glass matched the other windows nearly flawlessly, replaced after the old window was shattered by bullets Kyle and Aaron had to dig out of my living room walls for evidence. But it had been months since anyone shot at me—or Joey, which was a hefty point on the side of not rocking our newly quiet, very domestic boat with an execution-style murder and a potentially weird tattoo.

I unlocked the front door and put my bag in the closet, kicking my shoes off and stretching my toes over the cool tile.

"Nichelle?"

I followed Joey's voice and a positively mouthwatering smell to the kitchen, greeted by his dimpled grin and the semi-casual look he adopted after work: jacket and tie retired to the closet, shirtsleeves rolled up to his elbows, and his top two buttons undone. He guarded a large cast-iron pan on the stove, setting a lid over whatever was producing that heavenly smell. "No peeking." He winked.

I raised both hands in mock surrender. "That smells good enough that I am doing absolutely nothing to risk spoiling your surprise, lest you decide you don't want to share."

Darcy, my toy Pomeranian, raised her head at the sound of my voice and then flopped her chin back onto her paws with a contented sigh. She was never far from Joey when he was home.

"When have I ever been able to say no to you?" Joey switched the bamboo spoon to his left hand, extending his right arm to me.

"Hey there, Chef DiAmore," I said, snuggling under it and wrapping my left arm around his waist.

He planted a kiss on top of my head, only within easy reach because I wasn't wearing heels at the moment.

"Hi, beautiful." It never sounded like a platitude coming from Joey. He wasn't the type to say what he didn't mean. Hedge the truth, sure, but only ever for good reason. "Was I wrong to put money on you skipping lunch?"

Damn. "You even reminded me. I did have a protein bar this afternoon."

His end-of-day stubble rubbed against my scalp as he shook his head. "Whatever will I do with you?"

"Feed me, Seymour." My *Little Shop of Horrors* impression was sorely lacking, but he laughed anyway.

I turned away to open a bottle of wine, but Joey waylaid me by pouring a glass of red from a decanter. Another thing I never really did before he showed up in my living room: whether I was drinking white or red, I poured directly from the affordable, grocery-store bottle right after opening.

A self-described oenophile, Joey both knew and cared more about the finer points of wine consumption. He'd tried several times to explain why letting reds air for up to an hour before drinking brings out the more subtle flavors. I still didn't see the sense in opening a bottle an hour before we were going to drink it, just to glance longingly between it and the clock. But since he was the one forced to resist temptation today, I took the glass without a single teasing word.

"You really won't tell me what you're making?" I asked, taking a sip of the wine (the flavors really did explode across my tongue) and craning my neck to see around his broad shoulders.

"Linguine Carciofi." He smiled, his eyes glimmering.

"What...how...I cannot believe you remembered." I laid my head on his shoulder, stricken by the small miracle of having a person who would remember, find a recipe for, and then cook a dish I loved from a restaurant we visited almost two months ago. It was like he was tuned to my frequency, but in a different way from the days when he would show up unannounced at my house with dire warnings about threats to my life. These days, it was more like he could read my needs and address them before I could ever hope to articulate them. Work may have been a mess, but my home life—thanks to Joey—was better than it had ever been.

"Dinner should be ready in about," Joey glanced at the timer on the microwave, "half an hour. So maybe grab a snack."

"Copy that." I ducked into the refrigerator for some cheese to slice. You could never go wrong with charcuterie.

Joey passed me a wooden cutting board and knife. "The guys at the office can't stop raving about this new show on Netflix. Now I'm thinking we're going to have to watch it."

"I assume you're talking about the horror one and not the adaptation of the fantasy book series." I was up-to-date on the latest streaming shows; analyses and recommendations make for popular filler in a weekly.

"You assume correctly. Maybe we should try it out? Watch an episode or two until it cools off a bit, then go for a walk or something." Virginia summers are downright miserable some days. A Texas girl born and bred, I can take hundred-degree heat for months on end—the year I graduated high school it was a hundred and three at my house on Easter Sunday. But ten years on, I still wasn't used to the soul-sucking power of Virginia humidity. The air gets so thick it can sap the life right out of you. Twilight was the best time—the only time—to be outside if you didn't want to sweat and weren't in a pool. Well. Twilight and 4:30 a.m. and...no thanks.

"Are you sure that's the kind of exercise you're looking for?" I glanced over my shoulder at him as I turned on the tap to start rinsing grapes.

"I'm open to alternatives." His arm was warm and solid when he snaked it around my waist. With his other hand, he plucked a grape from the bunch in my hand and popped it in his mouth.

I put the colander down and turned, tipping my face up to his. "It seems I'm not as hungry as I thought."

Joey brushed his lips over mine, his shoulders shaking with laughter when I tugged on the back of his neck and tried to deepen the kiss. "You need to eat something," he said as he pulled away.

"Have you been talking to my mother?" I asked.

For half a second, I swear his face closed up into the stoic look he used to get when I asked him a question about a story he didn't want to answer, but it was gone so quickly I must have imagined it. He kissed the tip of my nose, shut off the faucet, and whisked the grapes to the table with the cheese and a box of crackers.

He told me about his day in between bites of food and checking on dinner—he'd been called out of the office to a job site near Culpepper where he'd managed to both repair an air-handler motor that wouldn't work right out of the box and calm an anxious client on the verge of canceling next month's half-million-dollar project.

"Talking people down when they don't have a gun trained on me is almost no work at all," he quipped, setting a plate in front of me.

The linguine tasted just as incredible as it smelled, and what conversation we had during dinner was casual. I'd been thinking about work all day, so it was nice to unwind some, give my brain time to recharge before I refocused on Troy, Holden, or Aaron's latest dead guy and his mystery tattoo.

We were washing dishes when I finally brought up what had been swirling in my mind all afternoon. "You remember Troy Wright? I did a feature on him a couple years back."

"Smart kid, wanted to be a sports announcer?"

"That's the one. He wrote a controversial op-ed for the school paper."

"Controversial?"

"The star football player was benched, and Troy took it upon himself to highlight the injustice of it—because the player had just come out as gay around the time he was benched."

Joey's face darkened. "Is Troy being threatened?"

"It definitely caught the eye of the campus internet trolls." I tried to shrug it off, but I wasn't feeling terribly optimistic about the situation myself. "It is just a school paper; it doesn't have a wide reader base." I wasn't sure which one of us I was trying to reassure.

"Until it ends up on The Athletic or BuzzFeed." Joey's right eyebrow went up.

Right.

"Damn. Even without that, there were hundreds of comments." I took a fortifying sip of my wine. "Some were just...horrible. Others shared personal information about Troy and Holden, the QB, with plenty of nasty threats sprinkled throughout—and I doubt whoever admins that site is used to policing this level of traffic."

Another sip, okay, maybe it was more of a gulp.

"Have you talked to Troy about it?"

"Yeah, I drove out to take a campus tour with him; he says he's being careful, but he also doesn't seem particularly worried." I set the last pre-rinsed plate into the dishwasher and turned to lean against the counter.

"Where do you fit into this?"

"That's the thing: Troy wants me to bring even more attention to it. Troy —or Holden himself—could try to report the school for discrimination, drag the whole thing into the national spotlight, even without my help. The NCAA is really big on equality for LGBT athletes, but the coach and local media are stonewalling everyone. The coach refuses to allow a new, witnessed, and impartial drug test, and Holden hasn't been interviewed at all. Not even by the school paper." I filled Joey in on the most notable statistics from my brief research. "These kids are already at risk: depression, bullying, suicide, self-harm, isolation, low self-esteem. They should be protected, not targeted."

"Sounds like they've found themselves a mouthpiece—and a protector." Joey's warm smile, the way he entwined our fingers when he reached for my hand, made me feel like the luckiest woman drawing breath—and like I could do anything. Help Troy, help Holden, find Aaron's hit man, save the whole damn world. It's nice to have a partner who can do that with a look.

Joey tapped the fine bones in my wrist with one finger. "Just don't forget to eat—and be careful. There's big money in college football. Nobody likes bad publicity, but people tend to get pissy when you start messing with their money."

"I'm always careful." I led him toward the couch and picked up the remote for the TV we said we were going to watch—though I had a feeling I might be about to scrap those plans. "But that's not the only thing I've got going right now. Troy has been running an LGBT youth group at the community center he used to go to when he was younger."

"In Richmond?"

"Would you believe I asked him the same thing?"

Joey sat back, shaking his head. "So he's been driving back and forth after classes to keep this up?"

"So far. He just started the group over the summer, but you should have seen him light up when he talked about it. I'm going in to talk to them on Tuesday, but I'm really hoping Troy can score me an interview with Holden tomorrow so I can slide that story in for this week."

"How very Nichelle Clarke of you."

"What?"

"Going from missing out on mediocre crime stories that frustrate you to scrambling to get two big features done back-to-back."

"Oh, and that's not all," I said, channeling my best infomercial voice. "But we'll get to that after we watch at least one episode. Got to give you something to talk to your coworkers about."

"Leaving me in suspense. Clever."

After a very artistic but rather boring first episode, we retreated to the backyard to appease Darcy with a game of fetch. It was definitely still too hot for a walk. Joey threw Darcy's stuffed squirrel first and then turned to me with an expectant eyebrow.

"Wait, you mean you need me to tell you about the dead guy in the woods this time? You don't actually know more than me already?" It was fun to tease him about how mysterious and omnipotent he seemed when we first met, but when his mouth turned down, I hurried on with my summary. "There was a hasty body dump out in the woods by Broad Rock Creek." I filled him in on the advanced decomposition from the rain and animal activity, the single gunshot wound to the skull as tentative cause of death, and my current festering concern—the tattoo.

"You said you got a picture?" He put his hand out for my phone.

I pulled it up, handed Joey my phone, and pitched Darcy's toy to the far end of the yard, much to her excitement. From the corner of my eye, I saw Joey tilting both his head and the phone this way and that, zooming in and out, and dragging his fingers along the screen.

He shook his head and handed the phone back to me. "I can't place it. There's just not enough there. And there weren't any other identifying marks?"

"I'm going to check in with Jacque first thing tomorrow, but she didn't mention anything else."

Darcy wilted quickly in the heat, and we trudged back into the sweet relief of the air conditioning. Lying in bed with Joey beside me, I pondered the privilege inherent in feeling truly safe. I wondered if the victim had thought he was safe. I wondered if Troy's youth group teenagers felt safe. Nothing I could do about the former, but the latter...maybe my article could change a few minds.

~

The next morning, I called Jacque's cell before I left the house. She was, of course, as much of a perky, morning-loving weirdo as ever. I wasn't sure I envied whatever sacrifice she had to make to the gods of caffeine for that to happen.

"Hi, Nichelle," Jacque said, the snap of latex gloves punctuating her words. "It's barely seven o'clock. You called me before even Detective White this time. What's got you so excited about this guy?"

I delayed answering by taking a sip of coffee, made fresh by Joey in some minimalist contraption I would never have the patience for but that he swore was the coffee equivalent of his wine decanter. No denying the product was delicious—I was down to only one pump of sugar-free white mocha syrup. But I could definitely lose the high-pitched whirring of the grinder first thing in the morning.

"I didn't realize calling during your normal office hours was considered unusual, Miss Morning Glory."

Jacque barked out a laugh. "Touché. Well, since I believe there's something to be said for early birds, and you got to me first—"

"And I'm your favorite," I interjected.

"And that too, my shoe sister." She sounded amused. And far, far too awake. "I'll give you the rundown and then the juicy bits."

I readied my pen.

"Cause of death is single gunshot wound to the head. Entered just above the left eye socket and took a down and back trajectory to exit out near the base of the skull."

"That's a sharp downward slope," I said, scribbling. "So likely the victim was lower than the killer, but upright—sitting or kneeling."

"Unless the killer is taller than, say, LeBron James, that's a safe assumption."

"Also probably right-handed?" I asked.

It was more of a note to myself, but Jacque answered anyway. "Yes, though the gun wasn't a small-caliber one. Based on the trajectory of the bullet through the brain matter I have left here, and considering that this guy was about five-ten and it's unlikely that the assailant was in fact an NBA star, I'm thinking the vic was on the ground, sitting or kneeling, shot by an assailant operating a .38 primarily with his right hand." There was some background noise from Jacque's end: metal pans clattering together, a hose powering on. She really had just finished the autopsy. "I did manage to get a pretty clear picture of the tattoo for you."

My phone buzzed, and I pulled it briefly from my ear, putting Jacque on speakerphone to examine it. There were a few thin, straight lines. It looked like a stylized tree or plant. Then there were some leaves off to the side. I saved it—I could call Larry about working his photo wizardry on enhancing it later.

"Got it, thanks, Jacque." I tipped my head to cradle the phone in the crook between my ear and my shoulder. "You mentioned a possible dental match yesterday; did those pearly whites get you a name?"

"You bet your favorite blue Louboutins we did," she said. "And White doesn't even have it yet. You have a pen?"

"Always."

"Mervin James Rosser."

Jacque filled in a few more details while I jotted notes, my brain racing ahead to the best road to digging up more. The basics were all there: a few minor defensive wounds, the gunshot wound, the tattoo, the guy's name. She'd given me just enough to make me more curious.

And I didn't have much of anything better to do than check out where Mervin lived this morning, as it happened.

"Thank you so much, Jacque. I owe you. And don't worry, I've already got an eye out for those slingbacks."

Journalism in any age, regardless of the internet, 101: always make the phone call. Because I was the only one who bothered to call Jacque to check in, I had a head start on what could turn into a big story.

I was under no assumption that I would be the first person to get the victim's name in print. Mark and Charlie would both have this out almost as soon as Aaron saw it, and their more frequent deadlines gave them a checkmate every time. But unless the PD came up with something interesting in Mervin James Rosser's home or background, his name was pretty much the end for Mark and Charlie. They'd be on to the next crime du jour, because today was a new day and they had a new deadline.

Which meant what I needed to find if I wanted into this story was the interesting thing Mark and Charlie would miss.

Journalism in the age of the internet 101: Google can tell you almost anything you need to know, as long as you're patient and know how to use filters and keywords correctly.

In five minutes, I knew that Mervin James Rosser was a driver for Coldtown Delivery service, a distribution company specializing in refrigerated and frozen foods for businesses and restaurants. According to an announcement I found on the company website, he'd only been working there for about three months. Facebook hits were sparse—only one in the greater Richmond area—and while it lacked a traditional profile picture, in its place was line art of a tree with crooked branches and three large roots surrounded by a circle of vines. I snapped a photo to compare to Jacque's photo of the victim's tattoo and clicked his name on my screen. His profile was set to private.

Strike one. Kind of.

A search through the DPS database got me an address in southside. Time for legwork. I put the address in my GPS app and hurried to my car.

5

The address belonged to a bungalow, though the building I faced wasn't at all what I'd have pictured if someone told me that: flaking paint, mold crawling up the bottom foot of the exterior walls, front shutters askew. It was painted the kind of drab gray that seemed to suck all the color out of everything around it. The only life in the yard was a scraggly plant that probably started its surprisingly long life as a weed. A sad-looking place, but a quiet one—no police or media presence. The street was crowded with cars, but they were all older models in various states of disrepair. And the spot directly out front was empty.

I parked a few blocks down, easing my car between an old Volvo that looked like Bigfoot had taken a bite out of its back bumper and a Honda with four very flat tires. My little red SUV isn't exactly new anymore, but the single paint color and lack of dents meant it stuck out all the same. Like I needed another reason to get in and out of Mervin's place quickly.

An eerie level of quiet on a sunny summer morning made the hair on my arms spring up as I closed the gap between my parking space and Mervin's house, the heels on my classic black Louboutins striking the pavement the only sound. Even the cicadas were silent here. I tried not to wonder how long it would take for the PD to lock this place down, or how the neighbors would react to police and investigators swarming the area.

I did a double-take when I got close enough to see a paper taped to the front door. An eviction warning, citing a ninety-day default on the rent, with a hearing date set for the following week. "Damn. Please tell me the landlord hasn't cleaned his stuff out of here yet," I muttered as I leaned in to peer through the glass—or, I tried to. It wasn't any cleaner than the moldy walls. I took a closer look at the eviction notice: the paper was slightly warped with smudges where the ink got wet and ran. That didn't tell me much about when it was posted, since we'd had an unusually rainy August. What it did tell me was that Mervin probably hadn't been in the front door since it was posted.

I reached for the doorknob with a tissue-covered hand. The PD wasn't here yet, but I knew they would be soon, and I wasn't about to give a detective reason to get on my case for compromising a scene.

Locked. I circled around the left side of the house, trying to get a look through the front windows (also filthy) into the dark house beyond. All I could see was the arm of a dark sofa between barely parted curtains.

The back stoop was poured concrete, cracked and stained with dirt and mildew such that I couldn't tell if the buildup was from frequent use or total disuse. The small, unfenced yard alternated bald swaths of bare dirt with patches of overgrown weeds, littered with a tipped-over, flimsy charcoal grill that looked like it had been rust-mottled since the Bush administration, old ashes forever trapped in the act of pouring forth, hardened into a paste by the rain and sun. My brain cataloged every detail, but my eyes focused on the jackpot: the back door leading into the kitchen was unlatched.

I stepped into the dim room, the red soles of my shoes sticking to the harvest gold and avocado sunray-patterned linoleum. Given the state of the bungalow's exterior, the kitchen was surprisingly tidy. Dated, with dark, oiled natural wood cabinets and laminate countertops, but neat. No dishes in the sink or clutter on the counters. Just the essentials: coffeemaker, knife block, microwave. I checked the cabinets and found pasta sauce, cereal, chips, and Pop-Tarts, then moved to the refrigerator.

The front showcased several papers held there with magnets—one of which definitely doubled as a bottle opener—and a Post-it note with "Coldtown" written across the top, over a list of dates and times. Mervin's weekly schedule, since he worked at Coldtown Delivery. Everything else was a takeout menu or a flyer of some sort, so I opened the fridge. My coffee immediately tried to come back up.

The vile stench of rotting meat seeped quickly to every corner of the small room, and I pulled the collar of my blue Donna Karan blouse up over my nose and mouth as I leaned in to see where it was coming from.

A package of what used to be hamburger before it turned gray and started to disintegrate sat on the second shelf, still in its Styrofoam grocery store tray but missing the plastic wrap. The milk on the shelf next to it was expired, the date more than two weeks past. Other than that, there wasn't much besides a few bottles of Coors and cans of store-brand soda.

"Mervin didn't leave here thinking he was never coming home." I snapped a photo of the fridge's interior as I whispered the words.

I closed the fridge but kept the blouse over my face, catching a flutter of movement as one of the takeout menus slipped to the floor. I bent to pick it up and saw a photo on the fridge door. A man—Mervin?—and a woman standing beside a pool table, cue sticks in one hand and beers in the other. Mervin didn't have any distinguishing features, and there wasn't any hint of a tattoo on his forearm, so it was obviously an old picture. He had the beginnings of a beer belly, a beard, and short brown hair. The woman looked very small next to Mervin, but her face was also slightly blurred as if she was caught in the act of looking away. I snapped a picture of the photo before covering it again with the takeout menu, as it had been when I entered.

I moved to the interior doorway and sucked in a sharp breath. Mervin's small, bland kitchen led directly to what could have passed as Hitler's own living room. A giant Nazi flag dominated the wall space over the sagging sofa, and placards emblazoned with white pride logos dotted the walls like needlepoints in a Southern granny's living room. It would've been dreadfully tacky if it wasn't already so far beyond offensive. My phone was in my hand with the camera app open before I could form the conscious thought that this needed documenting.

Holy Manolos, our vic was a Nazi.

A cursory peek into the bathroom revealed what I already suspected:

one toothbrush, one bottle of all-in-one shampoo/conditioner/shower gel, beard trimmings in the sink. Mervin lived alone; the woman in the photo on his fridge had no foothold in the house. Water spots dotted the mirror, and the tub had a ring around the inside and rust rimming the drain.

By the time I got to the end of the hall, I was a little afraid to look in the bedroom. But in my world, curiosity clobbers fear every time. More swastikas, a pair of Third Reich eagles, and Norse runes decorated the walls. The queen-size bed was unmade, the sheets faded on the left side from frequent use—though I wasn't about to get close enough to check if that also meant frequent washing—and the pillows were rumpled. The laundry lay piled in a hamper in the closet rather than strewn across the floor.

A thousand questions zinged through my head, not that I had anyone to ask. Were white supremacists known or frequent targets?

I realized as I turned for the closet that I hadn't seen a cell phone, laptop, or car keys. Nor was there any sign of gore. On first look, it seemed Mervin hadn't died at home, and Jacque confirmed that the site where the body was discovered wasn't the scene of the crime.

So the next big question was where did he die? And why was he there?

Mervin's shoebox of a closet did not possess a single business-worthy outfit. No slacks, no ties, no button-down shirts. Flannel and denim shirts hung in a short row, his jeans neatly folded. Tucked behind the hanging shirts was the long, gleaming barrel of a rifle. I gently pushed back some of the fabric.

A Winchester rifle sat propped against the wall. I wasn't sure why that startled me, given the state of the rest of the house—when I thought about it, the real surprise was that it was only a Winchester and not something with a high-capacity magazine. I was no expert, but having had a run-in with antique firearms before, I thought the thing looked old. Some folks—especially the kind with criminal records that bar them from buying or registering firearms legally—keep old rifles under the guise of "historical value," since antiques undergo different licensing processes than firearms. Age doesn't matter much, though—as long as it's well cared for, even an antique gun can still shoot.

I turned to the drawers: a nightstand and a bureau doubling as a TV stand. Inside the single drawer in the nightstand was a handgun—loaded, safety on. And, of course, in the underwear drawer (ick) there was yet another loaded handgun. Two boxes of ammo, some .22 caliber and some .38, were the sole occupants of the bottom dresser drawer. From where I stood, it seemed a man who might've lived a confrontational, possibly violent life had met a violent end—which, beyond maybe a cautionary tale, wasn't much of a story.

I wasn't ready to give up, but my hopes were significantly dashed—I could practically hear Bob saying, "Who in their right mind is going to give a rat's ass about a dead Nazi?"

Heading back out through the kitchen, one of the flyers from on the fridge caught my eye. There was an acronym I'd never heard of and a date and time from two weeks ago. I snapped a quick picture before ducking out the back door. Never had I been so relieved to step into muggy summer heat.

I'd made it halfway to my car when I heard an engine cut off behind me and snuck a glance over my shoulder, sticking close to the wall of vehicles lining the street. A police cruiser sat parked at the curb in front of Mervin's house. Both doors opened, and Detective Chris Landers and Officer Griffin Brooks stepped out.

I whipped my head back around and quickened my steps. Not that I'd hurt anything, more that I didn't want to waste a chunk of my day arguing with Landers about the trespassing statutes.

Landers was a good cop, we just had a fundamental disagreement about the role of good journalism in keeping the peace: he couldn't shake the belief that the cops should always know more than the press—or that they shouldn't have to share. Even after I broke multiple big cases for him. Sometimes I wondered if he was that secretive with other officers, too.

I didn't know Brooks as well and hadn't seen him in a while. My gut—and the day I spent with him on a ride-along through one of Richmond's poorest neighborhoods—said he was a good cop, if a touch idealistic, but staring down the barrel of his gun had prompted a policy of avoiding him when I could, which these days was pretty much all the time.

I sank low in the seat when I slid into my car, but neither officer noticed me before they circled around to the back of the property after they tried the front door, same as I had. Watching them disappear into Mervin's side yard, I couldn't completely squash a twinge of sadness that the murder might not be the big story I was hunting after all.

6

By the time Aaron called me at eleven, I was back at my desk with a bottle of Diet Coke and more than a few lines of notes about the symbols and slogans from Mervin's house.

"Jacque Morgan got ID on our victim from dental records this morning: Mervin James Rosser, age forty-two, lived out in southside. We haven't been able to find a next of kin, but I've got enough for a press release. Just wanted to give you a heads-up," he replied when I said "Good morning, Detective."

Sweet of him to call me first, and he didn't need to know I'd talked to Jacque hours ago. Besides, if he (or Landers or Brooks) knew I had been to Mervin's house before the detectives arrived, I would've at minimum gotten his patented "disappointed dad" sigh. Nobody but Aaron could effectively chastise me with a single breath—it always made me feel a little pity for his daughters, who weren't that much younger than me.

"Thanks. Any leads on who might've shot him?"

"Ballistics is backed up for two weeks if we can get a rush, and that's only if we find the murder scene and the casing. So—not a single one. I'll send photos to you if we find any. Maybe someone will call with a tip."

I hung up, ready to start refreshing the Channel 4 and *Telegraph* websites to see just how Charlie and Mark would spin this. Mostly, I wanted to see if anyone but me knew about the Nazi angle since Aaron hadn't mentioned it. Mark was way too lazy to go to the guy's house, and Charlie might not care enough to depending on what else happened today.

For once, Landers's aversion to talking to the press might actually work in my favor.

I tuned into Channel 4's noon broadcast, where Charlie was standing in front of a familiar stretch of trees beyond yesterday's crime scene. Her blond hair coiffed to perfection, with a stern expression on her face that gave her segment the gravity such a gruesome death deserves. The banner at the bottom of the screen read: "Body of ex-con found by hikers."

Ex-con. I hadn't seen that in my preliminary research. Thanks, Charlie. I made a note and opened a browser window, typing the state prison system's directory into the address bar.

"A pair of hikers found the remains of forty-two-year-old south Richmond resident Mervin James Rosser yesterday afternoon. Investigators have been unable to locate any next of kin or close friends." A photo—a mug shot of Rosser, maybe five years younger, glowering at the camera—floated next to Charlie on the screen as she spoke. "Richmond detectives have confirmed to News 4 that an active homicide investigation is examining the details surrounding Rosser's death. Cause of death, Detective Aaron White said today, was a single gunshot wound. If you have any information, please call Crimestoppers." She rattled off the hotline number, which was also displayed across the bottom of the screen.

Their broadcast pivoted to a spotlight on a local business doing significant charity work, and I closed the window, then typed Rosser's name into the prison database search bar.

Charlie didn't have much—she didn't even mention what he was convicted of. It was only a matter of time before the Nazi angle came up in someone's research, but I almost wanted to call Mark Lowell and inform him that I had not, in fact, lost my touch. If it wouldn't have involved tipping my hand, I might've done it.

I pulled up the photos I took inside Rosser's house, studying the symbols he kept on his walls: Norse runes, Nazi eagles, a stylized tree, swastikas, guns, slogans, memes. How could someone want to live surrounded by hate? I flipped through the images a third time—they felt like puzzle pieces, but I couldn't see how they fit together. Or where they might lead. But I couldn't shake the feeling that they mattered to how Mervin Rosser ended up in those woods. Maybe a reverse Google image search would help me find an answer. Or maybe...I glanced over at Bob's open door.

Journalism in the age of the internet 101: If you don't know where to start, ask someone who might.

I rapped my knuckles on the frame. "Got a second, Chief?"

"You, kid, can have a whole minute." Bob looked away from his monitor and folded his hands on the desk between him and his keyboard. I had his undivided attention.

I gestured to the Community Service Pulitzer on the wall behind his desk. "I was hoping to pick your brain about hate groups and maybe how to track down active members, since you might have known a thing or two about that once upon a time." The Pulitzer was from a series on this very subject twenty-five years ago. If anyone knew where to start, it was Bob.

"There's a nonprofit group that specializes in tracking hate groups in Virginia, and I'm pretty sure..." He turned to his old-fashioned Rolodex and flipped through for a moment before pulling a card free and handing it to me. "Vida was younger than I was when I interviewed her for that series," he waved a hand over his shoulder at the Pulitzer, "but I see her name on the internet often enough to know that she's still in the trenches. Tell her I sent you. But first, tell me why you want to know."

"Aaron White called me yesterday afternoon about a body dump his gut said was more interesting than average. I might have figured out before everyone else that the victim was pretty deep into white supremacy, and I want to see if that leads into why he's dead."

"Sharing crime stories hasn't really gone well for you on the whole since we started this venture." His brow furrowed.

"I know. And I'm not sure this story is right for us, either. But it's just interesting enough that I want to dig a little more before I make a call."

"Fair enough." He tapped one finger on the desk blotter. "You know what kind of folks you're digging around?"

"Not specifically, but I have a good approximation. I'll be careful."

"I know." He gave me a wink and then turned back to his computer.

My minute was up, then. But I had somewhere to start: Vida Rawlings.

When I dialed the number, her voice was chipper on the other end. "Stop Hate Virginia, this is Vida. How can I help you?"

"Hi, Miss Rawlings, my name is Nichelle Clarke. I'm a writer with *RVA Week*," I said. "I'm working on a story that's looking like it may involve hate groups, and my editor, Bob Jeffers, tells me that you're the local authority."

"I've seen your name in the paper," she said. "I figure you must be Bob's protégée since you're the writer he took with him when he left the *Telegraph*. How is that old badger, anyway?"

I leaned back in my chair and smiled. I liked her already. Bob's Pulitzer-winning series had been one of the handful of prizewinning series I covered in my capstone thesis at Syracuse, so I knew the story backward and forward—it was part of the reason I applied at the *Telegraph* after the *Post* didn't hire me way back when. I remembered Vida's name and hoped her expertise might give me insight into why someone might want to kill Mervin Rosser.

"He's practically an institution unto himself—and he seems happy here."

Her responding laugh was both graceless and genuine, making me like her even more. "Very glad to hear it. Tell you what, protégée, why don't you swing by my office and we can talk through what you're looking into, see if I have any insight or connections for you?"

I was on my feet and headed to the car before she finished talking. Cursing the heat for the entirely too-long it took for my car's air conditioning to actually condition any air, I lifted sweaty hair from the back of my neck with one hand as I merged into midday traffic with the other. Stop Hate Virginia was headquartered in an old spice factory downtown, so the drive wasn't long. I parked out front and hauled my bag out of the passenger seat, sighing as the first blast of cool air hit me when I opened the door.

I checked the building directory in the lobby and took the elevator to the sixth floor, where Stop Hate Virginia's airy office was hidden behind a bland door with a shiny but understated placard. A secretary stood and greeted me with a wide smile.

"You must be Miss Clarke," the young man said, already stepping back to open another door behind his desk. "Vida told me to expect you. Please, follow me."

He led me down a narrow hall lined with doors. Some were open, revealing studious-looking people behind cluttered desks piled with books and papers. The name cards by those doors were peppered with acronyms that indicated specialization in law, psychology, and social work.

Vida's office was at the end of the hall, her placard reading simply: Director. My escort knocked politely on the doorframe before he gestured me inside. I thanked him, stepping past him to greet a Latina woman who looked to be in her mid-fifties, with threads of gray in her sleek black ponytail and laugh lines around her mouth and eyes. She was wearing a slimming black dress paired with an utterly fabulous pair of Louboutins I'd drooled over for months. I might've even dropped a hint or two for Joey with my birthday coming up.

"I love your shoes," I blurted before even offering my hand to shake.

Vida let out the same deep, genuine bark of laughter I'd heard on the phone, turning her leg to show off the red sole. "Sometimes feeling powerful can be as simple as wearing really amazing art on your feet."

"I couldn't agree more." I stuck out my hand with a wide smile. "Nichelle Clarke."

Vida's hand was small but warm and dry, her handshake the kind of brusque and firm that said she'd had to speak volumes with such a small gesture so many times she had it textbook perfect: three seconds in the door and the routine action told me the woman taking her seat across a messy desk from me was strong, caring, and no-nonsense.

"You might've seen a story on the news last night about a pair of hikers who discovered a body in the woods near Broad Rock Creek," I said.

She nodded. "Charlie Lewis didn't seem to think it was significant from the time she gave it."

"The vic's whole house was decorated in an ode to white supremacy," I said. "Charlie doesn't know that, and I'd appreciate it if you could avoid telling her, but I'm curious about what it might mean, given how much of his personal space this man devoted to such ideas."

"I haven't spoken to Charlie in many years." Vida's tone said there was a backstory, but also that she didn't want to discuss it. "How much do you know about hate groups, Miss Clarke?"

"Call me Nichelle, please." I took a seat across the desk from her. "And definitely not enough. I studied Bob's piece in school; it's actually how I wound up working for him. At the time, it felt almost like...fate. I struck out with what I thought was my dream job, but Bob Jeffers had an opening on his staff, and he was exactly the kind of reporter I dreamed of being—with maybe a bit more politics."

"I'm sure this moment feels like coming full circle for you." Her smile slashed a dimple into one cheek, giving her an almost maternal air. "One of the biggest misconceptions about these groups is the demographic of their members. Yes, a majority of them are white, but socioeconomic status or location are not definitive factors for joining; indeed, thinking that people from lower social classes are more likely to join these groups only serves to enforce dangerous stereotypes that belie the sheer pervasiveness of recruitment for these movements. Everything has to be taken on a case-by-case basis, but the research suggests that one of the most influential events seems to be family upheaval: divorce, abusive parents, neglectful parents, parents who suffer from alcoholism or addiction, or incarcerated parents. But, of course, there are also those who join after being raised in stable and loving homes."

I scribbled so fast it was a wonder the pen didn't leave a smoke trail across my notebook, but I got every word.

"If you had to simplify everything you just mentioned, what would you say is the common denominator for members of these groups?" I asked.

"These are people who seek simplicity and clarity in a complex and murky world. They want a simple and universal explanation for things they don't understand, or someone to blame for their problems. These groups offer that: it's because of Black people, or it's because of foreigners, or it's because of transgender or gay people." She shook her head and folded her hands on the desk between us. "Can you imagine if the world were really so simple? Such broad generalizations are dehumanizing at their basest level, cutting out all of the layers that go into each person who's being targeted— a whole human is distilled to one thing that they have no control over and labeled 'the enemy' because of it. And the people who join these hate groups are often just frustrated or lonely or both, and then slowly manipulated and indoctrinated into the groupthink."

"What leads some of the members to violence? I know a lot of their insidiousness is just online conversations and secret meetings, but there are some violent extremists."

She nodded. "It's actually a relatively small percentage of people in these groups who are actually violent. It's important to remember that a lot of the members really just want to belong, they want to be heard, and they want to feel valued. But things can turn violent, and it usually happens when those feelings of need and protection are manipulated. Think of an extremist group like a small nation, and then you have the subgroup most predisposed to violence—these people are the army. Their talk, their meetings, their beliefs encourage something like nationalism, and any violence proposed is presented as being on behalf of the group and for the greater good. The violent talk is enough for many—giving them a 'safe' space for release without needing to resort to violence—but for some, the ratio of talk to action is too high and they can lash out, most often as individuals."

"How would you go about finding which group a person is a member of? Or if they're a member of any group at all?" I pulled a printout of Rosser's Facebook profile picture, the tree-like drawing, out of my bag. "Like, does this symbol have any hate group associations?"

Vida took the paper with one manicured hand, her nails flawlessly painted in a flattering, neutral pale pink. "This is a very common image of Yggdrasil, the world tree from Norse mythology." She dropped the paper to the desk and pointed at the trio of thick roots at the base. "See here, each of these roots leads to another world that is beneath our own, where gods and monsters of various orders live." Tracing her fingers over the runes circling the top of the branches, she continued, "These here are symbols of power, sacrifice, and strength. They're almost like a call to action."

"Is it significant in the world of white supremacy?"

"Yggdrasil, often translated as 'Odin's horse,' is named for the fact that Odin, king of the gods, sacrificed himself by hanging from an ash tree. In the context of white supremacy, we cannot consider nooses and hanging from trees without also thinking of lynching. But the myth imbues this tree with representation of the birth of the worlds and the passages between them, the making of the laws of the universe, and even the conjuring of the apocalypse. It's a symbol of power, justice, and stability. But, like most fixtures in myth and legend, it has a very bloody history. From sacrifices and rot to godlike creatures gnawing their way through the roots to escape into the human world and wreak havoc."

I jotted every word before I looked up with my brow furrowed.

"How did modern American white supremacists choose Norse mythology as a source for their power symbols?"

"Think about the image of Vikings in popular culture: tall and beautiful, while still maintaining their masculinity, they're presented as violent white men who paid for their place in society with blood. Many of these groups view the Vikings as the pinnacle of white power and excellence, and also as symbols of a simpler time when strength on the battlefield was enough to get everything you wanted. They think the era of the Vikings predates the mixing of races, immigration, and queerness." She leaned back in her chair and offered a wry smile. "They are, of course, wrong on all counts."

"This picture," I tapped the paper between us, "was the Facebook profile photo of the murder victim. There were multiple firearms in his home, though I know that not everyone who owns guns is a violent person."

"I own two myself," Vida said. "But something brought you here, and you have a decent track record for knowing where to dig for a story. What is it that has you wondering about this guy? Could it be just a general feeling of distaste for what you saw in his home?"

Great question. I sat with it for a moment before I spoke again. "What I really want to know is if there is some precedent for someone murdering him for his beliefs. Maybe a rival extremist group or something like that?"

"Why do you ask?"

"He was killed in a way that is often used by gangs, for example, to execute rivals or traitors. So far, the only thing standing out to me is his indoctrination into the white supremacy ideology, but it's like a glaring red flag, so it's all I can see." My mind went to the image of the swastika hanging above Rosser's sofa. "I'm trying to figure out if it's where I should be looking so that if it's not, I can move on to something else."

"Rival groups do exist. If you're too extreme or not extreme enough, if you have overlapping territories and take members for one reason or another. I can email you a list of a few of those." She tapped a few keys on her keyboard.

"Do you have files on members of these groups? If I wanted to look up someone specific?"

"It depends," Vida hedged. "We deal with a lot of reformed members who either have left or are trying to leave the lifestyle. Some of them will give us names, and we keep a list for reference, mostly. Violent talk, racist tattoos, white-power music, and gathering isn't illegal, so the police can't do much with this information, but it gives us a place to start if there's a hate crime. We have a separate database of anyone who was arrested for or accused of hate crimes."

"Do you have any records of a Mervin James Rosser?"

I spelled the name for her, and the click of her manicured nails on her keyboard was the only sound as she searched.

Vida shook her head. "I don't have a file on him, but I'll make note of his name and see if I can dig anything up. If I do, I'll let you know."

I stood and offered my hand for another shake. "Thank you so much for speaking with me. I learned a lot today." I passed her a business card.

"It was a pleasure, Nichelle. Please send Bob my best."

Back in the elevator, I checked my phone for missed messages. One from Troy stood out. *Hey Nichelle. I was able to secure an on-the-record interview with Holden. 2 pm at the Caller's office.*

The *Crimson Caller* was the campus paper. This time of day I'd have about an hour-and-a-half drive to campus, during which I could ruminate over Mervin Rosser and warring white supremacist groups before I needed to clear my brain and focus on Holden.

Perfect. Do you want me to call you when I get to campus so you can walk over? Having Troy in the room might make Holden more comfortable.

Buzz. *Thanks Nichelle. I'm actually in Richmond—want to carpool?*

The school was close enough for Troy to come home regularly for his youth group kids but far enough away that it was impractical to live at home and commute daily, especially when his scholarship covered on-campus housing.

At home? Pick you up in 10. Send.

See you then, he replied.

I texted Joey a heads-up: *Might be late home tonight; heading out for an interview.*

Joey's response was immediate. *Reservation is at 7.*

Damn. We had dinner plans. Dinner plans I was excited about, until I had two at least possibly interesting stories vying for my attention. Maybe Holden Peters was a fast talker.

I can make that. Send.

I hoped, anyway.

7

Troy directed me to a small lot beside the journalism department building and tossed his parking pass onto my dash when I parked in a shaded spot near the back. Weaving between students streaming out of classrooms, we made our way to a glass-fronted suite housing the *Crimson Caller* offices. There were two cubicles in the main room, lined on three sides by rows of closed doors obscuring what must've been offices and conference rooms.

Movement from the corner of my eye urged me to turn just in time to see Holden Peters rising from a seat along the window-wall to our left. He towered over me even in my heels, which put him at about six foot four— every inch of it the kind of toned muscle that could make Captain America jealous. His tentative smile revealed dimples the size of the Mariana Trench in his tanned face. Shaggy sandy-blond hair, an inch or two too long to be stylish, hung over his forehead—not quite in his eyes but getting close. He reached a hand out to shake, and I couldn't help but notice the corded muscles of his forearm. This kid was the Tony-Okerson-picture-perfect poster boy for the All-American quarterback.

When I did grasp his hand, his smile kicked up. "It's a pleasure to meet you, Miss Clarke." His voice was a smooth baritone, soft but intent. It was a voice that commanded attention without needing to be gruff or loud. The kind of voice that made you listen because you wanted to hear what he had to say.

"I wish it were under better circumstances," I said. "But I'm going to do as much as I can to make sure the truth wins out."

Troy nudged me with his elbow, pointing to one of the closed doors, labeled *Editorial*. "We're in here."

He reached up to clap Holden on the shoulder, a solemn nod passing between them before we filed into the room.

Before I got the door shut behind me, one of the doors across the way flew wide, a young woman rushing out so fast she practically materialized in the doorway of our conscripted office. She nodded at Troy and Holden, but her eyes stayed riveted on me.

"Are you Nichelle Clarke? Like, *the* Nichelle Clarke?" She leaned in, close enough that I could smell the coconut-scented product in her hair.

Um. I offered her my hand and a casual smile, though I wasn't sure I'd ever been referred to as "*the* Nichelle Clarke" unless someone wanted me dead. "That's me. Nice to meet you...?"

Leaving the hanging introduction meant the woman scrambled to fill in the gap. "My name's Amber—Amber Harvey. I'm the senior editor here. I'm a *huge* fan of your work. I've been following your career since I was in high school." She let go of my hand just this side of holding it long enough to make things awkward, returning hers to her side, where it seemed she didn't know what to do with it.

I'd seen more than a few people starstruck by meeting Grant Parker, but I'd never been on this side of the reaction myself. People I met in the field who recognized my name tended to react with exasperation—though, to be fair, that was usually because they were doing something shady they didn't want me to put in the newspaper.

Lacking the first clue what to say to her, I channeled Parker, flashing a big grin and ducking my head briefly the way he always did. "That's very kind of you, Amber."

"Honestly, I want to be just like you someday. Your story about the cancer patients a few years back really cemented my drive to go into journalism. Uncovering corruption, speaking out on behalf of the victims, not ever letting the actual people on all sides get lost in the story..."

At the last, I threw Troy and Holden a pointed look, because Amber and her staff not giving Holden the real estate to voice his side of the story was exactly the reason I was here.

"That's the main reason I overrode the professor's decision against publishing Troy's op-ed."

Oh. My smile was more genuine this time. "Sounds like you're well on your way to a stellar career."

Her cheeks flushed, a smile lighting her face. "I should probably let you get to it. I just had to meet you." She gave an awkward little wave before starting to take a few steps back toward the open door to her office. "Please don't hesitate to let me know if there's anything else I can do for you guys, okay?"

"Sure, thanks, Amber." That was Troy, reaching past me to close the door to our borrowed office. He turned back with a sheepish grin. "I may have name-dropped you to get us this space for the interview. I knew she was a fan, but I wasn't expecting all that."

I stared at the closed door. "I have honestly never considered anyone would follow my work. Not like that, anyway." I shook my head and turned to take a seat across the table from Holden. Troy took a chair off to my right, just barely visible in my periphery.

Holden sat ramrod straight in his chair. His hands were hidden by the table on his lap, but the play of the muscles in his biceps told me he was wringing them. His eyes darted back and forth between Troy and me, spending more time focused on me with each trip.

I took my time pulling out a notebook and pen so he'd have a second to settle, but it didn't seem to help. Clicking out my pen, I could see his pulse fluttering in the side of his neck, and anyone watching a heart monitor would've thought he was sprinting.

"Let's start with what got you into football." I ducked my head and caught his eye, offering a smile that said *tell me a story* better than the actual words ever could.

And that was all it took. Holden moved his hands on top of the table, and his shoulders eased down. "My dad played ball with me when I was a kid. He taught all the neighboring kids how to play two-hand touch, so we would do three-on-three matches in the backyard with him coaching both teams. From there it was peewee football leagues every year, travel leagues in middle school, and trying out for the high school team..."

The way he trailed off told me there was something there. "Were you on varsity your freshman year?"

He sat up even straighter, which I wouldn't have thought possible. "I was a really scrawny kid who lived at the gym but couldn't buy a pound of muscle. I could always throw a football and read the field like a book, but Coach flat-out told me that I was too small for varsity."

Hard to imagine, looking at twenty-one-year-old Holden: across from me sat a small mountain of a young man who I was pretty sure could bench-press my car without so much as breaking a sweat.

He caught my incredulous expression—even my face is lousy at lying—and laughed. "The summer before my junior year, I hit the mother of all growth spurts. It was almost like a cartoon. I couldn't stop eating, my mom had to buy new clothes every month, and my grandpa swore he could sit on the porch and watch me grow as a pastime."

"And that was your ticket to varsity?"

"Almost. I made the team, but I rode the bench for half the season. The starting QB was a senior who'd been on the team for three years and was a DI hopeful. In the fifth game, our big crosstown rival was pummeling us, and Jackson—the starter—suddenly couldn't seem to hit the broad side of a barn with a pass, when he could even get the ball off before he got sacked. I had to practically beg Coach to put me in, but he did. Their blitz game was strong, and I had almost no time in the pocket. But that also meant their entire defense was big, lumbering guys who couldn't run—and my buddy Trevon was the king of catching a screen pass and juking defenders until he had a clear field. And he could run like Usain Bolt. So a series of short passes ended up winning us the game."

I scribbled, mostly for background filler. Holden wasn't just athletic, he was smart—a high school kid who could read a field better than his coach and pull a win out of the jaws of defeat was a player who could go places.

And who he was attracted to wasn't going to stop him on my watch.

The tension in Holden's shoulders vanished, and he spread his hands palm up across the table. "And the rest, as they say, is history." He went on to describe starting the rest of that season and all through his senior year, leading his high school team to a perfect season and the state championship.

"I don't know if you follow college football, but we haven't always had a winning team here." Holden ran a hand through his hair. It didn't fall flat, instead sticking up in a way that made him look young and endearing. "My senior year of high school was Coach's first season with the team, and it was like he was a wizard or something. They came out of nowhere and started winning games, taking titles, making a name for themselves. And the school culture was one of acceptance and balance. I could see myself playing football here, finding my passions here, growing up here. It was my dream school in every sense of the word."

He slumped back in his seat; his rigid posture the last bit of tension to go, and weariness aged his face ten years in five seconds. He scrubbed a hand across his brow. "It wasn't supposed to go like this." The last word was softer, like it struggled out around a lump in his throat. "This was supposed to be my year. The Heisman talk started early; we have a solid team. We were on our way to a championship. Life had truly never been better. I felt safe enough to be myself, and look where it got me."

I took notes, trying to make eye contact and nod any time he would let me. He spent most of the interview staring at something behind my right shoulder.

Holden leaned forward. His arms were folded on the table in front of him, but I could see divots on his forearms where his fingertips dug into his skin. I could also feel the slight reverberation of his foot bouncing beneath the table.

"What made you feel unsafe about being yourself before?" I asked.

"Are you asking if I have some lurking childhood trauma?"

Kind of, I supposed. I held his gaze and stayed quiet.

Holden shook his head. "I had a normal, happy childhood. My younger sister and I got to go to Disney World twice before middle school. My sister —she's studying engineering at Georgia Tech—she's so, so smart. We used to always joke that she got all the brains in the family." The smile he quirked felt more genuine, if a little rueful. "I worked hard in school, but it wasn't as natural for me. I got decent grades, but football was..." He paused, took in a long breath. "Football was—football is—everything to me."

I nodded as I scribbled notes, the words he wasn't saying telling more of his story than the ones he did. Disney World and a wicked smart sister were great, but he hadn't said anything about friends, first love, or high school hijinks. I figured I knew why, but that didn't mean I didn't have to ask. "And what about the rest of high school, besides football and family? What was your social life like then?"

Holden's eyes were an arresting blue-gray that carried weight when they met my gaze. "It wasn't the time for me to be gay."

I furrowed my brow. I'd always had a terrible poker face and couldn't tell a passable lie to save my life. Well, once quite literally to save my life, but I still think that was pure desperate luck.

Holden clocked my expression and bit his lip again. "My parents aren't bad people, Miss Clarke, but they don't understand who I am. I've known I was gay since the third grade, when Katie Simpson told me she wanted to kiss me behind the equipment shed on the playground and all I could think about was how much I'd rather kiss her twin brother, Kevin. But my mom and dad wouldn't approve because they think it's something you choose, not who you are. I may not agree with them, but I do understand how they can think that, because they've never been gay. So I waited until I was out of the house to explore this part of myself more freely."

He chanced a quick glance at Troy, which he'd pretty much avoided doing for the entire interview so far.

"It's easier, in some ways, to come out when you look like I do—big, muscular white guy." His eyes settled on Troy again before flicking back to me. "No one is going to try to pick a fight with me, or even say anything to my face. Before my growth spurt, it was fear that kept me closeted. Growing up, I would see people getting bullied for who they were and who they loved, and I was terrified of bringing that down on myself."

"Why not stay the course until after the season?" I asked. "Football is a pretty macho, testosterone-heavy environment. What made you decide to rock the boat?"

"I wanted to help," he said, his eyes going to Troy again. "Seeing people plagued by that fear I had as that scrawny kid, I figured I could...I don't know...give them hope? Like letting the world know who I was might make other people feel safer doing the same. I waited until I had a solid future in front of me. My place on the team was secure—I thought. I had a coach who talked in the locker room about individuality strengthening the team, about seeking peace and seeing your game explode with the increase it brings to your focus. But I guess peace is reserved for folks who aren't quite as 'individual' as I am."

I believed him. This wasn't about trying to grab headlines or get attention. Hell, sitting here today, Holden had talked up someone else every chance he got. I made a note in the margin to see if I could ask Amber about why no one had talked to Holden before now. She'd mentioned overriding a professor's ruling on Troy's column, so why stop there?

"Let's talk about the drug test. The official line here is that you failed a drug test and that's why you've been benched."

Holden clenched his fist on the tabletop, a mirror of Troy's posture beside me. "I've never even tried anything. Not alcohol, not weed. Nothing. Football is everything to me, and my personal integrity means so much more to me than a few hours of fun."

I wanted his exact words on what he thought happened. "Then where did Coach Farrelly get a failed test with your name on it?"

"Coach must have switched it." He looked me straight in the eye, unflinching. "It's the only explanation that makes sense."

"That's a serious accusation—even more serious than the one against you," I said. "It couldn't have been anyone else? Or do you have proof?"

"The guys on the team...we're family. I was out to my team long before Coach got wind of it. They would never do anything like this. There's no way." He leaned back in his chair again. "Coach has a whole staff of yesmen; they follow him around everywhere and do anything and everything he asks. In their eyes, he's the sole reason for the recent success of the athletics program."

Interesting.

"Do you have any reason to believe any of these guys are homophobic? Have they said or done anything that would make you think that? Could one of the staff members have made the switch, with Coach Farrelly none the wiser?"

Holden answered with a shrug. "I can't say for sure, but not much goes on around here that Coach doesn't have a hand in. If someone really did switch and lie to him, I wouldn't want to be them when he finds out."

He sat forward in his chair, elbows propped on the table, leaning forward to stare right through me. "Look, I'll take another test. Anytime, anywhere. I will take a test every day for the rest of the season if it means I get to play."

"Were you serious about that last part? Because I can get a drug test run in Richmond—incontrovertible evidence that you're clean, certified by a third-party specialist—and we can bring that proof to whoever needs to see it."

Holden blinked. "How do you plan to transport it? And what about verification that it's legit?"

"I have a friend at the Richmond crime lab. She can get this all cleared up and verified with a few pieces of your hair. Hair, especially follicles, can show a much longer history of drug use—or not—than a urine test. Plus, no carting around bodily fluids."

I brandished a clean plastic baggie, a roll of masking tape, and a pair of latex gloves. I handed my cell phone to Troy and put on the gloves. Troy had shaken his head and grinned when I filled him in on this plan on the ride up. "Nichelle, do you have any idea how much of a badass you are?" he'd asked.

I didn't think due diligence was quite the definition of *badass*, but I'd take it. He started recording a video with my phone—which would be time-stamped—as Holden leaned forward, consenting for me to pluck hairs from his scalp. Troy kept recording as I put the hairs in the baggie, sealed it, rolled the top a few times, and taped it shut.

"Now, all three of us need to sign the tape here to show that the tape wasn't torn or replaced between now and when the sample is tested," I said.

We did so, with Troy recording the whole time.

"Thank you, Holden, for your time and for sharing your story." I handed him a card with my contact information. "If you could email me a couple of high-resolution photos—maybe from your Heisman PR shoot—to use with the article, I'd really appreciate it."

"Definitely." He pulled his cell phone out of his pocket and glanced at it.

"I have to get back. I'm moving out of my frat house this weekend, and the team is waiting to help me haul everything."

I well remembered that most fraternities were not exactly bastions of acceptance, but a rush of sadness washed over me at the thought of Holden getting kicked out of his frat on top of everything else. "I'm so sorry, Holden."

"I wish people were more accepting, but I can't control that. The whole house got hassled because I was a member. A handful of cars in our parking lot got defaced, we had people constantly ringing the doorbell and ditching. The brothers took a vote, and they blackballed me." He shrugged his broad shoulders. "Just another opportunity for growth. I'm moving to the queer floor of McGill Hall."

I had read about the LGBTQIA+ floor. It was featured on the school website as part of their diversity and inclusion initiative. The look on Holden's face made me glad there was somewhere on campus he could feel safe being himself.

"Troy was right about you, Miss Clarke," Holden said, shaking my hand again. "He said you're good people. For the first time in two weeks, I feel lighter, like things are looking up. Thank you."

"You're welcome." I squeezed his hand before I let go, glancing at Troy, who was knocking on Amber's door.

When Holden disappeared through the doorway, I noticed Amber trying to peer over Troy's shoulder at me. I stepped up beside him.

"You mentioned earlier that you overrode a professor who didn't want to publish Troy's op-ed," I said. She perked up at the attention. "But why didn't the original articles get Holden's reaction on the record? In order to remain objective, you have to get as many sides of the story as you can."

"I was thinking about that the whole time you were in there." Amber bit her bottom lip. "Dr. Nicks said someone else would run that down, just not as part of the original story. But then that story never made it to my desk— and, as a result, never made it into the paper." She wrapped her arms around her middle. "I didn't go out and get the story myself when it didn't come in." Her head dropped. "And that's on me. I know better. As soon as your article is live, I'll make sure it's referenced in our paper, with a sincere apology to Holden."

"It's okay to make mistakes." I leaned forward and caught her eye. "I've written stories condemning the wrong person; I've failed to speak up when I knew about an injustice because I wanted more information. The more important thing is that you recognize it and do better next time you're confronted with a similar situation. You're young. You have a long career ahead of you. It's okay to still be learning, because you should keep learning for the rest of your life. The learning is part of what keeps this job interesting."

"Thank you, Miss Clarke."

Troy and I were back at my car before I turned to him, my lips twisted to one side. "Do you think Coach Farrelly would be in his office right now?"

"Only one way to find out." His grin said he wanted to see me go toe-to-toe with Farrelly. "We should drive. It's a hike over there in this heat."

We turned the air to full blast as Troy directed me to the massive athletic department on the other side of campus. A newly Division I school with highly competitive football, basketball, baseball, and soccer teams—as well as up-and-coming tennis, field hockey, and lacrosse—meant big money spent on equipment, training space, gym space, and both indoor and outdoor fields. I'd covered news in cities smaller than the complex sprawling in front of us.

The path to Farrelly's office was like an homage to football: life-size portraits of players in Bulldog crimson and white lined both walls, broken up only by occasional glass cases filled with trophies, plaques, and signed footballs. It felt like walking onto a movie set. And Farrelly's door was open at the end of the hall.

Showtime.

"Excuse me, Coach?" I asked, rapping on the polished mahogany frame.

Farrelly looked more like a stockbroker than a football coach, dressed in a three-piece gray Armani suit even Joey would approve of, not a wrinkle or imperfection in sight. Both tie and pocket square were crimson.

"That's what it says on the door." Farrelly had a welcoming manner and a booming voice that dripped charisma. He stood and shook hands with both me and Troy before flagging down another man in khakis and a Bull-dogs polo. "Lawrence, bring everyone a soda, yeah?" Once Lawrence was gone, Farrelly winked. "We just landed a sponsorship with Pepsi, so it's all-you-can-drink around here."

I introduced myself and Troy, watching the coach's face carefully for changes. I didn't catch much. His eyes flicked a once-over when he turned to Troy, who held steady, lacking the frenetic energy that plagued him during Holden's interview. I knew he was nervous because I knew him pretty well, but I didn't think anyone else except maybe his mother would've been able to tell.

Lawrence returned with three bottles of Pepsi: regular for me and Troy and Pepsi Max for Farrelly. The interruption prompted Farrelly to speak for the first time since I said Troy's name.

"I understand the presumption that motivated your editorial, Mr. Wright," he said, his drawl coming through heavier than it tended to on TV. "But let me assure you that things are not always as simple as they seem."

"That's exactly what we'd like to talk to you about, actually." I stepped in before Troy could let his nerves—or his anger—get the better of him. "Holden's drug test—did you see the test results yourself?"

"Of course I did. The second I heard that my star quarterback had failed, I demanded to see it for myself."

"And did you yourself see the samples come out of the locker room and go into the lab undisturbed?"

His left eye twitched. "I have a few more important things to do than personally monitor urine samples, Miss Clarke."

Strike one.

"May I see the results of Holden's test?"

"That is confidential student medical information." He steepled his fingers under his chin, eyebrows shooting up. "You wouldn't want me to get in trouble for a HIPAA violation, now, would you?"

"That law actually applies to insurance companies and healthcare providers, not athletic teams or individual patients," I said.

Farrelly's face stretched into a slow smile. "You'll have to excuse me if I defer to the university's legal counsel on such a complex matter."

Strike two. But I didn't buy his simpleton-football-coach act for a hot second.

"I'll check with them for you." I didn't blink. "Was there anyone on your staff with access to the samples you tested who might have been bothered by Holden's sexual orientation?"

"No. And I'm not sure I care for that question."

Well then he really wasn't going to like the next one. "What about you, Coach? Do you have any personal issues with Holden's sexual orientation?"

Farrelly took a long sip of his Pepsi, leaning back in his chair. "My favorite uncle was a lifelong bachelor, Miss Clarke, and not because ladies didn't find him attractive."

I swallowed a "you ought to run for office" at his vague-yet-sound-bite-ish non-answer, jotting it down before I looked up with a smile.

"I personally collected a sample from Holden today for a more definitive test. I'll happily relay it to the state crime lab in Richmond and put you in touch with the scientist who reviews it. Would you accept the results of such a test?"

He tapped a finger on his desk, took a sip of his Pepsi Max, and held my gaze for three beats. "I admire your tenacity, Miss Clarke. Do give my regards to Grant Parker." His drawl got thicker when he was agitated.

My agitation got thicker when people deflected simple questions. "Will you accept the results of a third-party drug test?" I pressed.

"I cannot commit to that at this time." Farrelly's accent was so thick around his words I barely recognized them. And I'm from Texas.

Time to switch gears. "I spoke with Holden today. He said he felt safe in the locker room and accepted on this team and in this program. His teammates have spoken out on social media on his behalf—I can pull up the tweets if you want to see them—and are helping him move into his new dorm as we speak." I set my unopened Pepsi on the desk between us. "Why wouldn't you accept a second, more reliable drug test that covers a longer time period?" I took a moment just to stare him down, like Troy was still doing beside me. "I feel obligated to warn you that it's not going to look good if I print that you refused to accept verifiable test results from a crime lab. Not if you want to prove Troy here wrong."

Farrelly nodded, pursing his lips in a camera-ready "contemplative" expression. "You have to do your job just as I have to do mine." His hand moved to cover a spreadsheet lying in the center of his desk.

Troy rocketed to his feet, his chair screeching a protest against the floor.

Pulling his shoulders back and sticking his chest out, he glared down at the man across the desk. "It's all about the money, isn't it, Coach?" The words came out diamond hard and rapid fire, and Farrelly flinched, albeit so quickly half a blink would've made me miss it. "The kind words about inclusion in the locker room go right out the window when big donors have concerns. What bullshit." Troy turned and stalked out through the still-open door.

The look that flickered across Farrelly's face said nobody insulted the king here in his domain. Shifting his attention back to me, Farrelly stuck his chin out and folded his arms across his chest, holding my gaze.

Neither of us blinked. Nine ticks into a dead-still, you-could-hear-a-gnat-sneeze silence, Farrelly tipped his head toward the door.

I took the hint and stood. "Thank you for speaking with me, Coach." I offered my card. "If you change your mind about anything we discussed here today, just let me know. I'll be sure to give Parker your best." I strode out, the only sound the staccato click of my Louboutins on the marble floors of Farrelly's football temple—and, I hoped, his favorite uncle's voice making a cameo as his conscience. I still had four days for him to come around.

8

Troy pressed his forehead against the brick wall just outside the door, his whole body shaking. The door slammed shut behind me, making us both jump.

"You good?" I asked with a raised brow.

Troy pushed off the wall, and we started back toward the car.

"I swear, any time Farrelly opens his mouth these days, all I can see is red."

"I remember that feeling," I said. "It will fade as you get more jaded—and interviewing Farrelly's type on the daily for years will make you jaded. Though personal investment in a story still brings it out in me." I held out one trembling hand for his inspection as I unlocked the car with the other. "Coach is a piece of work. Everything he said was technically above board, but your instincts are good—he was careful about his words, and his refusal to commit to the more accurate drug test is the real story of that interview."

"Bigotry shrouded in pretty, politically correct words is the most insidious kind." Troy shook his head. "Give me a guy with a Confederate flag on the back of his jacked-up pickup any day over the suit-and-tie, smile-to-your-face-but-sabotage-your-entire-life-behind-your-back-because-money-rules-the-world guy. At least the Confederate flag guy is easy to spot and avoid—and rarely ends up in any position of major authority."

"No major university would hire that guy to run their biggest sports program," I agreed, sliding behind the wheel.

Troy folded himself into the passenger seat beside me. "That bit about his uncle was textbook tokenization. Even if he does have a gay uncle, that doesn't mean that he can't still be homophobic. It's the macho version of 'But I'm not racist, I have a Black friend.'"

"Here's what I don't get, though." I pulled out of the parking lot and veered toward the freeway. "I know Farrelly's type: nothing goes on in his program that he doesn't know about. If the other guys on the team knew Holden was gay, I promise you, Coach knew, too. But he didn't bench him until it was public knowledge. In my experience, macho assholes who hate gay people feel that way all the time, not just when other people might know someone they're connected to is gay."

"It's possible that it's not personal for Farrelly. Like I said—money rules the world. The problem may not be that Coach is homophobic, but that someone who donates money to the program is."

"That would explain the timing of his issue with Holden." I merged onto the interstate, punching the accelerator. "Doesn't it make him just as guilty if he knows how hurtful and wrong it is and still does nothing?"

"Yes and no. You're conflating the idea that he 'knows better' and the fact that he has queer folks in his life, which is the goal of tossing out factoids like the one about his uncle. At the very least, he's trying to use that relationship to absolve himself of suspicion here, and at worst, he's deliberately muddying the issue and the public's interpretation of his actions."

"I can imagine it's hurtful to run up against bigotry out of the blue," I said.

"The best protection is knowing how to handle it, because we can't stop it from happening. That's the importance of groups like the one you'll see on Tuesday. There are a lot of Don Farrellys out there—supposed allies who don't bother to consider their biases, hiding behind people they know or things they've done—rather than putting in the work to learn from the source what the real issues are. It's important for everyone to have a safe space where they can not only be themselves but also talk through the situations they encounter every day. For people just learning how to deal with situations like these safely, without compromising their mental health or sense of identity, having a group like ours offers answers and support."

His voice lightened as he talked about the group.

"Tell me more about the kids," I said.

"They're so great. They're inquisitive and protective, and so smart and so strong. When I started this group over the summer, I didn't know what to expect. Maybe the kids at the center would be more like I was: they'd never have given queerness a thought beyond playground insults. Like, nobody's got time to be soft in our neighborhood—you know? But instead they're..." He trailed off, staring out the window at the trees blurring into a palette of lime and kelly green outside his window. "These kids are ready to take what they deserve, not just accept what they're given," he finally concluded. "And it's fucking beautiful."

"What do you think makes their experience so different from yours?"

"The internet," he said without hesitation. "You don't really hear a lot about the good that social media can do, and while I know it has done plenty of harm to so many people in other ways, I think just in the past seven years or so, the way that some leaders and groups have figured out how to harness it has made a huge positive impact. Like, most people won't necessarily hear about anti-trans or homophobic legislation on the news because even though more things are covered now, it's rare for stories like that to make the front page or lead a broadcast. It might get a mention, but details and follow-up stories are seriously lacking." He shook his head. "On social media, though, queer folks from around the world share news, resources, safety guides, and more. They follow up and keep everyone informed as events progress. The past decade has seen some great networks grow online."

"Do you think these networks are providing the kind of security that helps kids today feel more comfortable with themselves than you did at their age, even though that wasn't so long ago?"

"Definitely. And in a progressive city like Richmond, there are more resources than just the internet, too. The public libraries now have a full stock of queer literature—and queer characters are being normalized in fiction for teens and young adults. That has downright exploded since I was their age, and it helps the people in their world understand and relate to them, to be better allies."

"Does your group help with that, too? Like, can straight kids attend to learn about these issues from the source?"

He touched one finger to his chin. "I hadn't considered that. We provide a safe space for queer or questioning young people to talk, learn, and be themselves. But there is an opportunity to educate the community and bridge gaps." He grinned. "Let me see what I can do with that."

"Because you're not already doing enough?" I laughed. "How are you keeping up with this during the school year, when campus is a good distance away?"

"Technology to the rescue again. The kids can WhatsApp me if they have an emergency, and they're good about keeping that to true emergencies, so I'm not constantly bombarded with messages. For everything else, they have my buddy Ben." Troy tapped out a drumbeat on his knees. "He's a member of the group, but he's special—big heart, smart—and he steps up to lead whenever I'm not there. Hell, even sometimes when I am. I've only been back on campus for three weeks, but I already know I've left the group in very capable hands."

I took the Richmond exit. First stop: the crime lab to drop off Holden's samples with Jacque. Troy waited in the car while I ran in. Jacque was, thankfully, in her office rather than, say, elbow-deep in some poor person's rib cage.

"Hey, Nichelle," Jacque said, peering up at me from behind a stack of papers. "No dead mystery men today, I'm afraid."

"I'm busy enough at the moment anyway." I brandished the baggie with Holden's hair sample. "Currently wondering if you could run a drug test for me?"

Jacque took the bag and squinted at the contents. "You even got follicles —good work." She winked. "I'll put it through; should only take a few days."

"Give me a call when you get the results?"

"You know I will." Jacque waved me off from where I was lingering in the doorway. "And don't forget about that shoe sale!"

"I would never," I called from halfway down the hall. I wouldn't forget, I also probably wouldn't have time to shop with so many stories bouncing around.

I pointed the car toward Joyce Wright's home, speeding and weaving through evening rush-hour traffic as I tried to keep from glancing at the dashboard clock every two seconds by changing the subject. "You know how we talked about threatening messages before? The comments on your op-ed, the emails you've been getting..."

"Yeah, what about it?" The blasé attitude Troy had taken to the comments only yesterday had dimmed somewhat. Something told me that it was finally hitting home what those comments actually meant, or at least what they could lead to.

"Are any of these people escalating? I'm worried about you."

He sucked in a deep, audible breath and let it out slowly. The quick glance I tossed his way revealed that he was absorbed in his phone. I gave him a moment to respond, but by the time he was done, I had stopped at the curb outside his house.

"There's...a few new ones." He handed me his phone.

On the screen was a picture of the outside of his house. I checked the time stamp—about an hour ago—and swiveled my head in every direction. "They took it from right over there." I pointed to the other side of the street, just a few yards further down.

"Swipe to the next one." His voice was smaller than I'd heard it since a sad, scrawny kid flagged me down at the hospital after his brother died, desperate for someone to listen to him, to help him.

I swiped. The second picture showed his mother's car, license plate clearly visible.

I clicked the sender's profile but found only a ghost with no connections or posts. Back in Troy's DMs, the photos stood alone with no accompanying text.

But the subtext was clear: *We're watching.*

9

Personal safety in the age of the internet 101: trolls and stalkers are entirely different animals. The vitriol I'd seen in the comments on Troy's opinion piece a couple of days ago could probably be attributed to the former, but the photos crossed a dangerous line to the latter.

He assured me he was taking the threat seriously. Running late for dinner, I took him at his word and headed home after promising to check in with him the next morning.

Richmond isn't like the DC suburbs, where whiplash isn't reserved for collisions thanks to traffic that slams from sixty to zero in less than a minute as gridlock spreads during rush hour—in Richmond, the problem is too many stoplights and not enough two-way streets. Alternate routes are mythical creatures on par with centaurs and unicorns. By the time I made it to the Fan and screeched into my driveway, it was coming up on 6:45.

I wasn't even out of the car when the front door swung open. Joey, looking sexy as hell in a blue-gray Armani three-piece suit, waved from the doorway. "Exactly what time do you call this, Miss Clarke?"

"Not late yet—that's what time it is." I winked and tugged on his tie as I slid past. "But of course you know picking something to wear takes the—" I swallowed "longest" when I walked into the bedroom, shedding my heels, and saw three outfits draped across our bed.

Joey followed, my sandals dangling from his fingers. "Feel free to veto any or all of them, but I figured I'd give you a head start." He fixed his tie with his free hand, tucking the sandals away in their place in my cluttered shoe armoire like he'd been doing it for a hundred years, not a hundred days and change.

And that was the best thing about my life right then: He just fit. In my arms, in my bed, in my house...in my life. It seemed silly now that I'd spent so much time and energy fighting my attraction to him.

I shot up on tiptoe to kiss his freshly shaved cheek before turning to the dresses on the bed. On the left was a deep orange floral that might have been perfect for an afternoon at a winery but was too casual for dinner. On the right, every girl's staple: the little black dress. It was slimming but also sexy, hugging in all the right places. If it was just going to be the two of us, that would have been my number one choice.

"The one in the middle is my favorite," Joey said.

I picked up the cloud-gray A-line dress he nodded to and looked it over. It would match Joey's tie perfectly, and since he didn't get to be my official plus-one at Grant and Melanie's wedding, we'd never had the opportunity to present a wholly united formal-attire front.

The gray dress was light—perfect for the weather—as well as flattering with its easy cut and understated color. I removed the hanger, shimmying out of my work clothes and tossing them in the general direction of the hamper.

"You know fashion at least as well as I do," I said. "And this way we match."

"Not counting shoes." He laughed as he zipped my dress. "You have the monopoly on shoe knowledge in this household." He grinned and stepped aside so I could get my shoes.

I grabbed a pair of black Jimmy Choos to highlight the black detailing on the bodice of the dress. A quick makeup check, a swipe of lipstick, and we were out the door.

"Record time," Joey said, opening the passenger door to his Lincoln, which looked pretty great parked in the driveway beside my SUV.

I slid into the seat, letting the smell of his cologne and the feel of creamy, luxurious leather envelop me. I would never drive a car this big and flashy, but I couldn't imagine Joey in anything else. It was a steerable symbol of the elegance and attention to detail he brought to everything.

"Busy day today, huh?" he asked once we merged into the sea of cars traveling through the city. "Were you out on campus again with Troy?"

"It was a nonstop kind of day." I waved a dismissive hand. "We can talk about it after dinner; maybe even at dinner, if that's okay—I think Kyle might have some helpful thoughts on a few things."

Special Agent Kyle Miller was the youngest acting branch director in the history of the Bureau of Alcohol, Tobacco, Firearms and Explosives. He was also my first love, and—thanks to the help Joey had provided toward the end of Kyle's years-long quest to take down the Caccione crime family —our close friend and half of the other couple we were meeting for dinner.

Joey parked outside our new favorite Mexican restaurant at a fashionably late 7:05. I spotted Kyle's Explorer in the next row over, because five minutes early is late to Kyle.

"They probably have a table already," I said as Joey held the heavy wood door, his hand on the small of my back guiding me into the lobby.

Joey gave Kyle's name, and the maître d' led us through a maze of wide tables set with colorful dishes to a secluded booth where Kyle and his date waited.

"Nicey!" DonnaJo Marsh shot to her feet as we walked up, pulling me into a hug. "Girl, it has been a minute. How are you?" She leaned close to my ear, her eyes on Joey. "Never mind. Nobody would be anything but amazing waking up next to that every day. Damn."

I coughed over a laugh and winked at my favorite hotshot prosecutor as the guys shook hands before we took our seats.

Kyle laced his fingers with DonnaJo's on the tabletop, watching her as she studied the menu like the sun was shining beneath her skin.

I smiled to myself and squeezed Joey's hand under the table, so happy we were all there—and all friends, when just a year ago I would've said it wasn't possible—I wondered if some vital part of me might actually burst.

The server recited the specials with a smile. Joey went for the seared adobo steak with rice and vegetables, Kyle and DonnaJo ordered the combo fajitas, and I settled—after more deliberation than normal—on chicken nachos over enchiladas.

"Our nachos are bomb." The server nodded as she jotted my order down. "You won't regret that."

"Not until you get to the gym tomorrow, anyway," DonnaJo said. Kyle laughed the kind of deep, booming, genuine laugh that had been missing for far too long. I met his gaze across the table and offered a nod so slight nobody but him would've seen it. He grinned a dopey lovesick grin I'd only ever seen on one other person—Grant Parker, after the first time I sent him out with Melanie.

Good for them.

Everyone deferred the wine choice to Joey, who picked a bottle of red for the table he said would complement everyone's food. We smiled and thanked our server as she collected menus before turning back to each other.

"So, Nichelle," DonnaJo said, leaning toward me across the table, "what had you two running in here ten minutes late to your own reservation?"

"Let me guess," Kyle said before I could open my mouth. "You bit off more than you could Jimmy Choos with a new story." He grinned the kind of self-satisfied grin that had me wondering how long he'd been waiting to use that one.

"Kyle Miller, making a pun *and* knowing enough about shoes to do it well? Color me impressed." I laughed. "I wouldn't say it's quite more than I can chew, but it's a mouthful for sure. I've got three stories going right now."

"How many dead people?" DonnaJo asked.

"Only one. So far."

"That's not even a busy week for you," she said.

"It's not the quantity of dead folks, it's how interesting they'll be to my readers," I said.

"Sure. Interesting vics are always fodder for juicy stories," DonnaJo conceded with an elegant wave of one hand.

"Y'all know I'll talk your ears off about this if you get me going, so I'll go last in the 'what are you up to' round robin, if you don't mind."

Joey's laugh rumbled as he patted my knee under the table. "I'll take this kickoff for the team." He nodded to Kyle. "We just got the ball rolling on some new government contracts thanks to Kyle's matchmaking skills."

Kyle shrugged. "It was the least I could do, man."

Joey had gone from running point on under-the-table deals and outskirts-of-the-law threats as a consigliere for the biggest mafia family on the East Coast to negotiating construction contracts and overseeing projects so smoothly you'd think he was born to it. He didn't have to change his wardrobe, except to occasionally don a hard hat for appearances' sake, and his head for organization and people had been a total game-changer for the company he took over. It wasn't exactly low-profile, which made me a bit nervous when he started there after his aborted stint in protective custody, but he hadn't run across anything worth being concerned about yet.

DonnaJo tapped her fingers on the side of her wineglass as she took a sip. "Wow. I'm glad we let Joey pick." She set the glass down. "As for me, no shortage of cases to prosecute around here, I'm afraid. The usual."

"She means kicking ass and taking names," Kyle added with a smug smile.

DonnaJo tugged playfully at his ear in mock retribution. "Stop it, you." She turned her attention to me and rested her fingers on the edge of the table, poised as if to start a piano concerto. "I will say, I miss having you beating down my door for the inside scoop on every single one of my cases. Even Shelby was better than that Mark guy; I never knew a reporter could be so condescending."

I couldn't say I was sad to hear she didn't like Mark any more than I did.

"Did you hear anything about why Shelby stepped back?" DonnaJo asked. "I never figured her for the type to let some guy take her dream job when she finally had it in hand."

Shelby Taylor was a reporter at the *Telegraph* who'd spent so many years chasing my cops and courts beat—stooping as low as to intentionally tip other news organizations to exclusives she heard I was working on, not to mention sleeping with first the managing editor and then the slimy publisher—that somewhere along the way she'd lost sight of whether or not she actually wanted the job. As it turned out, the creepier and more dangerous aspects that went with it weren't Shelby's idea of fun, and she'd scurried back to the copy desk as fast as her Nikes would carry her.

"The grass isn't always greener when you actually hop the fence to the neighbor's pasture," I said. "I don't think she realized being bulletproof was part of the job requirement. The pipeline story and some of the threats she got rattled her."

"They'd rattle most people," Kyle said, leaning back in his chair, his muscular shoulders straining against the lines of his dress shirt. I couldn't help thinking of Holden, who I'd noticed was sure to look a lot like Kyle once he aged out of the last vestiges of baby fat in his face. Holden was taller, but the two of them could probably go head-to-head in the muscles department.

"I guess that means it's my turn," Kyle said. "No word yet on my new boss, so I'm still in charge for now."

The ATF was probably taking vetting the new director very seriously after the scandal caused by the last one. Kyle, as the temporary director, was swamped with more work than he was used to, directing teams and projects while fighting his desire to abandon the paper-pushing of being the boss in favor of leading boots-on-the-ground raids.

I knew part of the problem was that he didn't want to let go of either thing—his trust in the agency and the people he worked with and for had been strained in the scandal that swallowed his old boss, which is a dangerous way to feel in law enforcement.

"Anything interesting going on there this week?" I asked.

"We're tracking a large shipment of guns." He rolled his shoulders in an easy shrug.

I waited for more, but he didn't offer it. "Vague much?"

His only response was to grin mischievously and then mime zipping his lips shut. "Your turn, Nicey."

"I do actually have a question for you two, related to one of my stories." I nodded to Kyle and DonnaJo. "Have you heard anything about infighting between hate groups?"

"What, we don't even get the story first these days? I feel so...used." Kyle rolled his eyes, but his tone was warm and playful.

"You probably saw Charlie Lewis talking about the murder victim from southside this afternoon."

They nodded in such perfect unison it was impossible not to notice.

"The vic was a neo-Nazi," I said.

Kyle's brows shot up. "You're sure?"

"The Nazi flag that was the centerpiece of his living room decor was a good tip," I said.

"That'd do it. Do you know what hate group he was a part of?"

Joey, who'd been listening to our banter with a polite but removed smile that told me he was thinking about something else, sat up straight and snapped his fingers. "That tattoo—can I see the picture again?" While I dug for my phone, he filled our friends in on the tattoo picture—and the gruesome way I went about getting it.

DonnaJo made a face.

"Before the food gets here and I ruin everyone's dinner..." I pulled up the picture and passed the phone around. Joey was last to look at it, and, just like before, he took his time zooming in and tilting the phone this way and that. "I'm not sure what group it is off the top of my head, but this looks like the Viking tree."

"Yggdrasil?" I asked, thinking back to my conversation with Vida this afternoon.

"That's the one."

"Don't they talk about that one in *American Gods*?" Kyle asked, waggling his fingers to ask to see the phone one more time. "Where the one god hangs himself to, what, prevent the end of the world?"

"I never pegged you for a Gaiman fan, Kyle," I said, impressed despite myself.

"Who? No, I binged the TV show on Starz last year." That was more like him.

"Either way, that part's based on real Norse mythology. I was talking to an expert on hate crimes this afternoon and she was telling me all about it. I didn't connect it to the tattoo, though. Good catch." I took my phone back, refusing to glance at the notifications before slipping it into my purse. "From what I gathered, not all hate groups hate the same things, and in fact some of them hate one another—but my source was more social justice than law enforcement, so I wanted to see if y'all had anything different to contribute."

"In theory, infighting among groups would be inevitable with tensions running as high as they are," DonnaJo said, "but I can't point to a specific case or anything."

Kyle shook his head. "Me neither."

The server arrived balancing a huge tray of large plates that all smelled amazing, and conversation dwindled as everyone dug in. For a while, the only sounds were the scraping of silverware and the soft, elegant background music playing through hidden speakers.

Kyle was the first to bring us back into conversation. "So, you have a dead neo-Nazi, but that's only one story. You said you had three."

I swallowed and nodded. "My old pal Troy Wright is running a group for LGBT teens at the local community center. I'm going to tag along to the next meeting and hopefully write a feature to run concurrent with the Richmond City Pride celebrations." Even though Pride Month was June, Richmond's parade and festivities were in September; we were just a little too close to DC to compete with their much larger events. "That'll hopefully be a solid feel-good piece to balance out my other story."

"And what's that one?" DonnaJo met my eyes over the bottle of wine sitting between us.

I filled them in on the basics of my interviews with Holden—"Damn," Kyle said—and Coach Farrelly—"What an asshole," Joey agreed.

"I think the coach is someone's puppet, but his whole vibe rubbed me the wrong way. I hope the drug test I was able to set up for Holden will be enough to put things right, but if they really want him gone, I can't run interference for him forever, either."

"Just making people aware should put the offenders in hot water, don't you think?" DonnaJo asked. "I mean, it's worked for you before—countless times."

"It's a little outside of my beat, but I'm hopeful. Especially since the editor at the school paper—apparently she's a fan of mine, as weird as that sounds—promised to amplify my story, whatever it turns out to be."

When I mentioned the photos and messages threatening Troy, all three of them went still and stiff. Joey's hand rested, warm and reassuring, on my thigh. Kyle laid his fork down on the side of his plate.

"You ought to let Aaron know," Kyle said. "The PD can keep an eye on Troy and his mom, or maybe track the sender. There's every possibility it's just kids being assholes, but it's safer to have the local authorities in the loop."

"I will call Aaron first thing tomorrow."

The wine disappeared along with the food, the conversation light and easy for another hour. DonnaJo completed several of Kyle's sentences and zinged home several sharp jokes that had us all laughing. I couldn't help marveling at how perfectly matched she and Kyle were, and Kyle's unabashedly lovestruck expression made my heart happy.

Things work out as they should. I could hear my mom's voice like she was sitting next to me. Joey snatched the check right out of the server's hand before Kyle could make a play for it, hugs were exchanged at the front door, and I paused to kiss Joey as he held my car door.

"You were right," I said when we were back in the quiet of his Lincoln with the AC blasting. "That was exactly what I needed tonight."

"Always happy to help, love."

"Thanks." I curled my fingers around his, my thoughts winding back to Holden and Troy and the photos. I hoped Aaron didn't have big weekend plans.

10

The high, keening whir of the coffee grinder woke me before the sun was up. Groaning, I patted the cold sheets next to me and dove under my pillow. I loved my Keurig, but Joey drank coffee like he drank wine—nothing but freshly ground beans in his French press would do. I was just fuzzy on why he was up at dark-thirty. Saturdays are for sleeping in—it's almost a commandment around here.

I squeezed my eyes shut when I heard Darcy's claws on the bedroom door, hoping she'd go back to her bed. The slight squeak of the hinge when Joey opened the door to shush her was my cue to sit up.

"Sorry, love." He disappeared but returned before I had all the sleep wiped from my eyes, a steaming mug in his hand. "Peace offering?"

I sipped the coffee. It really was good his way.

"Where are you running off to at such an ungodly hour on a Saturday?" I asked around a yawn, taking in his pressed slacks, crisp blue Oxford with the sleeves rolled up, showing off tan forearms, and gray tie.

"Site visit, remember?" Exhaustion lent his voice a sexy, gravelly note that made me want to wrap his tie around my hand and pull him close. It must've shown on my face—he stepped back and smiled. "Our big potential client is expecting me." He offered a slow smile. "Rain check, Miss Clarke?"

"Looking forward to it." I tried to make my voice a sexy purr, but it was too early for that so it came out more like a croak. I sipped my coffee, the cup a good cover for my burning cheeks.

Thankfully, Joey was either too in love with me or too distracted thinking about his meeting to notice. He leaned in for a kiss, lingering a beat longer than could be considered chaste, before backing out the door. "Until tonight, beautiful."

I took my coffee and wandered to the living room in bare feet and a soft cotton nightgown, settling on the sofa with my laptop. I sent Bob an email with an update on my stories as they stood, adding Vida's well wishes to the last line.

Darcy let herself in through the dog door, curling into a warm little fluff ball next to my hip and tucking her nose behind her tail. I stroked her fur as I turned Holden's story over in my head again, considering Farrelly's vague words from every possible angle as I finished the coffee. By the time I set my empty mug on the table, I went to the kitchen to get my phone. Sun streaming through the windows meant it was time to track Aaron down.

His cell went straight to voicemail. I opened my weather app and grinned when I saw the heat had broken overnight. Dumping Darcy's breakfast into her bowl on my way out of the kitchen, I pulled on cream linen shorts and a raspberry tank top, sliding my feet into a pair of low-heeled cream sandals because stilettos and boats don't mix. And Aaron White wouldn't be anywhere on a gorgeous late-summer Saturday except on his boat on the Appomattox with a fishing rod in his hand.

Two could enjoy the lovely weather as easily as one.

The warmth of the sun on my skin felt heavenly as I strode quickly up the dock thirty minutes later, spotting my favorite detective running through a check of the boat's exterior before heading out.

"Morning, Detective," I called when he waved. "You up for a passenger today?"

"How is it that you always manage to catch me right before I push off?" he asked, his smile softening his gruff tone.

"Could be because I know you pretty well after all this time. Got time for some questions?"

"You're welcome to come aboard if you're not here to stress me out. My wife has been worried about my blood pressure, and we both know you're the source of all the stress in my life."

"Oh, come on—Charlie is way more stressful than I am. And that's not even counting Mark." I took his proffered hand and clambered onto the deck of the *Alyssa Lynn*—named for his daughters.

Aaron laughed and started up the engine, pointing to the bench where he stowed spare life jackets. I buckled one on and took a seat in the corner, watching Aaron's brow furrow with concentration as he backed the thirty-foot craft out of the slip, making a tight turn feel almost effortless as we moved into the river. He eased the throttle forward, the wind whipping my hair out behind me, and I reveled in the cool breeze off the water, the warm sun on my shoulders, and the light tickle of spray on my arms. The Appomattox River was hemmed in on both sides by thick woods in peak green, but I could already picture the palette in October, when autumn settled in: fiery reds, oranges, and yellows as far as the eye could see.

"Does this mean I get to ask as many questions as I want while you fish?" I raised my voice to be heard over the growl of the engine and got a mouthful of my own hair for my trouble.

"Figured even you could use a break from the ground beneath your feet." He grinned, shouting over the wind. "You'll scare the fish away talking—we're just taking a spin."

A few minutes later, the engine quieted and Aaron guided the boat into a small cove off the edge of the river, pointing over the edge. I looked down and gasped at the silvery flashes of fish darting around the sandy bottom twenty feet below us.

"The water is still enough over here for silt to settle to the bottom," Aaron said.

"It's lovely." I smiled.

"I like the quiet," he said, waving a hand around.

I stilled; the leaves whispering against each other overhead, the water lapping at the sides of the boat, and our breathing were the only sounds. Living and working in the city, I very rarely experienced true silence. It was idyllic and peaceful—and brought a missing helping of clarity after a crazy couple of days.

Aaron dropped down beside me, cracking open a bottle he'd retrieved from a small Igloo cooler. "I'd offer you a beer, but seeing as how it's early and you probably have a lot planned for the day—don't give me that look." Aaron barked out a laugh at my puzzled frown. "I know you, Nichelle. No such thing as weekends when you've got your teeth in something." He shook his head. "Ask away, but you know I reserve the right to refuse comment."

I rolled my eyes at him, unable to keep a smile off my lips. I missed him. I missed this—our familiar banter was once one of the things I loved most about my job. Widening my areas of interest had not been everything I thought it would be when I started at *RVA Week*, but I didn't know what to do about it, so I focused on the moment. Right then, I had questions for Aaron that only Aaron could answer, and that was enough.

"Well, your blood pressure will be pleased that I'm not here about Mervin Rosser." I planned on keeping what I'd dug up about Rosser close to my chest, at least for now. There were a few more things I needed to dig up there before I'd know if he was worth writing about.

"In that case," Aaron leaned back and mock-saluted me with his beer bottle, "I am at your service."

"I'm looking into a discrimination case—a possible one, anyway—with a bright college quarterback and a powerful football coach at its center." I watched his eyebrow go up. Always a good sign. "Troy Wright put this one on my radar."

"Troy Wright? As in Darryl Wright's brother?" Aaron huffed out a sigh. "It still pains me to think about that kid." The hand not holding the bottle tightened like a claw on Aaron's knee.

I rested my own hand gently on his, feeling the cords of tension in his fingers ease at the touch. "You had nothing to do with that, Aaron." Indeed, Aaron had been instrumental in helping Darryl get the justice he deserved, even if he had been too late to save Darryl's life.

He grunted. It was impossible to tell whether he was protesting, acquiescing, or just acknowledging my statement. "How is Troy?"

"Doing well. Really well, for the most part. He's found some things he's really passionate about, and he's fighting hard for them." It wasn't my place to "out" Troy as gay, so I left that information out. "But he jumped headlong into this bigotry thing by way of a credited opinion piece in the campus paper, and he's getting some online threats. One in particular that has me worried."

"Start with that one." Aaron leaned forward, resting his elbows on his bare knees, tan from a summer of Saturdays on the water.

I filled Aaron in on the basics of Holden's story: coming out, failing the drug test, being benched, accusing Coach Farrelly (or his staff) of homophobia, the utter silence from local media showing Holden's perspective, and Troy's rise to his defense. "The one he showed me yesterday was nothing but photos of his house here in Richmond and his mom's car."

Aaron ran a hand over his face, the scratch of his calloused fingers over the fine dusting of stubble on his chin and jaw audible in the peaceful setting. "I don't like that, either—let me put our cyber unit on it. Depending on what they find, we'll figure out how to make sure Troy and his mom stay safe."

"Thanks, Aaron." The words came out like a sigh, the wave of relief so acute it surprised me. Even discounting his lingering guilt over what happened to Troy's brother, Aaron was a good cop. I trusted him to take care of my friends.

He sipped his beer, his face telling me he was thinking. Probably about perceived mistakes from long ago.

"So, while I have you, how's the Rosser case going?" I bumped his shoulder lightly with my own.

"Blood pressure," Aaron warned with a twinkle in his blue eyes. "This is off the record, of course." He waited for my nod.

"If I'm being honest, it's not going much of anywhere at the moment. There's a lot of...tangential factors we're taking into consideration."

He didn't want to tell me the guy was a neo-Nazi. Which also explained why Charlie didn't have it. She wasn't above traipsing around the woods, but quasi–breaking and entering and not-so-quasi-trespassing wasn't her scene.

"Mervin Rosser's background is much more interesting than Charlie let on in her report yesterday." Maybe showing a couple of my cards would get Aaron to admit a thing or two I didn't already know. I didn't need him on the record, I just needed to know where to look to get a better sense of why the guy was dead.

Aaron's head tipped to one side. "Interesting in what way?"

I raised my eyebrows but said nothing.

Aaron sighed. "How do you always know so much more than everyone else?" He raised a hand. "Never mind. Because you're not afraid to get in the trenches, same as every good cop I've ever worked with. That's why we get along so well, me and you—we do what it takes to get to the truth." He pulled the Saturday edition of the *Telegraph* from the pocket on the back of the seat across from us.

I scanned Mark's front-page story—it didn't get anywhere near the Nazi angle. So he wasn't the break-into-the-vic's-house type, either. Though with Mark I suspected laziness over scruples there. After all, was it really breaking in if the door was unlocked?

Mark did detail Mervin's arrest record (one assault, one charge of possession with intent to distribute), plus he went to Mervin's place of employment and spoke with the other drivers and the owner. Owner said Mervin was often late, so he didn't think much about it when Mervin quit showing up. The other drivers said he seemed standoffish, kept to himself.

All that fit the profile Vida had given me. Was Mervin actually quiet, or did the other drivers just not fit his idea of worthwhile social partners? Knowing a little more about how the group dynamics worked, I could imagine Mervin tossing out some white supremacy code lingo, testing the waters, and, when it fell flat, choosing to ignore coworkers who weren't like-minded. Any diversity in the group would likely have fueled Mervin's prejudice.

I kept those thoughts to myself, though, folding the paper up and handing it back to Aaron. "Well, I'll say this for Mark: he saved me an immediate trip to the Coldtown warehouse. I can chase other leads instead."

"This guy was not a popular fellow." Aaron held my gaze. "Anywhere, it seems."

I nodded understanding, twisting my lips to one side.

"Does this mean you want me to get you back to the dock so you can go back to saving the world?"

"Only our little corner of it." I grinned as he settled back into the captain's chair.

My hair was a little worse for wear thanks to the wind, but I'd gotten what I came for—with an interesting bonus, too. Once my feet were back on solid ground, I wished Aaron good luck with his fishing and turned for home.

My phone showed a missed call from Bob, who probably wanted more details and the official teaser for Tuesday's story on Holden and Farrelly. Thanks to Joey's early meeting, it wasn't even ten yet—I had practically all day to write up what I had, get Bob up to speed, and dive a little deeper into LGBTQIA+ statistics both nationally and in the Richmond area.

And if I got through all that, I had a dead guy with plenty of enemies that might make him a whole lot more interesting.

11

Almost half of LGBTQ youth seriously considered attempting suicide in the past year.

I started at the results of a sweeping survey of the mental health of America's LGBTQ young people on my screen, shaking my head as I copied yet another harrowing statistic into my notes file. In an hour alone with Google, I had found enough to feel confident in my ability to weave them into Holden and Farrelly's story, making the issue bigger than just one young man at one school.

Such was often the case with stories like these—if it was happening in one place, it was likely happening elsewhere, though the sheer pervasiveness of prejudice I'd found was downright unsettling. Every source I checked, from the Trevor Project to the ACLU to the NCAA to dozens of court records from across the country that I cross-referenced, told the same story: gay men aren't welcome in high-level sports in many places.

My job was to knit Holden's local story to the larger national scope in a way that gave my readers the same cold shock of realization I confronted while gathering the data.

I opened a blank file and started typing.

Holden Peters threw for 417 yards in the season opener, completing 34 of 46 passes without a single interception or sack. It's a record that builds on Peters's finish last season, a six-game winning streak fueled by what the Washington Post *called "laser-perfect precision in the passing game" that turned around a rocky start for his team. The strong start this year has Heisman chatter pinging around the internet, followed closely by musings of the Bulldogs' first Bowl appearance in more than twenty years—all of which would logically have Head Coach Don Farrelly using every bit of his considerable influence to back his star quarterback.*

Instead, Farrelly benched Peters in the second week of the season, citing drug test results he refused to share with RVA Week *pending the advice of the university's attorneys. Peters denies the allegation of drug use and contends that his decision to come out as a gay man playing Division 1 football is the real reason for his sudden demotion.*

"Seeing people still plagued by that fear I had as that scrawny kid, I figured I could...I don't know...give them hope? Like letting the world know who I was might make other people feel safer doing the same," Peters said. "I waited until I had a solid future in front of me. My place with the team was secure—I thought. I had a coach who talked in the locker room about individuality strengthening the team, about seeking peace and seeing your game explode with the increase it brings to your focus. But I guess peace is reserved for folks who aren't quite as 'individual' as I am."

I lost myself in the rhythm of the keystrokes, hearing Holden and Farrelly in my head as I worked, checking my notes occasionally for accuracy.

By the time I heard the kitchen door close behind Joey just before dinnertime, I had the first third of my story done. Bob had given the teaser a resounding thumbs-up, and I was pleased with what an afternoon in front of my screen had produced so far.

My productivity had also produced a rumbling stomach, since I hadn't eaten lunch. Which meant the prospect of some time with Joey—and Joey's cooking—took priority, even over the story I'd been lost in for hours. I saved my draft and stowed my laptop.

"Nichelle?"

I would never get over the sound of Joey's voice echoing off my walls, nor the warmth that stole through me at having someone who would walk in the door and want to see me first thing. It still felt so novel, and I never wanted to take it—or him—for granted.

I hurried toward the hallway, but Darcy beat me to it. I found Joey on his knees, completely unbothered that my very fluffy dog was shedding all over his Armani trousers. He really did treat her like a princess.

He caught me watching from the doorway and was on his feet and in front of me in a blink. His hand was warm and heavy on my waist, his eyes were all dark smolder, his lips on mine before I could catch the breath he always seemed to take right away.

"Well, hello to you, too," I said.

"You have it's-been-a-long-day face." He tugged my hand gently as he turned back toward the kitchen. "I'm not even going to ask if you ate because I know you probably didn't." He winked, ducking into the refrigerator. "I, for one, am famished, so I'll throw together something quick."

"Something quick" turned out to be pan-seared steak and asparagus with some sort of delightfully citrusy seasoning.

Not a combination I would have considered—if I knew how to make much of anything but Pop-Tarts, anyway—but holy Manolos, Joey could make anything work. Paired with a fruity merlot, the food was fantastic—and he took it from fridge to table in fifteen minutes.

"How was the site visit?" I asked once half my steak was gone and my stomach was quiet.

"The client definitely has a lot of big ideas, but I can work with him."

His face said he wasn't as excited about the project as he'd been earlier in the week. "Not too micromanaging, I hope?"

"I think he just wants to know his project is important to me. Which is why I meet all the clients and visit all of the sites on a regular basis." He swirled his wineglass in hand, laying his fork alongside his plate. "Keeps me busy, plus I enjoy talking to the people who are actually putting in the sweat out on the job sites. I went by the assisted living project in Church Hill on my way home, and those guys are busting their asses—they're almost a full week ahead of schedule."

I took another bite of steak and nodded a *go on* at him.

He obliged, telling stories of young men on their first big contract, of seasoned construction veterans, and everything in between as I finished my food. The lone constant was his obvious interest in each of them. After so many years of running interference for some relatively shitty human beings, Joey was in his element running the contracting company, and he liked being aware of and catering to the needs of his employees.

"How about your day? Do I need to be on the lookout for cars casing the house?" He turned to the window for dramatic effect, even though the kitchen window didn't face the street.

"Productive, yes. Dangerous, no." I scraped the last of the sauce onto my final bite of steak and popped it into my mouth before I laid my fork down and summarized my conversation with Aaron.

"I spent most of the day in front of my computer. But I'm chipping away at Holden's story, and it should be ready for Bob's review first thing Monday."

"And what about the dead Nazi? Does what White hinted at mean we still care about his murder?"

I took a fortifying sip of wine, because even thinking about Mervin brought me back into his living room and the walls plastered with hatred. "We damn sure don't care for old Mervin personally—not even a little bit. After going to his house and seeing what sort of person he was, I could never."

"But," Joey prompted, leaning forward to catch my eye.

"But I'm still waiting to hear back from Vida about what group he might be affiliated with, and I'd like to know just exactly who Aaron might have been talking about today when he said the guy wasn't well liked anywhere. Then I'll be in better shape to decide if there's a story worth pursuing here."

"You could always talk to Bob about it."

"I will if I find anything worthwhile. Both Charlie and Mark have already moved on, and I wonder if they're right."

"I know that look."

"What look?"

"The look that says your gut is telling you there's a story here, even if your brain is a little slow on the uptake."

"I have no idea what you're talking about." I feigned indignance.

Joey laughed, a sexy rumble that raised goose bumps on my arms even though we were talking about murder. "Sure you don't. Want to talk me through it? What's got you torn?"

"At face value, a dead white supremacist isn't all that newsworthy, at least not for the kind of in-depth coverage I do these days. It's the execution-style aspect of it that's keeping my attention. That part nags at my sense that there's more to this than face value. Jacque's likely scenario is almost Godfather-like." I paused, my lips popping into a soundless little "o."

"I swear to you I know nothing about this." Joey reached for my hand, his voice downright earnest. "If that's what you're worried about."

"No. Well. Not really." I flashed an apologetic smile and squeezed his hand. "I'm thinking more that if there really are rivalries between these groups and outbreaks of violence mixed up in that, that's something people would read about. Talk about. Maybe even learn something from. Plus, if that's the case, this guy may not be the last victim."

"By that logic, he may not be the first either."

I froze, my fingers tightening on his hand.

That's what I'd been trying to parse out of the puzzle running around my brain, but it just wouldn't come to the front.

"You okay, love?" Joey used his free hand to extricate his strangled fingers from my grip, appearing oblivious to the nuclear warhead of a revelation he'd just dropped into my lap.

I shook my head, smiling. "Sorry. Too many puzzle pieces. I'm fine." If I let on that I might even consider going hunting for other dead Nazis, he would lose his shit. I prefer to avoid that unless it's absolutely necessary. "Just trying to figure out some of his connections, but with no next of kin, no roommate or significant other, and locked-down social media profiles, I'm at a dead end until Vida gets back to me."

"I wonder if Chad knows a way to get around that."

Chad Rowe, my best friend's husband and my go-to for all questions computer-related, was a software developer and sometime hacker. He had helped me on multiple cases in the past where my own basic Googling skills weren't up to the task of rousing information from the depths of the internet.

I laughed. "Chad is smart, but I doubt he's smart enough to crack Facebook's security."

"Might be worth asking. Just...be careful, Nichelle." Joey reached across the table and laced his fingers with mine. "I know you always try to be, but sometimes the thrill of the chase gets you in over your head, and I worry. These hate groups are a nasty business. While I don't know much about people like that—I always found them desperate and demeaning and distasteful, and a good handful of other d-words, I'm sure—I do know that kind of hate can eat away at a person until it makes them dangerous." His voice was wistful and almost sad as he said that last part, his thumb making slow circles over my knuckles.

Probably thinking about his brother, but I knew better than to ask. We hadn't talked much about Jordan after the showdown in the Great Dismal Swamp last winter, and I didn't want to pry. Joey knew himself better than anyone I'd ever met, and had since the first time I met him. He would talk when he was ready.

"Let me clean up." I stood. "You go stretch out on the sofa—I think there's a baseball game on."

He brushed his lips over my knuckles as I picked up his plate, sending sparks skating up my arm. "Don't take too long." The look in his eyes turned the sparks into fireworks.

"Wouldn't dream of it."

Dishwasher running, I ducked outside to play fetch with Darcy when she scratched at my leg, her poor belabored squirrel in her jaws.

I threw the well-loved toy for the dog and touched Jenna's name in my favorites list.

"Hey, stranger—I was just talking about driving over there to check on you." The grin and wink were implied in her words, but I flinched at the sting anyway.

I knew I had kind of been neglecting our friendship as I got used to the ebb and flow of life with a live-in boyfriend, but I didn't realize it bothered her. And here I was calling to ask her for a favor rather than chat. Damn.

"I miss you, too." I chucked the squirrel toy to the far corner of the yard for Darcy to chase. "I'm sorry, honey. I'm juggling a couple big cases right now, and—"

"Finally!" She screeched loud enough to make me pull the phone away from my head. "It's been ages since you had a juicy murder, and Charlie Lewis just flat isn't as good as you at getting the nitty-gritty good stuff. Spill. Anything we can help with?"

I grinned, squatting to take the toy from the dog and scratch her ears. Thank God for good—and insatiably curious—friends.

"How's a dead Nazi for intrigue?" I gave her a brief rundown on Mervin, swearing her to secrecy on the white supremacy angle, before asking if Chad could do some extra digging.

"Sweetie, we'd be a lot more comfortable financially if he could hack Facebook, but he can effectively play internet Hardy Boys and string the guy's connections together until he gets to something that might be useful, if that would help." I heard rummaging followed by the click of a pen. "Can you spell his name for me? That was an odd one."

I did before turning the conversation to her kids and the bookstore, laughing at a story about a collector from New York who insisted on paying four grand for a canvas Carson had finger-painted in primary colors.

"Dude said he knew 'true genius' when he saw it, and who am I to argue?" Jenna laughed. "So, Carson has a college fund now."

"Auntie Nicey will get him some supplies in case the collector has friends." I giggled.

"He'll credit you in the program at his first gallery show." She hooted with laughter.

"Let's do something soon?" Girls' night would look a bit different with Joey waiting at home, but I'd figure it out. "Let me know when you're free."

"I'd love that." Warmth dripped from the words. "I'm so damn glad you're so happy, Nicey, but I miss you."

"Same. Love you, Jen."

Darcy disappeared into the house as I said goodbye to Jenna, so I followed. We piled onto the couch with Joey just in time to catch a grand slam that tied the score in the bottom of the ninth. We gave up on the game and went to bed in the middle of the thirteenth inning, not that the late hour meant Joey was too tired to make good on his earlier promises. An hour of fireworks later, I drifted to sleep with my head in the spot between his shoulder and chest where it fit so perfectly, thankful for everything in my life outside work and sure I could find a way back to happiness with my job with a couple more lucky breaks.

12

"It's six thirty in the morning, Aaron," I mumbled. "On Sunday."

"You are not the only one of us irritated with the time." The serious clip to Aaron's words yanked me fully out of half-slumber.

I sat up, sweeping my hair out of my pillow-creased face.

"What's wrong?" I asked.

"McNally in our cyber unit took a personal interest in your friend Troy yesterday, and he called me about ten minutes ago. He says most of the comments and DMs Troy has been getting are originating from university computers, which isn't terribly concerning—there are multiple profiles coming from a handful of IPs, so it's really only a small group of people hassling him. He's working on physical addresses, and once we have them, we'll share with the local PD there."

"That's great, thank you." I held my breath because I knew in my bones that wasn't why he called me at this hour on a Sunday.

"The one you showed me, with his mother's home and her vehicle in frame, is different." He sighed.

There it was. I shuddered. Joey's warm hand moved to my back.

"The IP address for that account traces to a guy with a record for assault with a deadly weapon. He ran over someone with a car after a bar fight, which he instigated." Aaron paused. "Nichelle, he has some possible ties online to extremist groups. I don't like this."

"Me, either." I shoved the blankets aside, trying to calm myself with Vida's words about how few of the people in the groups they tracked actually made the leap from talk to action.

Didn't work. All I could think about was Joyce, who had buried one son, and how we might be able to keep her from having to bury another.

"I need to go talk to them." Aaron's voice was softer now, the roughness smoothed under genuine empathy. "Will you come with me?"

"Of course. I'll meet you there in half an hour. The sun will be up by then." I gave him the address and hung up.

I got out of bed as the coffee grinder came on in the kitchen. By the time I was dressed in simple gray pants and a peach blouse with a pair of killer peach Manolos on my feet, Joey had coffee in my favorite pink travel mug and a packet of frosted strawberry Pop-Tarts waiting on the counter by the door.

He glanced up from the *Wall Street Journal* when I hurried past the table. "White didn't like whatever he found about the photos someone sent the Wright kid." He didn't bother with the inflection of a question.

I turned and kissed his temple. "Bingo. I'm on my way to meet Aaron at Troy's house."

He caught me around the waist before I could step away, standing to give me a much deeper goodbye kiss than I was prepared for. If it wasn't for his arm around me, I may have just collapsed into a puddle right there. "Have a good day." He tapped me on the nose with one finger, released me, and settled back in with his coffee and his newspaper.

"You too." I caught a deep breath.

I hoped that never got old. But right then, I had a friend who needed my help.

～

I pulled up in front of the Wright house twenty-five minutes later, carrying coffee for four in a tray. Joey had infected me with his coffee snobbery, so when I'd finished the to-go cup before I made it three blocks from home,

I'd veered a few more out of my way to get drinks from Lamplighters, a new place that even roasted their own beans. It felt a little weird to go to a high-end coffeeshop and order a white mocha, a caramel macchiato, a vanilla latte, and a cappuccino, but that's what I did. The mocha, latte, and cappuccino came complete with coffee art on the surfaces so intricate I almost didn't want to put lids on them. But I was in a hurry, so I complimented the barista, covered her designs, shoved the cups in a tray, and set off.

Aaron was out of his unmarked Crown Vic as soon as he saw my car pull up. I passed him the cappuccino as we approached the door. He gave me a solemn nod of thanks but didn't smile. His worry slid through me like ice in the middle of a muggy late-August morning.

"Nichelle Clarke!" Joyce beamed as she opened the door. "Girl, when am I going to get a chance to return some of the favors you keep doing for my baby and me?"

"Good morning, Joyce. I'm afraid we come bearing bad news, but I brought you coffee."

"Mrs. Wright," Aaron said so stiffly I turned my head and blinked. "Nice to see you again." It was the first time I'd ever heard his trademark charm fail him.

Joyce's smile faded when she recognized him, but she continued radiating hospitality, thanking me for the "fancy coffee" and enveloping me in a tight, maternal embrace when we stepped inside. She shook hands with Aaron and waved us into seats at her worn but spotless kitchen table while she went to wake Troy.

Aaron fidgeted with the cardboard sleeve on the outside of his coffee cup. His tension had all my alarm bells ringing. I took a sip of my white mocha. Damn. Maybe there was something to be said for snobbery.

"Hey, Nichelle." Troy dropped into the seat across from me, all smiles and long limbs. His eyes slid to Aaron, and he straightened slightly and gave a polite nod. "Detective." Watching Troy, one of the smartest, quickest-witted young men I'd ever met, react to Aaron's presence by immediately going on guard was unsettling. Especially given that I'd never felt anything but safe around Aaron. It made me sad—but I understood.

Joyce puttered around behind us, keeping her hands busy. Maybe to calm her own nerves? My stomach turned a slow somersault when she took a seat beside me, across from Aaron. The room felt much smaller with our little circle complete.

Troy took a massive swallow of his caramel macchiato. "Thank you, Nichelle."

I nodded. He didn't speak again. Joyce was silent too, holding herself perfectly straight and still, one hand wrapped around her coffee cup, the other on Troy's knee, which was bouncing under the table.

Aaron's gaze flickered between Joyce and her son, unsure where to begin. He straightened his shoulders, squirming like his shirt was too tight. I hated that his presence might be bothering them, but they needed him there. Aaron was rattled by what his cyber detective had told him, and he doesn't rattle easily.

"I asked Aaron for his advice about the messages you'd been receiving." I directed my full attention at Troy, trying to give a silent signal for him to stop me if I said anything his mom was unaware of. I caught his subtle nod and relaxed. "What the RPD cyber unit found was enough to worry him, and he needs to talk with y'all about the best way to make sure everyone is safe. Y'all know I'll help in any way I can."

Joyce's breath went in sharply, her head bobbing slowly as she met Aaron's gaze.

"You testified against them. At the trial," she said.

"And a verdict has never brought me so much personal joy," he said. "I only wish I'd figured out what was going on in time to save your boy." He blinked hard. "I have two girls, one about the same age as Darryl. I am so sorry for your loss, ma'am."

Joyce didn't blink, staring at Aaron for a good two minutes like she was looking straight through him. He held her gaze, unwavering, his face an open book on empathy and regret. Troy watched his mother. I watched Troy.

"Thank you, Detective White." Joyce's voice was warmer, both hands going to her coffee cup.

"Please call me Aaron, ma'am, if you're so inclined."

"Then we'll dispense with *ma'am* as well, Aaron." Joyce smiled, and the tension lying heavy over the room shattered.

"As you wish." Aaron returned the smile, his voice slipping closer to the easy, confident tone I was used to. "Troy, we tracked the sender of some of the more concerning messages to a local man with a history of assault and possible hate group affiliations. I'd like to put a patrol unit on the house for a few days, just to be careful."

Joyce's hand went to her throat, and Aaron reached across the table. She took his offered hand, letting out a shuddering breath. "How much danger is my son in, Aaron?"

"These guys usually have pretty short attention spans. He'll find something else to direct his hatred at and move along in a week or so most likely, but I think an abundance of caution is warranted here."

A protective unit was procedure, but the RPD hadn't exactly earned the trust of the folks in this neighborhood, and I wasn't sure how welcome the offer would be.

Joyce let go of Aaron's hand, sitting back in her chair and patting Troy's knee. His eyebrows drew down over the bridge of his nose as he watched his mother.

"With all due respect," Troy said, turning to Aaron, "I appreciate the concern, but having a patrol car just kind of lurking about might make the neighbors uncomfortable. This block is all good, hardworking folks who look out for one another, Detective. I'm sure we'll be just fine."

Aaron and I looked at Joyce, both of us sure she wouldn't risk Troy's safety.

"I know some of Darryl's old friends from the football team are still in the neighborhood," she said. "I'm sure they wouldn't mind keeping an eye on Darryl's momma."

Aaron nodded. He got it. I did, too.

"Maybe you should stay home for a while, too, Troy," I said.

"I absolutely will not leave my mom until I know she's safe."

I reached across the table and patted his hand. "Don't worry too much, all right?" But of course he was going to worry. I knew how his relationship with his mom was because it felt so much like my own relationship with my single mother—who I suddenly felt a pressing need to call.

Aaron interrupted my thoughts by pulling out his card and setting it on the table between Joyce and Troy. "If you see or hear anything, anything at all, that even just makes you feel weird, you give me a call, okay? Anytime, day or night."

"We'll do that, Aaron," Joyce said.

"Thank you," Troy said, looking at us both. "It was kind of you to come."

That was our cue. Aaron and I stood in a unison so perfect one might have thought we'd choreographed it. Aaron shook hands again with both Troy and Joyce at the door. I gave them each a parting hug.

"I'll see you on Tuesday," I reminded Troy.

He grinned back, his dimples out in full force. "My kids and I can't wait."

With the door shut behind us, Aaron visibly deflated. I could tell he wanted a moment to gather his thoughts, so we sipped our coffee at the end of Joyce's sidewalk.

"Thanks for helping them," I said.

He looked back at the house. "Like they said, their neighbors will keep an eye on them, and more if they ask for it." He nodded, like he was talking himself into the idea. "These are people who know the neighborhood: the familiar cars, the regular visitors. They would notice anything amiss without attracting the kind of attention a patrol car would."

"That makes me feel better," I said.

"It makes me feel better that I've already got a unit watching the guy who sent the threats, so odds are good that they'll be safe." He smiled. "I'll still feel better when Cyber tells me that activity from that particular IP address is directed elsewhere."

We crossed the street to our parked cars.

"Any updates on Mervin Rosser?" I asked.

"Off the record," he said, giving me a look that said he was about to share something interesting, "it's on a back burner for us as of yesterday. I know you already know Rosser was involved with a hate group. We have on good authority from a UC that it's likely that was the cause of his death. It may not be ideal, but the fact is we have limited resources, and if Nazis want to execute each other, I'm not sure that leaves the community worse off. Landers will stay on it when he has time."

I willed my face blank. "Thanks, Aaron."

"I know I called you about this guy, Nichelle, but knowing what I do now, I'm not sure there's a story there. And the kind of people who might know that for sure aren't the kind of people you want to go ask."

He climbed into his car and drove off. I did the same, my brain trying to arrange the new pieces of both puzzles. There had to be a larger story with Mervin: an underground world of hate groups with lines drawn and infighting that could lead to a kind of Al Capone gangster-style slaying. And I hadn't missed that whoever was threatening Troy was part of such a group.

I couldn't make anything fit together yet, but my gut said there were more puzzle pieces waiting to be uncovered.

Sunday's *Telegraph* had no further mention of Mervin, not even a bare-bones follow-up. I couldn't help smiling to myself on the drive home. Mark was already bored of this story, even though I knew there was more, potentially a lot more, than he'd bothered to dig for.

I texted Bob as soon as I pulled into the driveway at home.

Finally ahead on a crime story. Not a feature!! It had definitely been two exclamation points' worth of too long since I'd beaten out the dailies. *The Telegraph guy has zip on the murder vic today, cops are walking away, and I already know more than anyone else!* Three exclamation points, even.

Buzz. *Don't count Charlie out yet, kid.* Bob's first text was a cold splash of reality. But I smiled at the second: *But I'm cautiously optimistic.*

13

Bob called me into his office the second he heard my Louboutins on the tile Monday morning.

"I'm being caref—" The rest of the word got stuck in my throat when I rounded the corner to find Bob seated behind his desk, with Evan Connolly, the owner of *RVA Week*, propped against the corner, arms folded across his chest, watching the door. Irritation radiated off Connolly thicker than the amazing potato soup Joey had whipped up for dinner the night before.

"What's going on?" I shut the door without being asked, my feet widening into a defensive posture all on their own. It took effort to keep my arms loose at my sides.

"Breathe, kiddo," Bob said. "It's not what you think, but we do need to talk."

I sank into my regular burnt-orange velour armchair, which lived in the corner opposite Connolly's, glad for the space between me and my boss's boss. Despite Bob's assurances, I couldn't quite ease the spike of dread in my gut. Connolly was usually pretty hands-off now that the *Week* had been in Bob's capable hands for a year. In the early days, Connolly had been a staple in the office, often hosting all-hands meetings which felt silly when the staff barely numbered in double digits. Recently, though, he'd been more than a little scarce. Parker had heard a rumor he'd bought another paper in South Carolina and preferred Charleston to Richmond. "Fine by me," Parker had said. "Let him drive them batshit crazy for a while."

Connolly ran a hand along his jaw. "I got a...concerning call from one of our major advertisers on Saturday." He leveled his gaze at me. "He threatened to pull his entire account if we run this story about Don Farrelly and this quarterback controversy. Apparently, he's an alum—and the coach is a personal friend."

My jaw dropped. I wasn't quite sure I could speak if I'd wanted to, but any words I might have managed would probably have been shouted. Was this really what privately funded weekly newsmagazines would come down to? Pulling a story because of some advertiser's personal grudges? Wasn't that exactly the kind of corruption I spent so much time rooting out in my stories? Connolly was a wealthy and well-connected guy, but he'd done a lot of preaching about "unapologetically honest" reporting. Could I really have been this wrong about him? And what the hell was Bob just sitting there for?

"Are you serious right now?" I finally sputtered.

Connolly's face broke into a wide grin. "No, Nichelle, wait." His laugh was startlingly bright, like a clamor of bells. "I didn't come here to squash your story. We've been in the black most of this year, and fortunately for you and that young quarterback, I can well afford to lose this jackass's money. We'll pick up other advertisers for having the guts to run something no one else will." He shrugged. "That's the way business works. Besides, two things I know are that I hate a bully, and an investigative journalist is really doing her job when someone with as much power as the coach is trying to keep her quiet. Nice work, Clarke. This is why I wanted you here."

He clapped me on the shoulder on his way out. All I could do was stare at Bob for a solid minute. So much for my general ability to read a room.

"I thought he was going to fire me!" I burst out. "And then for a minute when he said the bit about the guy pulling his ads, I thought I was going to quit—warn a person next time, would you?"

Bob laughed. "I did warn you that it wasn't what you thought. And I'm slightly offended that you would think I'd stick around if he was going to run this place that way."

"I didn't. That's why I couldn't figure out why you were just sitting there."

"Sure, sure. I believe you." He didn't manage to suppress a chuckle.

"I don't need this. I'm going back to work." I stood.

"I want the coach played as the sort of guy who'd call up a friend to pressure a newspaper to kill an unflattering story," he called after me.

Check.

Parker looked up from his screen as I sank into my seat beside him. "What was all that?"

"Bob. Trying to take a decade off my life letting Connolly act all bothered that some jerk threatened to pull his ads over my college quarterback piece."

"That hasn't even run yet," Parker said. "Farrelly tried to kill it before we got it out by having someone he knows call Connolly?"

I nodded. "I know he's not your favorite person, but it is notable that he told the guy to piss off—says he doesn't need his money and we'll pick up other advertisers because of my story. So there's that."

"I don't hate that." Parker nodded. "Good for him. But you thought he was going to kill your piece, huh?"

"I have renewed resolve for becoming Don Farrelly's least favorite reporter now." I pulled my laptop from my bag.

Parker laughed. "Go get him, Lois."

I laid out my notes and lost myself in the writing in a way I hadn't in months.

Joey texted at 11:30 with a reminder to eat, because of course he did, and I hurried to the break room to grab the blue Tupperware container he'd shoved into my hands as I ran out the door that morning. Inside, I found a carved turkey sandwich on fresh sourdough with some kind of chutney, cheese, and...apples? There were thinly sliced apples on my sandwich.

And it was damned delicious—a thousand times better than limp old lettuce in a hundred ways. I devoured the whole thing in a record number of bites and sent my compliments to the chef via text message.

When my phone rang, I expected to see Joey's name. And the only one that could've possibly made me happier right then was the one that came up—Jacque Morgan.

"How is my favorite medical examiner this sticky Monday afternoon?" I said by way of hello.

"If you think you love me now, wait until you hear what I have for you." Jacque's tone was smug, the kind of self-assurance I only hear from her when she gets to tell me about a shoe sale first.

I gave it five beats of silence before I cracked. "Is this a guessing game? Because I generally suck at them."

"Holden Peters is clean, Nichelle."

"Hot damn. You're right, I do love you a little more." There was a pen in my hand and a notepad beneath it, almost without me having to put any real thought into the action. "How conclusive are your results?"

"This is a more definitive test, and there's not a trace of anything here. Not for at least ninety days. Putting things generously, it's possible that the original test was a false positive. Those do happen. But if I had to bet, I'd put my money on the 'somebody's lying' square."

"Jacque, you're a star. You're like a pair of Manolos at the thrift store with the tags still on and not an imperfection to be found." I jotted down a few notes. "And I can quote you, right?"

"Absolutely. I'll send you the official printout when I have a spare moment. I've got to run; I have really impatient patients."

"Nobody has more patience than the dead, Jacque."

"Tell that to the guy on my table. Bye, Nichelle."

Holden was clean. Holden was undeniably wrongfully benched. We had a case against Farrelly—or at least cause to get Holden back on the field. Which meant I had some phone calls to make.

First, I texted Troy: *Holden's drug test came back negative.*

The response was immediate: *Obviously.* Then a follow-up: *Thanks, Nichelle. I'll tell him.*

I couldn't suppress a grin as I dialed Coach Farrelly's office.

"Good morning, Coach, Nichelle Clarke at *RVA Week*," I said when he answered.

The line was silent.

"Coach?"

"What?" Yikes. That tone usually only came from folks who were afraid I was about to print something that would land them in prison.

"I'm very pleased to report that the state crime lab here in Richmond ran uncontaminated samples from Holden that determined definitively that he has not used illegal substances—or, in fact, substances of any kind —in at least the past ninety days."

"I cannot comment on lab results I have not seen."

"I'm happy to send you a copy when I receive the report, though I spoke with the medical examiner by phone and she relayed these results. Will Holden be able to play after you receive the report?"

He hung up.

"Damn." My fingers flew over my keyboard, hunting the number for the chancellor's office. Something told me I needed to get to him before Farrelly could walk over there.

I gave my name to his receptionist and told her it was urgent, curling the phone cord around my finger as I waited through what felt like nine years of hold music.

"Miss Clarke, what can I do for you?" The chancellor's voice was warmer than Farrelly's, anyway.

I relayed the facts of Jacque's report, adrenaline lending the barest tremor to my voice that I hoped he didn't notice.

"And you can provide us a copy of this report?"

"Yes, sir."

"And you're printing this when?"

"It will be in the cover story in Thursday's issue."

I heard computer keys clicking.

"You guys have built quite the little paper there," he said after a minute. "Is this the same Bob Jeffers who used to work at the *Telegraph*?"

"Yes, it is."

"Peters will be reinstated today, and the university website will have a home page apology posted by seven a.m. Thursday. You have my word. Good enough?"

I scribbled every word. "It's not my place to say. You'll have to ask Holden. But I have a feeling he'll be thrilled." All the kid wanted to do was play football.

"Have yourself a good day," he said, disconnecting before I could say, "You, too."

I put the phone down and turned back to my story, smiling and humming to myself as I typed.

Days when what I do can actually help someone are good days.

~

Tuesday morning passed in a blur of final checks on statistics and quotes, and the ones I pulled for Farrelly were harsh, to put it mildly. Bob peered at me over the rims of his reading glasses after he finished reading.

"You sure about this? The guy is relatively popular, and he comes across as an ass here."

"He's being an ass about this," I said. "Nothing there is untrue or even unfair. And sometimes a story needs a villain."

Parker read through the draft once the type was set. The more eyes on it, the better—especially former-professional-athlete eyes, in this case.

He shook his head at the section detailing my interview with Farrelly.

"It sounds like he's blaming other people for his bigotry—the sponsors, I presume, or whoever else might be whispering in his ear." He waved his hand vaguely, his wedding band catching the light from the overhead fluorescents. "Pointing to other people's bigotry does not change the fact that you're a bigot, there, Coach."

"You cannot imagine how angry I was when I walked out of that room."

Parker flicked his fingers at the computer screen in front of him. "Oh, I think I can imagine." He leaned back in his chair and laced his fingers behind his head. "It's a damn good story, Nichelle."

"Thanks, Parker."

"They really tried to screw this kid, and you made a difference here." He sat up. "Maybe in more ways than one." He grinned at me, his emerald eyes dancing, when I arched one eyebrow. "How about I introduce Holden to Tony?"

Tony Okerson was one of Parker's best friends—and a retired professional QB who had been the MVP of every big game there was over a storied career. He was a good man, the kind of guy who oozed charisma the way normal people sweat on a humid August day. Like Parker taken up a few notches. He also knew everyone who was anyone in professional sports

—particularly people who could help a talented young quarterback achieve his dreams.

"I'm sure Tony could do more for the kid's professional prospects with a ten-minute phone call to an old boss than a blowhard university coach like Farrelly could do with an entire Heisman campaign." I smiled. "I'm sure Holden would be thrilled. Thanks, Parker."

"What are friends for? I'll call him this afternoon." He cleared his throat, his gaze dropping to his tasseled loafers. "Speaking of friends, how are the plans going for Mel's baby shower? Anything I can help with?"

Crap. I couldn't exactly say, "Absolutely nothing because I've been so absorbed in these stories in the last week that I haven't even thought about it." But it was the truth.

He kept talking, giving me a minute to try to come up with something to say. "We've got the big thirty-six-week ultrasound coming up. Mel's all nerves right now—I hate seeing her like this, but I get it. Everything feels big and scary, probably more for her than it does for me, and I'm not exactly Joe Cool right now. She's jittery about the baby. She's at least as worried about leaving the *Telegraph*. She jokes that she's the last person there with any sense and that the whole paper will fall apart without her. At least, I hope she's joking."

Double crap. I certainly hadn't been keeping up with Melanie's mindset during the last few weeks.

"You know, I don't think she's joking," I added, hoping a quip would make my silence thus far less obvious. "I mean, have you met the new cops and courts reporter?"

"That bad?" His eyebrows went up.

"He gave a parking lot brawl that resulted in a death a cutesy serial-killer-esque nickname."

"He did not." Parker whistled, long and low.

"The Subway Slasher."

"We...we don't have subways in Richmond."

"The fight was in a sandwich shop parking lot."

Parker stared for two blinks to make sure I wasn't kidding and burst out laughing. "Where the hell is Andrews finding these people? I'm pretty sure the guy who replaced Spence when he moved to Colorado last summer has never actually watched a whole baseball game."

"Even Shelby is appalled." I nodded.

"Well, anyway," Parker said, "we can't save the *Telegraph*. Mel can't save the *Telegraph*. But I'm hoping the baby shower will cheer her up."

"It's going to be a great party," I said, pasting a grin on my face that I hoped looked more convincing than it felt. "Don't you worry about a thing."

As soon as he slid his chair back over to his desk, I snatched up my phone and fired off an SOS to Jenna. A mom twice over with the kind of head for party planning people have to be born with, she had to know a thing or two about baby showers. I myself knew maybe half a thing about them, and I definitely didn't have time to plan the kind of shower Mel deserved around digging into Rosser's suspicious death and writing about Troy's LGBTQIA+ group at the youth center—not in two weeks. Mel did not deserve the rush job of Nichelle-accidentally-procrastinated-planning-because-she-was-on-a-deadline.

I can totally take point on a baby shower while you hunt the Nazi killer. As long as you dish all the grisly details!

I sent her my thanks and breathed a sigh of relief.

Until I caught the time and realized I needed to leave for the youth group meeting, running out the door as fast as my heels would allow.

14

The youth center was a short trek from Troy's house and an even shorter one from the local high school. A squat brick building with dark windows, it didn't look like the kind of place kids would go for fun. I remembered Troy saying how he spent time here as a kid, when Darryl was too busy at football practice to watch him and Joyce was working her second or third job to support them.

Troy met me in the parking lot, all smiles and dimples and restless energy.

"Hey, Nichelle!" He greeted me with a hug that lifted me clean off my feet. "Come on in. I'll introduce you to the kids."

"Can you give me a little bit of background on where you got the idea to do this?"

"Really? I guess it started with me. Once I came out, I wanted to help other young people understand that it's okay to be themselves, you know?"

I pulled out a notebook and jotted along as he talked.

"I figure if my speaking up and being open can show even one person that they're allowed to be who they are...then I've done good."

I jotted a reminder that Holden had said something similar, about his driving desire to help others feel safe, seen, and accepted.

Troy cleared his throat and shoved his hands deep into the pockets of his jeans. "This is all relatively new to me. I didn't realize—or maybe *admit* is a better word—I was gay until I got to college. One of my favorite things about college classes is how specific they can get. The freshman writing class—which is required for everyone—has a max capacity of fifteen students per section. With thousands of freshmen, that means hundreds of classes taught by dozens of professors. I found a section that was all about the Black body in literature."

He let out a long breath, leaning back against the brick wall. "We read Toni Morrison, Alice Walker, even Octavia Butler. In high school, I couldn't imagine studying and analyzing a book by a Black author the way we looked at *Huckleberry Finn*, where the Black character is nothing more than a caricature, and my AP Lit teacher spent weeks tiptoeing around the N-word." He sighed. "I wish that just one day in that class, we could've had a discussion about that word and its use in literature. When is it acceptable? When is it not? When is the value of what's learned from the book outweighed by the harm done in letting kids read that sort of talk as 'normal'?"

He fell quiet when a group of kids burst through the door beside us, a basketball being passed between them as they raced toward the cracked concrete court with its lone net-less hoop, its metal backboard streaked with rust. Troy's eyes followed them, his face lighting with a small smile.

"It was reading Baldwin that really got me. There was something about how he described the male body, sexuality, and queer spaces in *Giovanni's Room*. This was a Black man—though his main characters were white—writing openly about the gay and bisexual experience in that time. He tackled so many issues other writers wouldn't touch, like toxic masculinity." Troy shrugged. "I talked with my professor about that book, and he pointed me to some of Baldwin's short stories, where the protagonists are Black and gay, and I just...felt seen."

"The magic of books." I smiled.

Troy grinned. "Indeed. I started going to the campus LGBTQ Center. Pamphlets and group sessions and just meeting so many people, pulling up links to resources from Tumblr, of all places. It's different for everyone, but for me, it was a bunch of little things...mostly learning that it was okay to not be sure. Like, I can't point to a moment and say, 'Here, right here, is when I figured out I liked men,' you know?

"One of the big things I've learned is that labels aren't always permanent. I'm gay, but I didn't realize it until a couple of years ago. Was I before that? Maybe, but I honestly couldn't say. And maybe at another point in my life it will be different: maybe I'll be bi or pan or even hetero. People change, sometimes because their understanding of self changes, and sometimes because they've grown through life experience and aren't who they were before. It doesn't mean they weren't born this way or that. Growing and changing is part of life for everyone, and so much of the community aspect of queerness is about embracing change."

I shook out the cramp in my hand from writing so fast once he stopped talking. "So what brought you back here?"

"I was thinking about how I wish I'd had those books, those resources, that safe space I found at college when I was a little younger. I'm not sure I would've figured anything out sooner, but I might've. When I was bouncing off the walls, feeling 'wrong' because I didn't quite fit, I could have used a space like this one."

"So you made your own."

"So I made my own." Troy grinned again. "I'd love to show you."

"I'm excited to see."

He led me inside and up a flight of stairs to a nondescript gray door. The only thing that set it apart from the other gray doors in the narrow hall was the big sign that read "Q & Q HQ" in large rainbow-colored block letters.

When I tapped the sign with a raised eyebrow, Troy chuckled. "Queer and questioning. It's a broad and inclusive way to talk about the community. Plus, it just sounds cool."

Behind the door lay a small room crammed with chairs in a tight circle, only some of them occupied, the center filled with piles of art supplies, a banner longer than I was, and a box of plain white T-shirts.

At the sound of the door opening, the group of young people gathered around the banner wielding art supplies all turned their heads toward the door. Beautifully diverse in ethnicity and clothing styles, they ranged in age from early teens through young adults.

"All right, folks," Troy said, clapping his hands once like he was a schoolteacher. "I did tell you that we were going to have a guest sometime this week, and here she is. This is my friend Nichelle, her pronouns are she/her, and she's a journalist."

"Like, a reporter?" One of the younger kids backed away from me as I took another step inside to stand at Troy's elbow.

"Yeah, but she's just going to sit in and watch what we're doing. If you don't want to talk to her or introduce yourself, that's totally fine. She won't be using anyone's name but mine in whatever she prints."

I took a seat off to the side, where I could listen without being a distraction.

"We've got a little less than two weeks left before the parade, so today's goal is to finish up the banner. Does anyone have anything..." Troy trailed off. He looked like he was counting the heads of the kids looking up at him from the center of the room. He even ducked out to do a quick glance up and down the hallway. "Anybody seen Ben?"

The question returned a chorus of "no" and a few shrugs. One of the girls leaned to whisper something in a boy's ear. I caught the word "weeks" but couldn't guess what they were saying.

Troy blinked, shaking his head. "Does anyone have anything they'd like to discuss?"

I felt a few pair of eyes on me. I may have been there at Troy's invitation, but I was still an outsider in their safe space.

"Well, I'm Sofia, and my pronouns are she/they." A young person with long, shiny black hair and wide, expressive eyes stood, turning to face Troy. "I just really want to hold my girlfriend's hand between classes. But my mom works in the principal's office, and I don't want word to get back to her." She pivoted to the girl still sitting on the floor. "It's not like I'm embarrassed about you or anything, but my family just...wouldn't understand."

I watched Troy circle the room, listening to fears and insecurities—and also little victories. One of the group members had come out as nonbinary on social media, changing their pronouns in their Twitter bio to they/them to a chorus of congratulations from their followers; the kids in the room broke out in raucous cheers at that story.

A lack of understanding of bisexuality no matter where she turned had one girl frustrated. "My straight friends keep asking me, like, am I gay or straight? Like, I'm neither—I'm bisexual. And I'm tired of having that argument over and over. They phrase it like I'm destined to end up with one or the other, so that will obviously be my future." She knotted and unknotted a lock of straight dirty-blond hair next to her cheek as she spoke. "But then on my blog, it's the lesbians who are like, 'Oh, but you're so privileged; you can just pass as straight,' when that doesn't even make any sense to me. I mean, can't most anyone pass as straight if they want? That's the whole thing about being in the closet, right?"

Troy squatted in front of this girl's chair and looked up at her. "It shouldn't be on you to educate your friends," Troy continued. "But you can certainly choose to do that, and sometimes when you help people understand, it benefits you both. If you want, I can recommend a few books to maybe check out from the library to read with them and talk about. Sometimes it's easier to step out of reality and focus on fiction." He stood up, addressing the whole group. "I'll text y'all a reading list. Totally optional, of course, and I'll also link you to some Instagram, Twitter, and Tumblr accounts that curate reading lists like this based on themes. I am a big believer in the importance of seeing yourself reflected in literature, but I'm learning that it's just as important for other people to see characters like you. Fictional characters at their best are a proxy for the reader, aren't they? We hunt a whale with Captain Ahab, we fight Nazis with Sam Train and the Buffalo Soldiers in Italy, we feel their victories and their heartbreak. Great fiction helps us understand each other as humans."

I almost wanted to applaud, seeing how at ease he was, hearing the passion in his voice, and watching the group as they watched him. I made a note to ask him to forward me the reading list texts.

Troy moved to stand over the group working on the banner—they sprawled all around it, coloring in the big block letters written in the same style as the sign on the door. It said *WE'RE HERE* in all caps. Nothing identifying the youth center or any of the members of the group. The verbiage was bordered in a bunch of rectangles with varying numbers of horizontal stripes. None had been colored in, but a few had penciled labels: ace, pan, trans, progressive, bi, intersex, sapphic were the ones I could see—I couldn't read them all without getting in the way.

After a few minutes of joking and talking with the kids, Troy moved on to a waifish young man who was sitting by himself, staring at his blank phone screen. Troy sank into the next seat, crossing his feet at the ankles and leaning back to appear comfortable and casual.

"Mikey, my man, what's on your mind?"

Thin enough that his skin stretched taut over the bones in his hands and face, with a buzz cut and startlingly clear blue eyes, Mikey might have been thirteen or fourteen.

"I think..." Mikey said, not looking up from his phone, which was still blank. "I think I might be...asexual."

"Asexual isn't a dirty word, Mikey," Troy said gently. "And if you're not sure, that's okay. Your understanding of yourself and your identity will likely change as your life changes, and that's okay too."

"Thanks, Troy." Mikey stashed his phone in his pocket and gave Troy a hesitant smile.

Troy brought the group together for some logistical talk about the parade, and the group talked a bit more, but it felt more like continuations of past conversations: crushes, friendships, school, sports, family. The flow of conversation between the teenagers, with Troy often but not always as a mediator, felt almost like group therapy, with anyone who was comfortable sharing a story or a thought speaking up like Kelsey had earlier.

"That's the end of our official meeting, folks." Troy's announcement felt sudden, but I checked the time and verified that the hour and a half was up already. "You all know that I'll stay here as long as any of you are here. But since Nichelle is here, if you're open to chatting with her, telling your story, whatever you're comfortable with, we'd both really appreciate it."

Most of the group scattered quickly. Sofia's girlfriend, the nonbinary kid who had come out on Twitter that week, and a boy named Garrett who had talked about toxic masculinity on the boys' soccer team at the high school stayed in the room with us. Sofia's girlfriend introduced herself as Alice. The nonbinary kid was Jay. Garrett and Jay wanted to sing Troy's praises, which I was more than okay with. I shook hands with and thanked them each before they left.

Alice showed no interest in me, but while the other three peppered me with kind words about Troy, she murmured to him a few feet away.

"I'm worried about Ben; I haven't seen him in eighteen days—not here, not at school, not anywhere," was all I managed to make out during a brief lull in my own conversation.

He patted her shoulder and she slipped out the door, leaving me wondering: Who was Ben, and why was she counting days?

15

Troy busied himself stowing art supplies once we were alone. I helped him drape the still-drying banner over a few chairs.

"Who's Ben?" I asked. "And what's significant about eighteen days?"

Troy pursed his lips. "Eighteen days means he hasn't been seen for two and a half weeks—so longer than you'd think for an illness or injury, and that's five missed meetings. I haven't been here in a while because of school, but I trusted Ben to hold down the fort. Something isn't right. He's not the sort of kid who would abdicate that responsibility without letting me know."

"You think he's in danger?" My voice shot up half an octave.

"Maybe? It's always a little scary when kids stop showing up; it might mean they've been found out and gotten in trouble." Troy curled and uncurled his fists. "And Ben's special to me. I've been friends with his older sister Evie since we were freshmen in high school. We still keep in touch even though she's going to school up in Pennsylvania now." He sank down in a chair. "Ben was one of my first regular attendees. I told Evie about starting this group, and she sent him my way. And when I had to go back to school and wasn't sure if I'd be able to swing driving back and forth all the time, Ben immediately stepped up to help."

"Could you ask the sister if she's heard from him?"

He nodded. "I know their family is pretty intense. And Evie is unflappable, but Ben is more sensitive. He's always seemed really dependable to me, though."

"Maybe he's just overwhelmed," I said. "If it's helpful, I can tell you from experience that the vast majority of reported missing persons are just fine and weren't ever in any jeopardy." I paused. "I can ask Aaron to poke around if you'd like some extra peace of mind. I know he'd be happy to help."

"Thank you. I know Evie keeps a close eye on things—as close as she can from school, anyway—and she hasn't said anything." Troy shook his head. "Anyway," he turned on his full-wattage grin, his eyes still betraying the worry over Ben, "thank you so much for coming. Did you get enough material for a good story?"

"Definitely. Can I also get a copy of that reading list you're going to send out? I think it'll give me an even better picture of what kind of resources are available and how LGBT issues are being talked about in popular media."

"Totally. As soon as I have that all written up, I'll let you know."

"And I'll let you know if I turn up anything on Ben. Can I have a last name?"

"Ben Winter," Troy said. He also gave me an address in a solidly middle-class neighborhood that wasn't particularly close to this youth center. I wondered why someone would go so far out of their way for a group like this, and what kind of reasons they gave to "intense" parents.

I was ten minutes from home when my phone rang. "Clarke," I said after I picked up.

"Hey, Nichelle, it's DonnaJo. I think I might have some new information on your murder case. I overheard some state troopers in the courthouse elevator."

She could've been a professional eavesdropper, however unintentional. "Do I need a notebook? Because I'm driving."

"Nah, I'll email you notes. But listen, they were talking about a cold case that just wound its way into their office from out in Fluvanna County. The remains were found over a year ago and never identified; there were no prints by the time of discovery, and no luck with a local effort at a dental. But the state lab was able to get a more advanced dental scan, and one tooth was an implant replacement, the screw obscured by bone. The serial number gave them a name, and they traced some disturbing hate group activity online. Cause of death was a single shot to the head, likely with a high-powered rifle from the bone splintering."

"Must have been a long elevator ride for you to get all that."

"I might've followed them down a hallway. Or two."

"You're my hero, do you know this?" I laughed.

"Trying to keep up, my friend."

"There are enough similarities to give me pause," I admitted. "You said this guy was found a year ago?"

Jesus, how many more could there be?

"Could we have some kind of vigilante Nazi executioner on our hands?" DonnaJo mused.

"Or something," I said.

DonnaJo laughed. "I know that tone. I could probably paint the expression on your face right now if I was any kind of artistic. Listen, these guys didn't say the victim's name, but it was a statewide cold case if you want to send an FOI for cases received in the past three weeks. Give them a buffer just for grins. If anyone can get to the bottom of this, it's you, Nichelle."

"Thanks, DonnaJo. I'll let you know what I find out."

"You do that. Bye, darlin'."

I hung up, remembering just before the bridge that I was supposed to meet Joey at the river near Belle Isle. A scenic walk beats the hell out of the same old neighborhood route, so we'd made a new press-day-end tradition that I looked forward to. New habits—the good kind—are great to settle into. I even had a pair of sneakers stashed in my car because I'd forgotten mine once and lost a heel on the uneven paths.

I parked next to Joey's Lincoln in the River Road lot and opened the tailgate on my SUV to change my shoes.

Joey climbed out of the car and stole a quick kiss between my lacing and tying. He had stopped by the house on his way; he was dressed down in a fitted T-shirt and basketball shorts. Before he moved in with me, I had never seen him in casual clothes, and he made them look every inch as sexy as his expensive suits. Another perk: it felt like he was an entirely different person when he wasn't dressed to impress. He also had Darcy's leash in hand, and my best girl was more than excited to see me.

"Hey, beautiful." Joey grinned as Darcy tried her hardest to *101 Dalmatians* us by circling our legs, leash wrapping this way and that. "How was your day?"

"Good, but long," I said, looping an arm around his waist and breathing in the crisp scent of his cologne as I rested my head on his chest. "You go first. I need a few minutes to decompress."

A deep, sexy laugh rumbled under my ear. "Just remember you asked," he said. "Your day-to-day is much more exciting than mine." He described a day of meetings, including a customer who was determined to be dissatisfied with everything, and lunch with a new round of contractors for a new project. He'd made a habit of treating new employees to lunch and getting to know them from his first day on the job, and I loved that he was a conscientious boss who cared about the people working for him—especially when construction can be such a dangerous and thankless business.

We walked the park trails as he talked, the air heavy with a heady mix of late summer blooms, loamy earth, and the sharp scent of the river. Darcy milked the longer walk for all it was worth, strutting down the trail with her head high. She knew the way to her favorite stretch of field and always hurried us there for a game of fetch. The breeze off the river was just enough cooler than the rest of the city to take the edge off the death-by-southern-humidity weather, knocking the feel down to slightly-too-warm-for-comfort.

"So the quarterback is back in Saturday?" Joey laced our fingers together, signaling my turn to talk with the question.

I nodded and filled him in on my day, ending with DonnaJo's overheard revelations. He stayed quiet, offering the occasional nod or squeeze of my hand. We listened to the river burble over the rocks for thirty yards or so when I stopped talking. I was pretty sure he wanted to say something but was trying to decide how to word it.

"I think the first question is, did both of the victims belong to the same group? Or maybe to groups with a history of conflict?" He paused as a jogger swerved around us. "But Nichelle, these aren't like street gangs or organized crime. These people tend in general to be much more paranoid and given to embracing conspiracy theories. There's a very real chance that they will not take kindly to a reporter poking around in their business—or the business of their dead members."

"I wondered if they belonged to the same group, too, but why would you take out people who agree with you?" I focused on the first part of what he said, mostly to try to keep the last from scaring the hell out of me because I knew he wasn't wrong, but it didn't make me less curious.

"What if it wasn't them killing each other?" he mused. "You said execution-style killings. What if it was a professional?"

"A hired neo-Nazi hunter?" I tipped my head from side to side, both of us falling quiet as Darcy tugged forward toward her favorite field. I claimed her squirrel from Joey and, as soon as Darcy was unclipped from her leash, let it fly. Darcy took off like a high-powered rifle shot, blurring into a coppery-gold streak as she chased the toy. The mindless ritual of the game gave my brain a chance to zigzag through theories.

"I don't hate that. Because why kill each other when you could easily target the kind of people groups like that blame for all the world's troubles: gay people, Black people, people from other countries..." I bent to pick up the toy and passed it from one hand to the other as Darcy bounced at my feet.

When she barked at me, Joey took the next throw, sending the little squirrel soaring. He shrugged.

"Hell, maybe it's a bona fide criminal outfit; those supremacist types rub me the wrong way, and Don Mario loathed nothing more than he loathed a bigot."

"I would not have guessed that about him," I said.

"You didn't see his best face," Joey conceded, stooping to get the toy from the dog. "Look, love, you know I get nervous when you're poking around in stuff I can't protect you from." Joey's jaw flexed as his eyes followed Darcy's route, his Adam's apple bobbing with a tense swallow. "I'm trying here, but the more I think about this, the less I like it."

I popped up on tiptoe to kiss his scruffy cheek as Darcy came bounding back. "I'm always careful."

His grim façade cracked with a sardonic smile. "I'm not sure that word means what you think it means. But I am well aware that all I can do is warn you and trust Aaron and Kyle to have your back."

"You know they do."

"It could be random," he mused, clipping Darcy's leash back to her harness. I watched his jerky movements, the stress I saw in them raising a pang of guilt. Not having an ear to the ground constantly had to be hard for him—especially since this was the first murder I'd worked in months.

"It could," I conceded, keeping the "but I doubt it" to myself.

"Hate group affiliations aren't exactly common knowledge most of the time. It's easy to see a pattern when you know that common thread, sure, but people who belong to groups like that often have the kind of personality that rubs all kinds of people wrong, from little old church ladies to loan sharks. They might've just been assholes who got themselves killed, and both happened to ascribe to the same warped worldview." He nodded like that made him feel better, so I did, too.

He wasn't wrong. It may well have been their sunshiny dispositions that got them popped rather than anything directly related to the hate groups.

Then again...following my gut has gotten me more than one story no one else thought to chase. And I was a firm believer that true coincidences were rarer than Jimmy Choo on a barn hand. This thing had a whole damned myriad of them—two white supremacists, two clean shots to the head, two body dumps in the woods. I didn't want Joey to worry, but I would follow the trail until I was sure it didn't go any further.

16

My first call Wednesday morning was to Aaron.

"Detective White." He didn't exactly sound chipper, but it was early. He was probably only on his second cup of coffee. I could empathize.

"It's your favorite reporter." I winked at Parker when he started laughing from the next desk.

"Morning, Miss Clarke." Aaron's tone was both more relaxed and more reserved. He'd been at the receiving end of my wheedling phone calls enough times to know that caution was always warranted—at least until he knew exactly what I wanted. "What can I do for you?"

"I ran across something yesterday I could use your help with." I tapped my pen on my desk, searching for the right phrasing.

"You have something else on your plate? Is this week like the Thanksgiving dinner of reporting for you, or does it just seem that way from here?"

I laughed. "I suppose there's been a lot—but as long as there's sweet potato casserole coming up here somewhere, I'm happy; that's my favorite."

"Noted. What're you into now?"

"Welfare check," I said slowly. "Kid by the name of Benjamin Winter. He's fifteen years old and hasn't been seen by his friends in at least eighteen days."

"Eighteen? That's oddly specific."

"Just relaying what I was told."

"Huh. That's a stretch of time to be out of his usual circles, even for a teenager. Let me see what I can find. Got an address?"

I recited it.

"I'll let you know what I find. And hey, while I have you—heads up, Charlie's been asking about hate groups. She called me yesterday."

Crap, crap, crap. That meant my lead was dwindling—as soon as Charlie had enough information to make an educated guess, it would be all over Channel 4's six o'clock. Then even Mark snappy-headlines-but-no-substance Lowell would catch on. Okay, maybe that was uncharitable; he did have one solid follow-up to an arrest back in June, scintillating reading he crafted by paraphrasing the suspect's lengthy affidavit and sharing as many gruesome details as he could possibly include.

"I have a week until press day. Which means I guess I'm writing two cover stories and hoping Charlie gets bored before she kills the one with the dead guys?"

"Solid plan, but I'm not the one you need to convince." Aaron chuckled.

"Thanks, Aaron."

"I'll get right on this missing kid. Good luck beating Charlie."

I hung up and clicked my email open. Right at the top, I found a note from DonnaJo with a quick rundown of what she'd told me the night before. Most notable was the name she'd gone to the trouble to get from the state police: Aryk Lee Larsen. There couldn't be but so many of those in Virginia, so locating records and information should make for an easy morning.

Unlike Mervin Rosser, Aryk had a Facebook profile with no privacy restrictions, even if he wasn't particularly active. There wasn't anything obviously problematic about his posts—a few dubiously sourced shared articles about politics and half a dozen fishing pictures. It wasn't much to go on.

I flagged Facebook for further review and went back to Google. If there wasn't anything recent and more interesting, I'd go back to digging through the older Facebook posts.

The fourth hit was a trucking company—not refrigerated foods like Mervin at Coldtown, but concrete with Michaelson, Inc. Coincidences and

I don't get along as a general rule, and four was just flat too many to believe.

"I suppose trucking is a solitary job, which might appeal to white supremacists who sometimes don't work well with others," I muttered, jotting the name and phone number for the company down.

Moving to the state police records database, I ran Larsen's name and found an arrest record. Two counts of assault in the last two years but nothing before that.

Back to Facebook, then. I flipped through his photos: football game, hunting trip, fishing trip, shooting range, barbecue. Every photo featured the same handful of (white, which seemed significant in this particular case) guys doing stereotypical-guy activities. The other men in the photos were either not tagged or had their profiles locked down with privacy settings that didn't let me see tags. Going back farther, I noticed a woman and baby in a few pictures, but, again, I couldn't see a tagged account.

The very first photo Aryk posted in 2019 was a photo of the woman, pale and gaunt, grimacing and clutching the baby in her arms. Aryk wasn't pictured; he must have been behind the camera. The caption read *Bonnie, wee lassie.*

Vida had told me that a lot of white supremacists in America latched onto the culture of "great" older nations, particularly ones where, historically, physical strength and battle prowess were highly valued. Generally, this meant Vikings and Norse mythology, or, I'd read, even the Greeks and Romans, but the old tales of Scottish clans could also be viewed similarly. Bonds of brotherhood and fealty, paired with historical battles, rebellions, and insurmountable odds would fit the same sort of narrative. Modern Scotland was fairly liberal—but it probably wouldn't do to tell the bigots that.

Something about the photo nagged at me. Not just the woman's expression, which lay somewhere between haunted and exhausted, but the caption. *Bonnie, wee lassie.* The comma was throwing me. Was it just that Aryk didn't know grammar? Normally it would be all one phrase: bonnie wee lassie. Beautiful little girl.

But Bonnie could also be a name.

Back to Google I went, with a handful of fresh ideas.

Three hours and a grumbling stomach later, I surfaced from my internet deep-dive knowing considerably more about Aryk Lee Larsen than I knew about Mervin James Rosser. Things in common: truck driving (kind of), hate group affiliation (not confirmed in Aryk's case), cause of death, and arrest records for assault. The ties were tenuous—especially after my long conversation with Vida in which she couldn't stress enough how common hate group affiliations had become thanks to online forums.

The crown jewel of my morning, though, was Bonnie's identity: the woman from Aryk's old Facebook photos was his ex-wife, Bonnie Medina. I found her address with my paid subscription to the DMV's records service and yelped when I saw it wasn't far from Richmond.

Jumping to my feet as my stomach let out a louder sound than my yelp, I stuffed a notebook and pen into my bag and tossed the strap over my shoulder.

"I have never in my life seen anyone that excited for lunchtime," Parker said through a mouthful of buttered and seasoned noodles, which smelled amazing.

Crap, it really was lunchtime. I hightailed it to the kitchen to grab whatever culinary-creation-in-sandwich-form Joey made for me that morning and snagged two massive bites before ducking my head into Bob's office. I remembered to chew and swallow before I opened my mouth to tell him I was off to chase a lead.

"Go on, kiddo." Bob waved me off before doing a double-take. "Just finish that sandwich first before you choke on it, okay?"

I didn't need to be told twice.

17

Goochland County, Virginia, stretches from Richmond to the Shenandoah mountains like a greedy hand. On the map, it's a strange, elastic shape, a narrow slice of foothills between the capital and the mountains. The rolling hills and farmland make for a beautiful driving backdrop, compared to the city.

Aryk Lee Larsen's ex-wife lived in a tiny single-wide trailer with her three-year-old daughter (the aforementioned "wee lass" now much larger than in those old Facebook photos) and three cats: a rangy gray one with a scarred face, a fat orange one that lingered near the littlest human, and a tuxedo missing half of its tail sitting on the roof of the trailer.

"Bonnie Medina?" I asked, walking slow to avoid turning an ankle with the winning combination of loose gravel and five-inch heels.

"Who's asking?" Bonnie's sharp brown eyes ranged over me, down and then back up, lingering slightly on the shoes. They were eye-popping: bright red and high gloss.

I offered her my press credentials. "My name is Nichelle Clarke. I'm a reporter with *RVA Week* in Richmond."

Bonnie glanced around with raised brows, as if to say, *This look like RVA to you?*

I scanned a field of trailers propped up on cinder blocks, some starting to sink into the damp ground, the silence marred only by music blaring through poorly sealed windows next door. Across the dirt lane that cut up the middle of the neighborhood, old men sat smoking on the warped steps of adjacent double-wides, and a woman with pink curlers in her hair that matched her floral housecoat sprawled across a plaid woven lawn chair with a tall mason jar of iced tea, waving a paper fan, her curious eyes on me.

"It's about your ex-husband, actually," I said. "Aryk Lee Larsen?" I pronounced Aryk like *ah-rick*, and Bonnie laughed.

"Oh yeah, I was married to that sonofabitch back when his name was just Eric, E-R-I-C, and he worked an office job. His middle name was Michael." She rolled her eyes, sinking down onto the stoop. She glanced at her daughter, making mud pies under the watchful eye of the orange cat. "And back then he didn't rant nonstop about whatever entire group of folks he hated today." She scoffed, rolling her eyes. "A-R-Y like Aryan and Lee like Robert E. It was some white power nonsense; I can't believe a judge let him get away with that shit legally."

"Can you tell me how that happened?" I pulled out a notebook and pen to make sure I got her words exactly.

"Once upon a time," she began with brows up for irony, "we lived in a nice house in a subdivision with a neighborhood pool, sidewalks, and an HOA." She huffed like an HOA was something almost mythical: a dragon, a unicorn, and a magic wand that shot out money all rolled into one. "I'll be honest, I'd rather raise my daughter here." She waved her rail-thin arms at the surroundings. "At least the meth dealer next door is a nice, sane man."

Her daughter screeched in delight at her inedible confection, and we both watched her for three beats—until she smashed her artwork flat to start again. The cat leaned in to sniff the wreckage and then sat back on its haunches, tail swishing through yellowed grass.

"What changed?" I prodded, drawing Bonnie's attention back to me.

"It was a neighborhood cookout, of all things. Some guy from two streets over had one beer too many and started talking about how good-paying jobs were being stolen from hardworking Americans by illegal immigrants. My guess? This guy got laid off and someone on his team who stayed through the cuts had an accent. That's all it takes for some people."

She shook her head. "I didn't pay him too much attention. Hannah was a newborn at the time, so all my energy went into her. Plus, what kind of sane person pays any mind to that? Like, aren't most illegal immigrants so desperate for a better life that they take on the jobs a majority of 'hard-working Americans'"—she waggled her fingers in air quotes—"don't want anyway?"

I nodded, taking notes.

Journalism even before the age of the internet 101: if someone gets to talking, do not interrupt. Whatever questions I might have could wait until I had heard everything she was going to say that I might not even know to ask about.

"So my husband takes up with this dude, they started texting or whatever—which, fine, you want to have friends in your neighborhood. A few weeks later, this guy invited Eric to a 'community meeting.'" She nodded when I looked up, her lips pinched into a thin white line. "It was all downhill from there."

She gave a half-hearted wave, as if to brush off what exactly she meant by downhill, but I could guess: he lost the office job, got his first arrest according to the records I'd found earlier, started going to more meetings... generally spiraling further and further away from the man she married. I wondered when he changed his name but figured I could trace that myself; legal name changes always leave a long paper trail behind them.

"Six months later, when I left, I wouldn't have batted an eye if I'd found a damn white hood or a swastika—or both—in my house."

"Do you have any idea what Aryk got up to after the divorce?"

Bonnie raised a brow. "Well, I'm guessing you're not about to tell me that he won the lottery and I'm entitled to half of his winnings."

Had the police not contacted her yet? Maybe she was no longer listed as his next of kin. At least this death notice was unlikely to end in tears; it didn't seem possible that Bonnie could care any less about Aryk than she already did.

"He's dead. He's actually been dead for about a year now." I went on to describe the cause of death, where and how he was found and identified—the only detail I left out was Mervin Rosser.

She was completely unfazed by her ex-husband's fate. "At least now I don't have to worry about him wanting to see her none." She jerked her head in the direction of her little girl. "Not that he ever paid a nickel of his child support, anyway. I figure he was probably too busy giving all his money to whatever nut jobs the internet hooked him into and their never-ending need for weapons. The last thing he said to me when I was walking out was that I better keep a rifle handy. I asked him if he was threatening me, and he said I needed it to keep me and her safe from 'the others,' not from him."

"Do you have a firearm, Miss Medina?" I asked.

"Absolutely not. I'd never listen to a word that man said to me. Not again." She jumped up to keep her daughter from shoving a fistful of mud into her mouth. "What's a reporter care about a dead asshole like him, anyway?"

"I'm honestly not sure yet," I said, pulling a card from my pocket. "But if you hear anything about what happened to him, say, maybe from the state police, will you give me a call?"

"No problem." She pointed to the stoop, and I set the card down while she wrangled her toddler—little Hannah was now covered head-to-toe in thick gray mud. Even the orange cat didn't make it out unscathed, globs dotting its fur. I thanked Bonnie and excused myself, the tuxedo cat's eyes on me until my car was out of her yard.

18

"Hey, Siri, call Kyle Miller." I set the cruise control once I was back on I-64.

"Calling Kyle Miller, mobile," my phone said from the little rack Joey had attached to my air vent so I could see maps and answer calls more safely. It was the middle of the day on a Wednesday, but Kyle usually made time for me. And Bonnie's comment about guns had me wondering a few things Kyle was in a good position to help answer.

"Nicey, you okay?" Tension thrummed in Kyle's voice when he picked up, like he expected me to say I was in the middle of a shootout between the cops, the mafia, and a street gang and needed backup. It was getting to be a regular enough tone from him that I was a little offended.

"Have you guys had an eye on any massive gun purchases into or out of Fluvanna County? Maybe in the past two or three years?" That was the county where Aryk's body was found rather than the one where he lived, but part of my theory was that maybe Aryk had gone out that way for a weapons purchase that went terribly wrong. Anything major should've at least been on the ATF's radar.

"Fluvanna?" Kyle hummed a toneless rhythm that told me he was thinking. "It doesn't ring a bell, but I'll look into it."

"Thanks, Kyle."

"You're not going to tell me what this is about?"

"I'm not really sure yet. Just following a hunch."

Kyle chuckled. "A hunch related to DonnaJo's eavesdropping in the courthouse elevator?"

"She told you about that, huh?"

"I'll take that as a yes." Kyle's voice took on an edge. "Be careful, Nichelle."

Why was everyone in my life always telling me to be careful? I'd never gotten into trouble I wasn't able to get out of. Well, okay, maybe I occasionally called in the cavalry...and maybe the cavalry sometimes got shot...and maybe I also sometimes got shot, cavalry or no.

I suppose that's why they keep the warnings coming.

"I'm always careful," I said, trying to play flippant.

"Right. I'm a phone call away. And please don't wait until you're in too deep to ask for help."

"Let me know if you find anything about guns in Fluvanna." I ignored his last comment.

Kyle sighed. "You got it."

"Thanks, Kyle." I touched the red button to end the call.

I had a few more minutes left in traffic before I'd arrive at the *Week* office, which gave me plenty of time to puzzle over what I'd learned. If Aryk was hoarding guns and even telling his wife—as she was leaving him—that she needed to keep guns around, then he probably fell in with similarly gun-obsessed and paranoid people.

Maybe a deal went south. Maybe Joey was right, and there really was nothing more connecting Mervin and Aryk than a hatred of people who weren't like them.

Second Star to the Right blared, and I touched the talk button, switching the call to speaker. "Clarke."

"Hey, Nichelle."

"Aaron, how's your day?"

"Oh, I've been better. I just talked to Mr. and Mrs. Winter—Ben's parents. I drove over there when I couldn't get anyone on the phone."

"What did they say?"

Aaron took a long moment to answer. "They say he's been sick—like, really sick. They didn't say with what, but..."

"Did you see him?" I asked.

"No, they said he was asleep. Something felt off about the whole thing, but I'd need a warrant to search the house. You want me to try for one?"

A police officer—worse, a detective—shows up to your door and you act cagey. That's not exactly a ringing endorsement of good citizenship. Then again, people hide things from the cops all the time; acting guilty doesn't necessarily prove guilt.

I pulled into the garage that the *RVA Week* office shared with the rest of the building. "Let me talk to them first. Maybe they'll let something slip to me that they wouldn't to you."

"I'm here if you need me. I might even know a judge who owes me a favor."

"Thanks, Aaron."

I stayed parked for only as long as it took to tap the Winters' address into Waze. I watched the city slide by: office buildings, then smaller homes crowded together, then houses that started getting bigger and farther apart. More streetlamps, wider sidewalks, taller homes with fresh paint.

The Winters lived in a cul-de-sac with other suburban-style homes that felt out of place just outside of downtown. The lawn was vibrant green and freshly mowed; I couldn't help comparing it to Bonnie Medina's trailer park or even Troy's neighborhood. But evil and pain can hide just as easily behind a white picket fence as a plywood-covered window.

The door's center was entirely inset frosted glass, and, after I rang the bell, I watched a muddy silhouette materialize and linger for a moment before the door opened. A tall, older man—tall enough that I had to look up to meet his eyes, and I touch six-two in my heels—filled the doorway.

"Can I help you?" His voice was softer than I expected, almost mild.

I offered a hand. "My name is Nichelle Clarke. I'm a reporter for the *RVA Week*."

"Your name sounds familiar." He gave my hand a firm squeeze. "Nathan Winter. What can I do for you, Miss Clarke?"

"I was actually hoping to talk to your son, Ben. Is he home?"

Nathan Winter went still. I watched the transformation come over him slowly, radiating out from the base of his spine until he was stiff as a statue.

But then he smiled. "You know, you're actually the second person to come asking about Ben today."

"Really?" I played it casual. It wouldn't do to have him thinking Aaron and I were in cahoots.

"Ben is sick, has been for a little while." Nathan's tone was still mild, his manner conciliatory.

A blond woman appeared behind him. "Nathan? Who are you—" She stopped when she spotted me. "Oh, hello."

"Honey, this is Nichelle Clarke. She's a reporter." He pursed his lips in a weighted pause. "She wants to talk to Ben."

"Miss Clarke." Mrs. Winter didn't smile. "I'm sure my husband has made you aware that our son is sick. He's also a minor and shouldn't be speaking to...a member of the press." She gave a haughty sniff, like a "member of the press" was something she would pry off the bottom of her shoe.

"I understand that some of his friends expressed concern, said they hadn't seen him in a while."

Mrs. Winter gave a sharp bark of a laugh. "He shouldn't be going to those gay meetings at that youth center in the ghetto, anyway."

I fought to keep my face from giving away my shock. I have always been a terrible liar, but I'd learned to, at the very least, maintain a blank expression.

Mrs. Winter read me like a book anyway. "Of course we know about the meetings. You think my son hides anything from us?" Her laugh sounded less like a weapon this time. "It's just a phase. He wants to lash out, be rebellious, try out something new. He'll get over it, given time."

Nathan wrapped an arm around his wife's waist, holding her to his side. "He really is quite seriously sick, Miss Clarke, but don't worry, we're taking very good care of him."

"Why do you care, anyway?" Mrs. Winter asked.

"I have a friend who is worried. And the foundation of my job is to help people."

"We appreciate your...*concern*, but our son really is none of your business." Mrs. Winter was a brick wall in my way.

I nodded, leaving my card with Nathan, and retreated to my car. Aaron was right—something was off. I just couldn't tell exactly what.

I dug my phone out of my bag and dialed Troy, shifting the car into drive.

"Hey, Nichelle."

I summarized my conversation with Ben's parents. "Something about this doesn't feel right. Honestly, something about this feels very, very wrong."

"I trust your gut." I heard papers rustling in the background on Troy's end. "Keep your phone on you. I'm calling for reinforcements."

19

It was my third time in the parking garage under the *RVA Week* office today, second time in the elevator, and first time getting a wave from Bob when he heard my heels clicking on the floor as I rushed to my desk.

I sank into my chair, and Parker craned his neck over the half-wall. "No coffee? You okay?"

I laughed. "It's almost four thirty."

He raised his to-go mug in a mock toast. "Never thought you were the type to care what time it is when it comes to coffee."

"It's too hot out for coffee in the afternoon."

"That, Clarke, is why God invented air conditioning." He shook his head, and I laughed again as I pulled out my notebook and flipped my laptop open.

The notes from my conversation with Bonnie Medina practically wrote themselves, but my anxiety over Ben had my foot tapping double-time as I worked. Troy's worry was bleeding into me—and waiting for his call was inching my blood pressure higher by the minute.

"You're shaking the whole office, Clarke," Grant said. "Maybe it's a good thing you didn't get more coffee."

I made a conscious effort to sit still. "Sorry. I'm waiting on a call."

Parker's voice immediately went softer. "Is your mom okay?"

My mom was a force of nature—she raised me all by herself, and when she was diagnosed with breast cancer almost five years ago, the whole world stopped for both of us. I live in low-key terror of getting that call a second time, the words "it's back" often haunting my dreams.

"She's fine, thank God." I shook off the panic that came with the mere idea, pulled out my phone, and tapped out a text to my mom: *Just thinking of you and wanted to remind you I love you because I don't say it enough.*

The phone rang in my hand before I hit send. It was Troy.

I sent the text and answered his call. "Your anxiety is rubbing off on me."

"I wish I could say I'm probably worried for no reason." His voice was tight, the words clipped. "I called Evie, and she's on her way down."

My fingers tightened on the phone against my ear. "Doesn't she live in Pennsylvania?"

"Yeah, and she's dropping everything to drive home right now." He sucked in a sharp breath. "She should get into town at around six or seven, and I think you should talk to her."

"Bring her to the *Week* at eight thirty. We should have the office to ourselves, and maybe she can get something out of her parents beforehand."

"Thanks, Nichelle."

"Try not to worry too much until you know for sure there's something to worry about. Maybe he's got mono or pneumonia or something."

"Sure." Troy's tone said he didn't buy that any more than I did. But all we could do was wait.

Evie Winter was the spitting image of her mother, but her eyes were the same soft blue as her father's and she had his height. There was a dynamic energy about her, like a coiled spring waiting to be released.

Her blond hair pulled up in a messy bun, she bounced on her toes, eyes darting around the office as if Ben were hiding under Parker's desk to jump out and surprise her. She gripped the fingers of her left hand in her right fist tightly enough that her fingertips were turning red.

Troy, reading her distress, gently rubbed between her shoulder blades. "Evie, this is Nichelle Clarke. She's the lady who got justice for Darryl, way back when." His voice was low and smooth, offering his friend a calming touchstone for her anxiety, but I noticed a tightness in his jaw. "Nichelle, this is Evelyn Winter."

"God, please don't call me Evelyn." The blurted statement was automatic enough to seem instinctive—and served to center her slightly, the grip on her fingers relaxing as she rolled her eyes at Troy.

"Hi, Evie," I said, reaching out a hand. "It's a pleasure to meet you, though I wish it was under better circumstances." I led the way to the conference table and walked to the far side so I could sit facing them.

Evie pulled in such a long breath she should've doubled in size. Her eyes were dry but restless, bouncing from me to Troy and around the room. "Ben's phone and computer are gone. He's not home holed up in bed or whatever bullshit story my parents fed you."

"And the cops," I added.

"They lied to the *cops*?" Evie's voice rose an octave, and her hands went to her head, fingers digging into the base of her bun. "Jesus..."

"I asked a detective friend for a favor, just a welfare check. They won't necessarily be in trouble for lying." I actually wasn't sure if that was true, but it was more important to get Evie calm for the moment. "Let's just talk about what we know right now, okay?"

Evie hissed in a breath between her teeth, bobbing her head in a series of small, sharp nods. "Okay, okay." She dropped her hands to the tabletop and looked right at me. "Troy can tell you, Ben's a pretty quiet kid, at least to talk to. He loves fantasy books and playing online games, but more recently, he's been...discovering himself."

"The coming-out process isn't just one-and-done," Troy added, leaning his shoulder against Evie's. "It's a very personal experience, a journey of discovering sexuality and self, beyond simply saying 'I'm gay.' It seemed to me that Ben has made some deep dives into who he is and who he wants to be this summer."

Evie nodded. "He wasn't exactly out to our parents, but he was out to me, and right before I left for school, he started pushing back at problematic things my parents say. I don't know what the day-to-day has been like this past month, but dinners when I was home in July were...tense, quiet."

"When did you first notice a change in your brother? And in your parents' relationship with him?" I asked. If he'd run away, we needed a timeline. If anything more horrible than that had happened, we also needed a timeline—but I wasn't ready to think about that just yet.

Evie looked down at the table, her gaze going unfocused. "He started talking to me about his sexuality the summer before my freshman year at Penn, so I've known for a while. I tried to get resources to him whenever I could. We talked through Instagram DMs so Mom and Dad wouldn't see it."

Their parents routinely checked texts between their own kids? I was just old enough that social media and frequent texting wasn't yet a big deal when I was Evie's age, but that seemed very Big Brother-y to me. I jotted a note.

Evie raised an eyebrow at Troy. "So, when this guy came out to me last spring and started telling me about his plans for a youth group, I sent Ben his way. I think it was good for him, to get to see someone he knew, even a little bit, going through the same thing he'd been struggling with."

"Ben really opened up with the group," Troy said. "He has a natural command of a room and an easy way about him that made him the perfect choice to lead things whenever I couldn't make it to Richmond for a meeting."

"And he was regular at the meetings until now? He hasn't disappeared before?" I asked.

"Never missed one," Troy said.

"But he has disappeared before." Evie's eyes popped wide. "When I was home for winter break last year, he had gone off the grid. I couldn't even get him through Insta."

"And your parents didn't report him missing then?" Aaron would've found that in five seconds.

"Mom said he was at camp, but I still don't understand who would go to camp during the winter. Ben hates skiing. They never explained, though. They just didn't seem..." She trailed off, her jaw hanging slack in horror. "Worried." She finished in a whisper. "They didn't seem worried."

Troy went ramrod straight in the chair next to her, looping an arm over her shoulders as she buried her face in her hands. I scribbled *conversion camp* on the page in front of me and put stars by it, noting the dates she gave.

"He never told me." Evie's voice came through her fingers as a muffled squeak. "God, I'm so stupid. He was quieter after he got back, holed up in his room for most of spring break, and not much better even when I was home over the summer. My brother is a reserved guy, but he has been known to talk my ears right off about his favorite shows or his latest book obsession—except lately. I knew he was going to Troy's meetings, though, and that they were good for him, so I've tried not to worry too much. But a couple weeks ago, he went completely radio silent. He wouldn't answer texts, calls, or DMs on Insta. My mom said she took his phone when I asked, and I just...believed her."

Troy met my eyes across the table, the whites visible all the way around. He had no idea. He'd been missing the last few weeks of meetings himself.

"Of course you believed her, honey, she's your mom." I clicked my pen in and out, my brain racing through possible scenarios for the most likely one. I wasn't sure what the hell had happened to this kid, but I knew in my bones Troy wouldn't sleep well until he knew Ben was safe, and Troy had enough to worry about right now. I had hit my limit of ability to keep him safe from the assholes threatening him online, but I knew how to help them find Evie's brother.

"Ben and I, we're close." Evie sat up, sniffling as she let her hands drop to the tabletop. "Closer than your average siblings of different genders with a few years' age gap usually are. My parents are lying. They lied to your detective friend, and they lied to you. Whatever is going on here, my brother is not sick. He's not even home."

"If he left, and I'm not saying I think he did, do you have any idea where he would go?" I asked.

"He's fifteen years old; he can't even drive yet, and he's always been a quiet kid. The only real friends he talked about were the others in Troy's group. But they would've said something to you, wouldn't they?" She turned to Troy.

"Alice is the one who told me Ben was missing. No one else said anything, but I'll ask around."

"If he did leave of his own free will, there's no way he wouldn't have told me. He wouldn't want to worry me like that." Evie balled her fists on the table and stood up. "I'm almost twenty, a legal adult, and since my parents won't do it, I will. I'll go to the police tomorrow and file a missing persons report. Ben's safety is more important than whatever lesson my parents might think they're teaching him by shutting him out and keeping people from looking for him."

I walked them to the elevator. "I'll do everything I can to help you find him, Evie."

Back at my desk in a silent room, I stuffed my laptop and notes into my bag, my thoughts racing through puzzle pieces. Where was Ben? And why were his parents covering up his disappearance?

20

Five hours of fitful half-sleep later, I was showered and dressed and on my second cup of coffee, waiting for Aaron in the lobby when he walked into Police HQ.

Evie had mentioned filing a missing persons report, and I wanted Aaron to snag it before the sergeant assigned it to someone else.

"I've never pegged you to be the early bird type," Aaron said, accepting the coffee I handed him with a grateful smile and waving me into the elevator. "If I didn't know any better, Miss Clarke, I'd say you've missed me the way you're hanging around this week."

I stuck out my bottom lip and blew a stray hair off my forehead. "I know you missed me, too, so don't even try to pretend you're not thrilled to have me underfoot again."

"Maybe. Just a little." He sipped the coffee as we hurried through the maze of detectives' cubicles to his office. "What brings you by bearing gifts this morning?"

I moved a stack of manila folders and dropped into one of the black plastic chairs facing his desk. "I wanted to fill you in on the Ben Winter situation." I told him about my conversations with Ben's parents and then with Evie.

He set the cup on the desk with a loud clap and turned to his computer, tapping keys. "Miss Winter put through that missing persons report just an hour ago at the third precinct."

"She means business," I said. "It's not even seven yet."

"That means she's worried about her brother," Aaron said. "And gives me a good reason to go back to the parents. This time, I'll press harder."

"Thanks, Aaron."

"I'll keep you posted, Nichelle."

"Enjoy that coffee." I waved on my way out the door. A surefire way to start the day in Bob's good graces was to be early for the staff meeting. And I had a cover story to pitch.

~

"What've you got cooking this week, Nichelle?" Bob turned to me last after making the rounds of the conference table.

"A couple of things. I have a cover story in the works: an LGBT support group at an underserved youth center downtown. The group is participating in the Pride parade next weekend. That one can run anytime this month, really, but I should have it done by Tuesday."

Bob nodded along, tapping his chin thoughtfully. He didn't look super intrigued, but he hadn't shot me down—yet. Before he could poke any holes, I played my ace.

"But there's potential to switch to a story about a missing kid from that group or maybe even rivalries between hate groups turning deadly. I'm chasing both, and you'll be the first to know if one or both prove interesting."

"Richmond Pride is next weekend?" Bob turned to Larry. "We have photo there already?"

Larry nodded. "I'm going, and so is Lindsey. Nichelle, let me know what you want for your story, and we'll make sure we get it."

"We can't publish their faces," I said, raising one hand when Bob's brows shot up. "It's a public event, but especially after what I heard about the missing kid last night, I can't cause these kids trouble at home."

Bob and Larry nodded.

"Fair," Bob said.

"We'll shoot around faces, especially on teenagers," Larry said.

"Keep me in the loop when you know what you're going to focus on," Bob said. "I don't want to deal with a last-minute switch if I can help it. Especially on the cover. It's expensive to change it after Saturday, and Connolly has already taken a hit for us this month."

"Watch your ass with the Nazis, Clarke," Parker said. "I know nothing about baby showers."

The room erupted in laughter.

As we filed out, my desk phone bleated. I jogged over to answer, shouldering past Parker with a grin.

"Clarke."

"Good morning, again." Aaron's voice sounded far away. I pressed the receiver harder against my ear.

"Now it's starting to seem like it's you who can't get enough of me," I quipped.

"Ben's parents were...cagey, again. I think they're feeling the heat about Ben." Road noise rumbled in the background. He hadn't even waited to call me when he was back in his office. "They did let it slip that Ben has run away before, just after Thanksgiving last year, but came home after a few days."

"Evie didn't mention that." I bet she didn't know.

"You think she should have?" he asked.

"She said they're super close," I said. "Or they were, anyway."

"With his sister away at college, unable to intervene, maybe Ben didn't feel like he could confide in her like he used to," Aaron said.

"Or maybe he thought that if she couldn't do anything to help anyway, it wasn't worth worrying her," I mused. "Thanks, Aaron. I'll keep digging."

"I'm going to hang onto this file. Let me know if you find anything."

"Back at you."

I hung up and opened my computer.

If he'd run away before without telling his sister, then her assertion that something sinister was at work here didn't carry nearly as much weight. Assuming that was the truth—the parents had already shown themselves to be the kind of convincing liars who didn't regard Aaron's badge as worthy of their honesty.

For now, the smartest move would be to try to build out a timeline including Thanksgiving and the December "camp" and anything else we could find. Maybe a pattern would show itself.

I reached for my phone and opened a new text, copying Evie's number when Troy sent it to me.

Hey Evie, it's Nichelle Clarke. Can you meet for coffee?

She answered right away and said she'd meet me at Lamplighters.

I sent Troy an update. He was catching up in his classes online, having been granted a two-week leave of absence from campus because of the threats to his mother. *I'm waiting to hear back from my group members who know Ben best. I'll let you know what they say.*

When I arrived at the coffeehouse, Evie sat behind a confection of a drink piled high with whipped cream. Instead of drinking it, she was using the handle to slowly rotate the mug on the wood tabletop. She jumped when I greeted her, then slouched in her chair and tucked a lock of hair behind her ear.

"Hey, Miss Clarke." I think she tried for a smile, but it came off as more of a grimace. "I went to the cops this morning, like I promised."

"I know. My friend already went back to your parents, and he got some new information out of them." I paused, watching her face. Expectant, maybe even hopeful. "They say this isn't the first time Ben's disappeared."

"What do you mean?" Genuine confusion furrowed her brow. "Of course it is. If you mean the camp—"

"Before that. They said in late November or early December, probably before you finished finals for the semester. They told Aaron he ran away from home right after Thanksgiving."

"No, he didn't." Evie's response was immediate, instinctual. Her voice cracked on the last word, stinging betrayal written in every line of her face. "He would've told me. Hell, I would've picked him up myself and brought him to my dorm." Her blue eyes swam with unshed tears. "He knows he can tell me anything."

"They said he was only gone a few days before he came back. That's why there wasn't a missing persons file opened then. But I wonder if that's what triggered your parents to send him away later in the month?" I wasn't going to say the words *conversion camp* out loud. "Moreover, I want to know if any of this could lead us to where he is now. We need to trace his movements from last time. If he has run away again without telling you, he may be following the same pattern."

"How can I help?"

"The shortest road to an answer here may well be his friends," I said. "We should start by working through his circle, see if anyone can give us more information about where he went and how long he stayed."

I took notes while Evie reeled off names. Most of them were familiar from Q & Q HQ. Even though the group hadn't started until after the December incident, news about it probably spread through word-of-mouth, so it would make sense that many of the members knew each other beforehand.

I sent the list of names to Troy, followed by a list of questions: Did Ben stay with any of them back in December? Had anyone heard anything from him that concerned them around the holidays? Outsourcing interviews isn't my usual MO, but the group members trusted Troy, and speed was paramount here.

I turned my attention back to Evie, who was now stirring melted whipped cream into her drink. "You said last night that you and Ben kept in touch mostly through Instagram, right?"

"Yeah," she said. "Our parents would sometimes read his texts—he has an Android, so they can see them all through the phone nanny app they have with their cell company." She shook her head. "Which is why I got off their plan as soon as I could sign a contract of my own."

"Does he have a public Insta profile I could look through?" I asked.

"No, but I can log you into my account so you can access his feed, if you want."

I pulled my laptop out of my bag, opened it up, and pulled up Instagram. I didn't have an account—I used Twitter for work and Facebook for my personal life but neither consistently enough to be particularly social media savvy. I turned the laptop around and slid it to Evie.

She typed in a few short bursts and then turned it back around to face me. "You're logged in as me, and I brought up his page so you can look through it."

"Would you be able to access his messages?" I asked, giving a cursory scroll.

"Without his phone or computer, I don't have access to his saved passwords. I can try to guess it, but if he has two-factor authentication, it's game over." Evie already had her phone in hand, typing rapidly.

Ben's account, @wynterigreen, was what I'd expect from any boy his age: a few group shots with friends, most of whom I knew from the center; artistic shots of flowers, brick walls, or empty streets with a handful of selfies mixed in. The photos had a smattering of likes—never more than thirty or so, but he only had eighty-four followers. I clicked his followers list. A few struck me as odd: no profile picture, the username a string of seemingly random numbers and letters, and no posts.

My phone buzzed with a text from Troy.

Ben stayed at Alice's house for two nights in December. She said her dad was out of town for work and he needed a place to crash. He was quiet and she didn't ask too many questions but he left that Monday morning. She lives in Scott's Addition.

Scott's Addition was a ways from the Winter house, closer to downtown. Was he moving that direction on purpose, just looking for somewhere safe to sleep, or both?

I thanked Troy and went back to the sketchy Instagram accounts. If Ben's account was private, he had to accept follow requests.

So why would he accept these?

The mark of an interesting—if frustrating—story is the propensity for new questions to pop up as fast as I can find answers for existing ones.

I wanted to see his DMs, but from the set of Evie's jaw as she tapped a finger on the edge of her phone across from me, she wasn't having immediate luck guessing his password.

I wondered if there was a way to get any other data on the people behind the accounts.

I texted Jenna's husband. *Hey Chad, Looking at some sketchy Instagram accounts for a story I'm working. Can you find any details on who might be running these?* I went back to Ben's account page and sent Chad a photo of the followers list with the odd handles circled. There were only a few, but in a sample size as small as eighty-four, those few stood out.

The time on my laptop screen read 11:58, so I opened a new tab and clicked my saved link for the Channel 4 website. Charlie was onto something if she was asking Aaron about hate groups. I popped in an earbud just in time to catch her teaser for the six o'clock slot: "An already gruesome murder could be more than it first appeared," she intoned in a somber voice. "News Four at Six has what you need to know to keep your family safe."

"Dramatic much?" I muttered, setting a reminder on my phone to tune in later. I suppose her teaser worked—on me, anyway.

The station's decision to hold the story for the evening broadcast meant Charlie thought she had an exclusive. I imagined her cat-that-ate-the-whole-flock-of-canaries grin when she saw our cover story that morning on hotshot college quarterback Holden Peters, no mention of Mervin Rosser, Nazis, or murder to be found in seventy-two pages.

Dammit.

I knew better than to panic before I was sure what she had, though.

Back to Instagram. I clicked through Ben's friends—the real ones with actual posts to their accounts—working my way out a layer to close friends of close friends.

I wasn't sure what I was looking for, but I generally figure it out once I see something interesting.

Halfway down the fifth profile I clicked to, I found it: a photo a young woman had posted from her bed in a homeless shelter downtown, Ben clearly visible standing behind the girl on the next cot. The post was dated December 22, which put the post outside the runaway window but around the time of Ben's mysterious camp visit. But people don't always post photos immediately, either. I noted the partial name of the shelter painted on the wall in the distant background and glanced over the top of my screen. Evie chewed what nails she had left, staring at her phone without seeming to see it. I spotted a dot of blood seeping along the cuticle of her ring finger.

I'd never before been concerned about someone actually worrying themselves sick.

"Hey," I said, snapping my laptop shut. She didn't need to see that photo until I knew more about what it meant. "Let me get you some tea. Maybe head over to Troy's. Sit, breathe, try to think positive thoughts. I have plenty to go on for now—if you crack that password, I'd be interested to know what you find, but it's not time to panic, and you coming apart isn't going to help your brother." I tucked my notebook and laptop in my bag and stood. "This kind of stuff is what I do best. I have smart friends. We'll find him."

At Evie's nod, I went to the counter, dropping her untouched drink in a dirty dish pan on the way. Texting Troy to tell him she was on her way because I didn't think she ought to go home right then, I waited for her lavender London fog and my white mocha. Drinks in hand, I walked her out into the late-summer sunshine and watched her sit in her car, chin to her chest, for several beats before she drove off in the direction of Troy's place.

I started my own car and cranked the air, searching through my Google app for a place named with the letters I'd made out on the wall in the photo.

Good Graces Kitchen and Shelter was on Franklin, not far from where I sat. I touched the blue phone number on my screen.

"Hi there," I said when a volunteer answered. "My name is Nichelle Clarke, I'm a reporter with *RVA Week*. I was wondering if I could make an appointment to speak to the director about a story I'm working on."

"You don't really need an appointment, ma'am," she said. "We don't stand much on formality around here. She's here all day, drop by anytime."

"I'll be there in"—I checked the map—"ten minutes. Thank you so much." I ended the call and pointed the car east.

Would these people remember a boy they might've only seen for a few days nine months ago? Long shot, probably. But sometimes long shots are worth taking.

21

"Forgive the mess," Natalie Snyder said with a self-deprecating smile, clearing a spot on the threadbare sofa in her cramped office at the shelter for me to sit. Her curly brown hair was secured in a sort of French twist by a clip and a pencil, her jeans and fitted button-down well worn but classic enough to be stylish in any era. "This is one of the busiest times of the year for us because of the heat, so paperwork takes a bit of a back seat to the people streaming in the door."

"It's no problem at all," I said, perching on the edge of the cleared cushion. "I just had a few questions for you. And then if I could maybe talk to your staff and a few regular residents, I'd sure appreciate it."

"Ask away. I recognized your name when Susan told me you were coming. I've always admired your work."

I smiled, feeling a flush creep up my neck. Was this how Grant Parker felt every day?

"Thank you very much." I pulled a picture of Ben up on my phone. "Have you seen this boy? Not recently, but maybe over the holidays, sometime in December?"

Natalie chuckled. "Our other busiest time of the year." She leaned closer, peering at the photo. "He looks familiar, but we don't shelter unaccompanied minors. Maybe he was a volunteer? A lot of local high school students get their volunteer hours dishing out meals for me."

I was stuck on the first thing she'd said. "What do you mean you don't shelter minors?"

"Unaccompanied minors," she corrected. "We take in full or partial families temporarily before rerouting them to the correct resource, usually a women's shelter or domestic violence shelter. This place is usually the first step on a longer journey." She leaned back in her chair and settled her gaze on me. "We might take a kid with a CPS file for a night as a favor to a social worker, but no parent or guardian and no CPS case means no bed."

"So where would you direct a kid? You said you reroute families and people with specific needs to places that can help them."

Natalie's lips disappeared into a thin, pale line as she shook her head. "There really isn't anywhere in Richmond. Youth shelters are a pretty novel thing. We would direct them to CPS."

"Why?"

"Harboring runaways is illegal. We could lose our license to operate."

I made a note to look into that. Where the hell were kids who didn't feel safe at home supposed to go?

"But you said you recognize him," I said.

She tossed her hands up. "I think? He's a good-looking kid, seems familiar, but we see a lot of people on a daily basis."

"Can I talk to some of your staff, see if anyone remembers him?"

"Be my guest. You're welcome in any of the common areas—just stay out of the rooms off this hall and the curtained areas on the main floor. When it's very hot or very cold out, we set up as many makeshift rooms as we can."

The large, open common room functioned as a combination cafeteria and hangout space, the walls lined with cots that would provide extra beds once the sun went down. Most people seated at the tables had some kind of food in front of them, whether they were eating it or not. The three women moving about the room picking up trash and cups from empty tables both wore khaki shorts and blue polos, as well as large "VOLUNTEER" or "STAFF" badges. I flagged one down.

I showed the staff member—her name was Anisha—Ben's photo, and she nodded. "Sure, that's Ben. He volunteered here last year, came in a few times around Christmas and Hanukkah time, which is perfect because that's when we really need all hands on deck. It was a bunch of kids from one of the high schools. Might have been a club or something? I don't remember."

"Did you see him outside of his volunteering?"

"Now that I think about it..." She hefted a stack of olive army surplus blankets onto her hip. "I did notice him lingering outside after his volunteer shifts. Right up until we closed the doors for the day. I figured he was waiting to get picked up by his parents. Some people work late." She paused. "There was one night, I was walking out and he came running in right as Annie closed the doors. He said he forgot something. But I heard the next day they had to go looking for him when he didn't go back out within a few minutes." She shook her head. "I had almost forgotten about that...Annie said she got the impression he didn't want to go home."

I made note of that. "Is there anyone else here who might have noticed him or talked to him back then?"

Anisha pointed out a few regulars who had been in and out of the shelter around that time, and then she and her stack of blankets disappeared through a door marked "Staff Only."

I made a circuit of the common area, showing Ben's photo around. I was met mostly with shrugs and indifference, but at the seventh table I stopped by a man perked up. He introduced himself as Irish. "Oh, I remember him!" he said in a fantastic brogue as he pointed at the picture. "He was outside talking to Nora."

"Who's Nora?" I asked.

"She volunteers at a bunch of these places." Irish gestured around to encompass the room. "But she's not, like, a normal volunteer, if you know what I mean. She's always looking closely at anyone who looks too young to be about by themselves." He shook his head. "Of course, these places don't take kids who're on their own, but you hang around enough, darlin', and you'll see quite a few with the run-down look that says they don't have anywhere to go. We know it well, don't we, gents?"

The other two men at the table grunted agreement.

"Do y'all know of anywhere that kids who need a shelter can go around here?"

"Around here? No. Kids gotta stay with friends or family—or go to the State."

"Thanks." I jotted a few notes.

"The boy matter to you?" Irish asked.

"To a friend of mine," I said.

"Seems you're a good friend to be down here looking for him, then. I hope you find him. And I hope he's all right when you do."

"Me too. Take care of yourself, Irish. It was nice to meet you."

I added a question about the woman Irish had mentioned to every subsequent interview before I left the shelter. Everybody knew Nora, and they all said the same thing: she was in her fifties, occasionally volunteered at multiple shelters downtown, and always seemed interested in the younger crowd—especially young men. The folks who knew Ben said he was a quiet kid who served food for a handful of weekends in the fall and winter. Several people had been to the shelter before, and two middle-aged women in shorts and tank tops explained that most stays at this particular shelter were short-term unless one of the other shelters was being overrun. Which was often—especially in winter and summer.

I was almost back to the front doors when I saw a woman come out of a hallway. She had the rounded shoulders and darting eyes of someone who was trying to see everything at once without being noticed herself, and she moved in jerky bursts, almost like she was in pain. Her face was marred by a smattering of a half-dozen healing abrasions. Something about her tickled my memory.

Oh my God. I clapped my hand over my mouth when I got it.

Mervin Rosser. Rather, the photo from Mervin Rosser's refrigerator. I dug for my phone, hunting the photo I'd snapped of the front of his fridge. Double tapping the picture in the center, I looked at the woman hovering near the end of the hallway and gasped.

It was definitely her.

Anisha paused on her way to the kitchen with a tray of dishes, following my gaze. "Sad story, that, she's been here for four weeks because the DV shelter is overbooked right now." DV was shorthand for domestic violence. "She came right here after being in the hospital for a week; word is her boyfriend beat her almost to death."

I shook my head, my eyes wide, as I put my phone away. "I think I recognize her... Could you introduce me?"

"Sure, come on."

Her name was Julianne. When Anisha introduced me as press, she nodded. "I been expecting a reporter to come calling if any ever found me." Julianne's voice was quiet and a little raspy, like she was recovering from a cold—which also happens to victims of strangulation. "I saw the story about him on Channel 4, that he'd been...murdered." She leaned forward suddenly, latching onto my arm with two surprisingly strong hands. "Is he really gone?"

"I saw his body myself."

"He can't find me. He can't finish the job. I don't have to be afraid anymore." Her whole body shrank as she let out all of her fear in the form of a long sigh. She whispered the words on replay like a mantra.

I waited three cycles before I gently extricated my arm from her grip.

"Julianne, do you know if Mervin was part of any kind of club? Like maybe one that had to do with the tattoo on his arm here?" I made a circle on my forearm with one finger.

"He was gone a lot. Sometimes for work, sometimes not. Sometimes he was mad when he came home. Real mad." Her hand went to her throat, and I made out healing bruises. "He didn't talk about where he went. And I learned real quick not to ask."

She nodded to me, patting my arm with a grateful smile and watery eyes before she shuffled off in the direction of the small television in the common room.

Sounded like Mervin was Julianne's personal boogeyman. Which was interesting, but not surprising, and didn't put me any closer to finding his killer. That I could see yet, anyway.

22

I made it back to the office just in time to catch Charlie's story on Mervin. She had the hate group connection but not which group—and if she knew, she would have said. Most of her report was an interview with a local psychologist about how people connect with those organizations.

The psychologist said a lot of the same things Vida had: hate groups are not inherently violent but can escalate if provoked or if enough people are loud and clamoring for action. The more inherently violent people in a group—or the more people who feel directly wronged and victimized—the easier it is to get a whole group to boil over out of control. The psychologist also mentioned that the popularization of internet chat rooms and coded messages online allowed for more people to secretly indulge in hate speech as a release valve for everyday stress.

I made a few notes to follow up with Vida about.

"Nothing I don't already know, Charlie," I said to the screen, hoping she was done digging and moving on now.

Since I still didn't have enough information to blow Mervin's case out of the water—and my continued silence there would make Charlie and Mark think I'd lost interest (if Mark even remembered Mervin)—I set aside the murdered white supremacists in favor of Troy's youth group. I spent some time looking up LGBTQIA+ programs at community centers around the state—very few that weren't at colleges or part of counseling centers were advertised specifically for youth.

"Wow." I sat back in my chair.

"What gives?" Parker asked.

I scooted my chair back so I could see him. "Say it's like fifteen years from now. If this baby grows into a teenager who comes home and tells you they're gay, what would you do?"

He blinked. "I mean, I never thought about that, but...I'd say okay and ask what they want for dinner, I guess? Seriously, coming down to the wire here, all I want in the world is for this kid to be healthy and happy. Gay, straight, short, tall...whatever." He touched one index finger to his chin. "I'd hope by then my kid wouldn't get picked on for that, I guess. Kids can be mean."

I nodded.

"Troy Wright's mother isn't...?" Parker's brows went up.

"No, God no. Joyce is amazing. So much like my mom. It's this other kid from the group Troy is running."

"The one who's missing?"

I pointed to the computer. "Turns out, the shelters here won't take unaccompanied minors, and there aren't many programs I can find like the one Troy started here. Which has me thinking about kids who don't have accepting families. They really have nowhere to turn."

"Maybe there's some sort of like, off-the-books network for them?" Parker mused. "Like that they could find places on the internet or something?"

I nodded, rolling my chair forward to note that so I could see if it was true.

"You're going to be a good dad, Parker," I said to the wall.

"You think?" He stood and looked down at me.

"I really do."

"I hope so." He grabbed his mug and wandered off in the direction of the break room.

I reached for my phone and dialed my friend Emily. She was a practicing psychiatrist back home in Dallas, and I wondered if she might know something about a safe-house network for teenagers.

"Nicey! How is it that you always manage to catch me between patients?"

"It's a reporter's gift," I said. "That, and a clock that tells me it's nine minutes to the hour. I'd ask how you are, but I only have nine minutes and I've got a question for you."

"I'm always good, friend. Fire away."

"I'm working on a story about LGBT youth, and I'm wondering about where they go to find help if their families don't accept them."

"You mean like, are there halfway houses or something?" she asked.

"Exactly that, yes. I checked shelters here, but they don't take unaccompanied minors."

"No, they don't. And unfortunately, the best answer I can give you is... not officially. Harboring runaways is against the law in most states, so someone would have to be willing to risk arrest, jail time, fines...you'd have to have someone both really committed to the cause and either independently wealthy or like, totally off the grid. In which case, how would anyone in need find them?"

I scribbled down every word, nodding.

"It's not a terrible idea, though, if there were a way to pull it off," she mused. "Kids whose sexual orientation and gender identity are affirmed and supported are significantly less likely to attempt suicide."

"I read that." I wrote it down again, my whole body going cold. It hadn't occurred to me until she said it that Ben might be... Nope. I didn't want to think it. "Are suicide rates in LGBTQ kids really that much higher than the general population?"

"Yes—especially if they are transgender or people of color. But it's such an unnecessary tragedy: the presence of just one person who they view as having authority, usually an adult like a parent, teacher, or mentor, who respects their pronouns and identity brings down the rate of suicide attempts significantly."

"So you'd say that it's very important for people to be accepting."

"I'd say it's life or death for a very vulnerable population."

"You're the best, Em. Thank you."

"You know I'm always glad to help. But I'm afraid your nine minutes are about up. I need more coffee, and my next patient is in the lobby. Love you, girl. Come see me, and bring that sexy new guy of yours. It's been way too long."

"It has. Love you too."

I hung up and rested my chin on one hand. I couldn't believe Evie's brother was dead. But finding him was the only way to completely banish the thought at this point.

What Em said about acceptance stuck in my head. Troy's youth group was definitely a safe place, but the shelter where Ben tried and failed to stay was not. How many kids like Ben were there in Richmond, and how easily could they find a sense of community outside of their home or school? Absent shelters and community centers, would there be enough demand to sustain something like a teen club? I clicked my search bar.

Swing and a miss. I found a few gay bars and clubs in the greater Richmond area, but nothing for the under-twenty-one crowd—at least not anything with an official website.

I flipped through my notes.

Nora. I tapped my pen on the notebook. A person volunteering across several shelters, seeking out young people enough that everyone noticed, was odd. What was she after? I mapped routes to the two closest shelters and checked the clock—I still had time to get to both before five.

Just like Natalie at Good Graces, both shelter directors cited similar policies about not accepting unaccompanied minors. Both also described a woman, an occasional volunteer but frequent visitor, who focused on speaking with teens who came by for meals or spent time lingering outside the doors. Older, shoulder-length gray hair, soft-spoken. It had to be Nora.

I was on my way back to the office when my phone buzzed from its position in the rack.

"Nichelle, it's Evie." She sounded frantic, and I could hear Troy in the background trying to calm her. "Oh my God, oh my God."

"What's wrong?" I kept my voice level and calm.

"I got into Ben's Instagram account." She sobbed. "His inbox is flooded with DMs, all from one account. It seems like a bot or something, not an actual person—the handle is sketchy, and there's only one photo in their feed and it's their profile picture." She said all of this in one breath.

"Define flooded. Ten messages? Thirty?" Easy to be calm when all I could think was thank God she wasn't calling to tell me the kid was dead.

"A hundred? Hundred fifty? I didn't count, but whatever this is has been messaging back and forth with Ben for months."

"Are they threatening him? Bullying him?" I asked.

"No, it's not like that. It's weird, but not mean. A lot of these are worded the same way: 'just checking in on you,' but...I don't know, exactly. I know I don't like it, and neither does Troy. Ben has told this account a lot of personal information, but there's nothing identifying here about who or what he's talking to at all. He's just a kid, Nichelle. This feels almost predatory."

"How did it start?"

"That's weird, too—with directions to an address downtown. I looked it up, and it's a homeless shelter."

"What's the address?" I wrote it down as she read it to me.

Good Graces.

I slumped in the chair, looking at the address I'd written down for the second time that day. If someone led Ben there, was he being targeted somehow? And was Nora the someone behind the account that had Evie so freaked out?

"I need you to send me screenshots of that entire conversation. And of the page associated with the sender's account."

"Sure, but there's more," she squeaked.

"What is it, Evie?"

"The last message on the chat is one Ben sent. Three weeks ago." Another sob.

Oh, hell. "What did it say?"

"Come get me."

23

I needed Holden Peters.

If Troy had any insight into what Ben's Instagram buddy might be up to, he would have told Evie, and she would have told me. Which left Holden. A young gay man who grew up—closeted but knowing he was gay—in the age of the internet and, I hoped with everything in me, might be more familiar with online LGBTQIA+ resources and contact points.

"Hello?" Holden answered on the third ring, the clinking of barbells loaded with heavy plates in the background telling me he was at the gym.

"Hi, Holden, it's Nichelle Clarke. Sorry to call you out of the blue like this and interrupt your workout."

"Are you kidding? I read your article this morning, Miss Clarke," he said, still breathing a bit heavily. "I really want to thank you for everything you wrote. And, of course, you know Coach reinstated me after the drug test came back. You can call me out of the blue anytime you like. You want tickets to Saturday's game, too?"

"So glad I was able to help, Holden. And thank you for the kind offer—I'm happy to buy a ticket, but I would love to see you play." I merged onto the freeway, heading north toward campus. "Actually, I'm working on another story that I think you could help me with. Do you mind if I swing by for a chat?"

"Not even a little. I'll be at the gym for a while if you don't mind talking while I lift. I'll send you a pin when I hang up."

The drive was quicker than normal, helped by my Lead Louboutins—Evie's panic and Ben's last message had me anxious to unravel the mystery surrounding his disappearance.

When I walked into the gym, I found Holden sitting on a bench with a towel draped around his neck. Two of the other guys about his age in Crimson Football T-shirts stood at either end of the bench joking with him. Coaches and trainers floated around the room, spotting heavy lifts and adjusting form.

Holden jumped to his feet and grinned when he saw me. He held his hands up when I approached. "I'm a sweaty mess, so I won't shake your hand, but thank you again. You saved my ass...uh...bacon."

"I'm not easily offended." I winked. "And don't thank me yet, I'm about to make you talk through the rest of your workout." I followed him to an unoccupied tall rack in the back corner.

He loaded the bar with the ease of frequent practice, double-checking the clips with what I counted as nearly four hundred pounds resting on the rack. Tightening his belt and setting his stance, he eased the bar onto his shoulders and lowered himself into a squat. "So, what do you want to know?" he bit out, standing back up and racking the weight.

"I've got a high school boy, a regular member at an LGBT youth group, who has gone missing."

Holden nodded, catching his breath and settling back under the bar. "You're worried."

"His sister is about to lose her mind. Ben has had difficulties at home—his parents know he's been going to the group, and they don't approve. His sister is supportive, but she's a sophomore in college up in Pennsylvania and isn't present in his day-to-day life." I slowly relayed the tangled web I'd followed over the last few days: from the suspected stint at conversion camp, to the homeless shelter, to the messages from the mysterious Instagram account.

Holden listened as he completed two sets of squats, occasionally nodding but not interrupting or asking any questions. After the second one, he racked the weights and sank down onto a bench. He ran a hand through his sweat-soaked hair, making it stand on end, before he pulled his phone out of his pocket and started typing.

"I don't know what kind of social media presence Ben had, but there are corners of every platform for queer and questioning resources." He showed me Reddit threads, Tumblr blogs, Twitter feeds, and Instagram accounts—as well as some lesser-known message boards that appeared to be password protected. He saw my raised brows at the last one and shrugged. "I couldn't be out at home, so I did a lot of my discovering, exploration, and learning online. I was super paranoid about my search and internet history. My folks are afraid of the internet—my mom is a news junkie, and therefore thinks every chat room is harboring pedophiles or axe murderers. But when it's not safe to be yourself at home, someone who might be an axe murderer but will accept you and listen to you is better than nothing."

"But have you ever met any of your online friends in person?" I asked, thinking about Ben's *come get me* message.

"Oh sure. There are lots of ways to be careful now, if you know what you're doing." Holden walked me through some actual resources for LGBT youth and then showed me some spoof accounts. Just like with anything else, the warning signs were similar: misspelled words, links with previews that looked like gibberish, pay walls, obviously stolen infographics (watermarked for different accounts, blurry text from a screenshot, or strangely cropped). He pointed out code words that people would use in posts to signal that they needed help—these were agreed-upon in other forums and passed around in secret. "Is Ben good with computers?"

"I'm not sure," I said, pointing to his screen. "This is all very elaborate."

"It kind of has to be. People's lives are in danger. People like your boy Ben, whose families are negligent or dismissive or actively abusive, people who cannot be true to themselves out of fear." He rolled his shoulders and neck. "There's another layer for people who are in the closet, because if people from your real life discover a different you on social media, it can out you. So you can never be too careful."

I pulled up the screenshots that Evie had sent my way after our last conversation and passed my phone over to Holden. "This is what I've got to work with."

I gave him a moment to read, but he was interrupted by the occasional teammate clapping him on the back or offering a wave and a congenial nod. Holden obviously had a supportive community in his team, and if the smile teasing at his lips was any indication, he knew it, felt it, and was grateful for every shoulder smack and high five.

He returned my phone and went back to his. "So yeah, Ben was definitely more active on social media than big sister realized." He showed me three forums where accounts existed with the same handle as Ben's Instagram, @wynterɪgreen. "From what I can see here, he was being bullied at school." He showed me several text posts on a Tumblr account. "Just the start of this year—someone saw him at a meeting and outed him, it looks like? With his sister off at college and parents who weren't accepting, these posts show a kid who's feeling increasingly desperate to find somewhere to be himself."

"Does it say anything about Troy's youth group?"

Holden grinned. "Ben's one of Troy's kids? He was definitely in good hands, then. Troy is a good man." His brows drew down as the rest of that sank in. "Is Troy doing okay with all this?"

"He's worried. Ben's sister is an old friend."

Holden scrolled. "There's a mention here from July of a group being helpful, even though he had to hide the fact that he was going from his parents. And another one from a couple weeks ago about someone posting on a ghost account at school about him being there. Things at school rolled downhill from there."

"Could this have started with him asking to stay home from school?" I muttered.

"Could what have started?"

"Earlier this week, Ben's parents lied to me and the police, saying Ben was home sick," I explained. "His sister came home from school and told Troy he wasn't home at all, but now I'm wondering if his parents told the school he was sick because he didn't want to go, and maybe they thought the school sent Aaron that first day I asked him to go by there."

Holden growled in the back of his throat. I had never heard anyone do that in real life before. "I couldn't say, but from what I see here, it sounds like his parents were getting more restrictive: reading his texts through their cell provider, tracking his movements, randomly checking his browser history..." He shoved his phone back in his pocket. "Sounds to me like Ben ran away."

I nodded. "I checked a bunch of shelters in town looking for him."

"You know they can't take kids in those shelters, right?"

I was bewildered. "Is that common knowledge? I had never heard that before today."

"I mean, youth shelters do exist," Holden said. He pulled out his phone yet again and navigated to another webpage. When he turned it my way, I saw the heading Oasis Center. "Like this place in Nashville is specifically geared toward youth—they have beds, counseling, community-style groups, and workshops to help kids recover from crises. There's even resources specific to queer kids or kids from abusive homes."

"But there's none around here, I'm guessing?"

Holden shook his head. "The closest would be DC."

"I really think there's a bigger story here. Because what do kids in situations like Ben's do? They can't stay in shelters, they're isolated from peers, they feel like they have nowhere else to turn...where do they go?"

He raised his eyebrows. "Where else would they go? They live on the streets. It sucks, but at least they aren't being suffocated by an oppressive home situation."

"That's better than waiting a few years until you're an adult and can get an apartment?"

"If you were being abused, which would look better to you? Just because no one is hitting them doesn't mean it's not abuse."

"I didn't think about it that way," I said. "But I get it now. And I'm so sorry this happens to so many kids."

Holden stood. "I know you'll do these kids justice. You don't know what you don't know, you know?" He winked at this last part and turned to move to a leg press machine.

"Thank you for this, Holden," I said, visiting all the pages we had discussed and bookmarking them while he set up for his next exercise.

"No problem. I hope Ben is happy—wherever he is. I hope he's one of the lucky ones."

∼

Safely ensconced at my kitchen table with my laptop after dinner, I went through the forums Holden had shown me. Four years of posts, comments, and links to other sites and resources led me to five other teenage boys who'd gone missing from across the state. From their names and aliases, I traced back to public-facing social media profiles left up like graveyards.

Scrolling through the feeds, I saw the occasional plea from a friend or family member: "Are you there?" and "Please come home." There were also several long-winded stories of friendship or kindness from people who knew them only in passing. Almost like a memorial site. I shuddered as I compiled a list of links to send to Troy. *Honest question: Do you think Ben and these other boys could have run away willingly? Or is he in danger?*

It took him a minute to reply. *Both. It could always be both. Just because you get yourself into a situation doesn't mean you're able to get yourself out of it safely.*

I thanked him and touched the phone icon. It was time to call Bob.

"Hey, kid, what've you got for me?"

"I've been looking into a missing boy, and I think I've found a really good story."

"I thought you were working on a youth group and maybe looking into hate groups. When did you have time to run across a missing kid?"

"It's a spinoff of the youth group, and it might be a better story than the hate groups."

I pitched Ben's story to Bob: a gay boy in a strict and disapproving household runs away from home but has nowhere to go, his sister is desperate to find him and has no way to tell if he was preyed upon, and his parents seem intent on misdirecting any investigation.

"Okay. I'm intrigued. Now—where is he?"

"You'll be first to know when I find out."

"Keep after it, not that you'd drop it if I told you to." He chuckled. "But it has to go all the way. This isn't a cover story if you don't find him."

24

"Hey, Nichelle." Troy's voice was thick with sleep. Was it really that early? "Have you heard anything?"

"Nothing new about Ben, but I do have a question for you."

"At your service."

"Are there any other kids in your group who've been...quieter lately? Or maybe anyone who has disappeared for a chunk of time without any explanation in the last few years?" Evie said Ben had retreated even from her in recent months. If I could find a pattern, I might find a potential victim who could lead us to Ben's mysterious online friend.

Troy hummed into the receiver. "Not that I know of, but the group is still pretty new. I'm not sure they tell me everything."

"What about the boy who was sitting alone staring at his phone the other day?" I asked. "Is he always that quiet?"

"Painfully shy, that kid." Troy sighed. "I keep trying to draw him out of his shell, and I think he's starting to trust me, but yeah—I bet he hasn't said a dozen words in, like, four months of meetings."

I heard his fingers snap. "You know, there was a guy I knew in high school. He wasn't out when I knew him, and while I would never want to assume, in hindsight, the signs were there. I remember seeing an Instagram post, more than a year ago, that he'd disappeared without a trace."

"Can you check that profile to see if there have been any updates?"

"Sure, hang on." He was silent for half a minute. "Damn."

My phone vibrated against my jaw, and I looked down to see a text notification from Troy. It was a screenshot of an Instagram post: a cross-shaped headstone with a rainbow flag draped over one side and the tagline #RestInPeace.

"Oh, Troy. I'm so sorry."

"An old friend tagged him in this photo. I'm not sure what happened—all the comments are just condolences."

"Can you try to get in touch with whoever posted it?"

"Yeah, I'll see if she knows any more details. There's not much here."

"If you don't mind sharing his name, I'll see what I can find, too."

"Trevor Mathis."

"Thanks, Troy. I'll be in touch with whatever I find."

"Same here. Have a good one, Nichelle."

I jotted Trevor's name on the list I'd started the night before, a whole page in my notes now filled with the names of boys who identified as members of the LGBTQIA+ community between the ages of fourteen and eighteen—all of whom had disappeared.

Maybe something about one or all of them would get us closer to finding Ben.

I opened a map on my laptop and searched local records for each name, placing a color-coded pin for each boy's home, school, and workplace if there was one. As I worked my way through the list, searching everything from small-town newspapers to social media profiles, the links between them multiplied. I was able to find three of the social media profiles via Holden's private, password-protected forums. All three had stories like Ben's: unaccepting families, bullying in school, a lack of close friends that they could lean on, and a lack of financial independence.

The other five were more of a mystery—lacking a strong social media presence in LGBTQIA+ spaces, only known through the internet grapevine. I put a star by each name, not ready to drop them from the list, but unsure where they fit in the story.

Copying the online handles they used across multiple websites, I texted the list to Chad followed by a plea: *If you have five minutes today, can you see if you find anything interesting around these handles, particularly anything they have in common? I checked major social media and these forums already.* I added a list and hit send.

My phone buzzed with a text message too fast for him to have even read all that, my eyebrows shooting up when I checked the box on the screen—and saw Charlie Lewis's name in it. I touched the alert.

Are you ready to go back to the Telegraph *yet?*

I laughed right out loud. And clicked the emoji for it on my screen before I started typing.

You bored, Charlie? Or did someone swipe your phone?

I miss real competition.

Before I could think of what to say to that, the phone buzzed again.

Who is this joker with his fake monikers for one-off hoodlums in parking lots and lazy lack of research?

I sent her another laughing smiley face.

Quit laughing at me, Clarke. There's more to this Nazi wannabe who got himself executed, and I hope to hell you're holding your cards until you can throw down a royal flush. Bring your A game. I'm ready.

I nodded at the phone, typing just two words.

Game on.

Charlie was smart. And she knew my style as well as I knew hers. We'd always been a little too evenly matched—but having Mark in the mix was good for our egos, anyway, given that we couldn't take his lazy bumbling seriously.

A small smile played around my lips as I finished my research on the missing boys so I could get back to Mervin and Aryk's story, at least long enough to see if there was a story there.

I flipped to Mervin's name in my notes. "Thanks, Charlie. It really has been too long."

25

Journalism in the age of the internet 101: you're never too old—or too good —to pick up new tricks. Troy's use of a web of social media profiles to discover the death of an old classmate had me flipping through social media profiles for people Mervin worked with at Coldtown so I could see if anyone had tagged him in their photos when my phone rang.

Kyle. I crossed my fingers for interesting news.

"If it isn't my favorite federal agent," I said by way of hello.

"I would say you're my favorite reporter, but, you know, that Charlie Lewis is pretty great." He laughed.

"Ha-ha, Miller," I deadpanned. "I'll forgive the insult if you're calling with something interesting, though."

"Well, I may have a lead on those gun purchases in Fluvanna you asked about. Will that get me out of the doghouse?"

"I knew you were my favorite agent. What kind of lead?" I picked up a pen. Kyle's voice had the edge it only got when he was hedging, but he'd called me.

"Not a hundred percent sure yet—I called in a favor from an informant, but he's suddenly very reluctant to talk. I'm going to give him some space and then maybe lean on him again in a few days."

"You called me to tell me you're still waiting?" That wasn't like him.

"No, I just know you and figured you'd be wondering if I forgot before long—I was actually holding just a bit so I could tell you both things at once, but since my stooge is getting jumpy, I figured I'd share the thing I do have—which is some interesting footage from a parking lot camera at the address from your dead guy's refrigerator."

"No kidding? In all the craziness of the past few days, I flat forgot about that," I said. "I meant to check it out and got distracted by a dozen wild geese that need corralling."

Kyle laughed. "I know the feeling."

"So what's at that address?"

"A restaurant. That shares a parking lot with a gay bar."

"Curiouser and curiouser," I said.

"We're not out of Wonderland yet, Alice. Check your email."

I opened up my inbox and found Kyle's name at the top. The message had a video file attached. I clicked play.

The time stamp was 10:37 p.m., the black-and-white footage showing a mostly empty parking lot between two catty-corner buildings. On the left side of frame was the gay bar, where most of the cars were parked. I wouldn't call it busy, but there was a decent handful of cars and a trickle of people going in. On the right side of frame was the restaurant, which appeared to be closed for the night, with only a couple of cars.

The time stamp slipped past 10:40, and a figure emerged from the gay bar. As he moved out into the light of the parking lot, I recognized Mervin Rosser. He walked with a lopsided gait, obviously unbalanced. My first thought was that he was blitzed.

"He wasn't at the restaurant," I breathed.

"He was not," Kyle said.

"What was he doing in there?"

"The two likeliest scenarios are he was looking for a hookup or doing some kind of recon for his group."

I kept watching. A small sedan pulled up, parking at an angle that worked to keep both plates obscured from the camera's view. It was impossible to tell what color it was in the monochrome camera footage. The person who got out was wearing a hooded sweatshirt, keeping their face hidden. Considering that even after 10:00 p.m. it was still too hot in Richmond to comfortably wear a hoodie, this was suspicious. The figure approached Mervin, its back to the camera the entire time. They left together in another car.

"I'm not sure what I just saw." I started the playback over to take notes. "Walk me through your thoughts while I run it again?"

"This is from the last day Mervin Rosser was seen alive in Richmond. He comes out of the bar, presumably drunk, and gets into his own car with a person whose identity we can't confirm at this time."

"They left in Mervin's car?"

"Yeah, if you zoom in at the end of that clip, as they're leaving the lot, there's a clear shot of the plate. Vehicle is registered to Mervin James Rosser. But that camera doesn't reach the road, so we have no way of knowing which way they went."

"And what about the stranger's car? When does that one get picked up?"

"Not for at least twenty-four hours after this, but we're still going through the footage. I'll keep you posted on that."

"Thanks, Kyle. I'm going to that bar to see if anyone remembers old Mervin."

"Let me know if anyone does?"

"Sure thing." I saved Mervin's mug shot from the state prison records, plus two other low-resolution Facebook photos I'd been able to find of him and a screenshot of the plate on his car from the security tape to my phone, then made tracks for the gay bar where, as far as anyone could tell, Mervin Rosser was last seen alive.

26

The daytime scene in the parking lot of Valentino's Lounge and Bar was the opposite of the surveillance footage I'd watched—the neighboring restaurant, a Tex-Mex place called Poblano's, was surrounded by rings of cars, while Valentino's was a ghost town despite the neon sign above the door proclaiming it open for business.

I pulled the slightly cockeyed wood door open, hoping the daytime bartender was lonely and felt like talking—and remembered Mervin.

The entryway was dark and narrow, with fabric-covered walls that would dampen sound coming from the bar. To the right of the front door, a set of stairs led up into darkness, and straight ahead, a short hallway dead-ended into the main room. There was a small stage set up on the far wall, a bar along the left sporting protest and Pride parade photos—mostly in black and white—laminated onto the surface. Tables dominated the center of the room: tall, standing tables near the entrance giving way to shorter tables with mismatched chairs by the stage. The right-hand wall was lined with booths. The stairs near the entrance apparently led to a mezzanine, which ringed the room in a big U-shape about a foot and a half over my head. The seating upstairs, from what I could see, consisted of couches, chaises, and armchairs, the kind of overstuffed that invited people to stay awhile.

"Help you, miss?" a man called from behind the bar, his torso covered only by a waistcoat left partially unbuttoned to expose his waxed and well-defined pecs. A top hat tilted jauntily on his head, surely pinned in place since nothing else explained its defiance of the laws of physics. Gold wire-frame pince-nez glasses perched on his nose, completing the old-timey look as he dried and stacked glassware.

I flashed my most winning smile. "I sure hope so. I'm Nichelle Clarke, and I work at *RVA Week*." I showed him my press credentials. "I was wondering if you recognize this man; he came in here two weeks ago and, as far as we can tell, that was the last time anyone saw him."

The bartender sucked in his cheeks, making the planes of his face and jaw appear even sharper. "Now, normally, the guys who come in here, they value their privacy. Wouldn't be good for business for us to be telling anybody—wives or press or whoever..." He gave me a once-over. I held the smile and met his gaze straight on. He offered a small nod and finished, "Whether or not we've seen someone. You know?"

"I do. But you can't get Mervin here in trouble. He's dead."

"Dead?" The lighting wasn't great, but I could swear most of the color drained from his face.

"I have a couple of photos from the body dump site, but they're pretty gross."

He shook his head. "No, that's okay. I believe you."

I held out my phone. "This is a mug shot, so it gives you a good look at his face."

He peered at it for a full minute. "Sorry. I can't say he wasn't here, but I can say with certainty that I don't recognize him."

"Is there anyone else around I could ask? I'm trying to trace his movements in his last days."

"Marco's in the back somewhere. Give me just a second to fetch him—make yourself comfortable."

Marco was a server, shorter and thinner than the bartender, but attractive in his own right. Again, no recognition of Mervin's mug shot.

I also spoke with Julian, then Hani, then Lou, then Michael. No one recognized Mervin, whether they were bouncers, kitchen staff, or waitstaff. Maybe the place was busier than I gave it credit for. Maybe it was just the wrong group of employees, because I was here at opening rather than at 10:30 p.m.

I settled into a seat at the bar, and the bartender glanced up at me, the lenses of his glasses flashing in the light.

"Fancy a drink?" he asked, conversationally.

"Unfortunately, I'm on the clock."

"Me too, sister." He elegantly twirled a glass between his fingers and filled it with soda water from a gun, setting it in front of me with a wink. "Close enough, right?"

"Cheers." I raised the glass to him.

"You know, I can only really be certain of regulars."

I swallowed a mouthful of the water. "Sorry?"

"Your guy," he said, nodding at my phone where it was sitting on the counter. "He wasn't a regular. We're very big on regulars here, but there are occasional lookie-loos who pop in to see what it's all about and never come back."

"You ever have any trouble with violence here?" If Mervin was here to scope the place out for his hate group, there was no reason another group wouldn't think to as well.

He arched a brow. "I mean, this is a bar; occasionally folks get a little rowdy, but it's pretty rare and we've had nothing remarkable lately." He turned his back to me, setting a bottle on the counter behind him. "We have seen an increasing number of nasty comments on the bar's Facebook page over the last year or so."

"Just on Facebook?" I asked.

"Yeah. Instagram and Twitter are pretty tame. Younger users there, Marco says."

I made a note to check the Valentino's Facebook page to see who'd been leaving hateful comments.

"Thank you so much," I said, knocking back the last of my water.

The bartender laughed. "Sorry we couldn't be of more help." He took my glass and waved goodbye as I turned and left.

The change from dim and cool interior to hot and bright exterior had me blinking away stars when I stepped outside. I heard the sound of a car door closing nearby, and my attention flicked to it immediately. My vision settled just in time to see a leather-jacketed man walking right for me. Who wears a jacket in ninety-plus-degree weather? Especially since he was driving a car, not a motorcycle. I took a step to the side and caught sight of a patch on the arm of said jacket when he walked past me and opened the door to the bar.

The patch was the same stylized Yggdrasil symbol Mervin had as his Facebook profile picture. By the time the association clicked in my brain, the door had already shut.

I couldn't exactly go back in after the guy without attracting attention, but I had a minute to watch the door. I snapped a quick photo of his license plate and went to sit in my car—doors locked. Better paranoid than dead.

I nearly jumped out of my skin when my phone rang.

Chad.

"Hey, thanks for getting back to me so fast." I pressed the phone to my ear. "Any questions?"

"Fast is a relative term. I hit a pretty solid dead end, but you might be able to do something with the one thing I did find." His words were punctuated by the rhythmic clacking of keys. "I have a GoFundMe page that a few of your missing boys donated small amounts to before dropping out of the public eye, same handles as their other accounts. There's not a whole lot about the GoFundMe organizer, but I was able to trace it back to a nonspecific LGBTQIA+ organization whose address is a PO box in Winchester. Not much, but I thought you'd want to know."

"No, no, that's great," I said. "Can you text me the details?"

"You got it." A buzz heralded the text's arrival.

"Thanks, Chad. You're the best. Give Jenna and the kids my love."

"Will do." I ended the call and put the phone in its holder on the air vent, checking the clock.

I could make it to Winchester before the end of the workday. I told Siri to call Joey and got his voicemail.

I left a message giving a quick rundown of my status, both so he wouldn't worry and so someone would know where I was headed.

Kyle answered my call on the second ring. "I didn't expect to hear back from you so soon. Did you get good intel at the bar?"

"Something like that." I quickly filled him in on both what I learned from the bartender and what Chad said about the GoFundMe. "So I'm heading up to Winchester now to see if I can find the owner of the PO box the GoFundMe is registered to or maybe get the cops talking."

"Let me know if you run across anything I can help you with."

"Actually, I might already have one of those. Can you run a plate for me real quick?" I rattled off the license plate for the Yggdrasil-patch man.

"On it. Drive safe."

"Always."

The drive from Richmond northwest to Winchester was a scenic one, which was good because despite being the northern Virginia equivalent of "the middle of nowhere," traffic into and out of Winchester was rough on a weekday afternoon. Commuters between DC and its myriad of ever-growing suburbs kept strange hours to try to avoid traffic, which only served to turn "rush hour" into "rush half-day."

I made it to the sheriff's office just in time to see all three patrol cars go tearing out of the parking lot, lights flashing and sirens wailing.

27

Three cruisers running code in a rural community doesn't always guarantee the city definition of big news, but it was interesting enough for me to hook a U-turn and chase after them. Trees pressed in from both sides as they roared down increasingly narrow and winding roads, all veering onto a wide shoulder bordering dense woodland. I parked fifteen yards back—it wouldn't do to crowd cops who didn't know me.

Before cutting the engine, I took stock of the scene. Standing at the side of the road, greeting the sheriff and his deputies as they emerged from their cruisers hats first, were a pair of hikers and their dog. The hikers looked agitated, waving their hands as they spoke. The dog, shaped like there was more than a little German shepherd in its blood, lay calmly at its owners' feet, gnawing a large stick gripped between two massive paws.

Press credentials in hand, I got out of my car and strolled over, listening intently. A deputy stepped toward me with one hand up, and I stopped and smiled, in comfortable earshot of the distraught hikers.

"Barnabus likes sticks, as you can see, so he was trying to pull one free back there, but then we saw a license plate hidden behind it." The hiker shook his head. "We gave him a new stick and called you guys."

Maybe fifty yards from the road in the direction he pointed, I spotted a mound of debris about the size and shape of a car. Several large branches—

or maybe even saplings—covered in full summer plumage lay laced together in what looked almost like a hunter's blind. But in the light from the steadily drooping August sunshine, I saw glimmers beneath that weren't native to the forest.

"Did you check the vehicle at all?" The sheriff—I guessed he was the sheriff, anyway, because his hat was the biggest—had a gravelly voice that projected an air of importance.

The hikers exchanged glances. One barked out a strained laugh that sent the dog's ears up. "Absolutely not. I watch *Law and Order*. People who come across weird shit while exercising always find a dead body. Especially if there's a dog with them. No thanks. I walked straight out here and called 9-1-1."

"I'll just need your contact information, then, in case we have any follow-up questions."

I stepped closer when their voices lowered. The deputy who'd been eyeing me met me halfway.

"Ma'am, this is the site of an active investigation. I'm going to have to ask you to keep your distance." She hooked her thumbs into her gun belt, her voice polite but authoritative and firm.

"Actually, I'm here about the possible crime scene." I was now, anyway. I showed her my press badge. "I'd love to talk to the sheriff when he has a moment."

She looked me up and down, her gaze lingering on my shoes. "Come on, then."

I kept my eyes on the ground as we walked, looking out for soft spots and rocks.

"You didn't have time to get here from Richmond on this call," she said. "It's been ten minutes since the phone rang."

"I was in the area," I said.

She shot me a look that said she knew I had another reason for being in the area, which made me wonder what she thought I was interested in.

Before I could ask, she touched her boss's elbow and pointed to me as she murmured something.

The sheriff barely turned his head, spatting a gruff "No comment" before turning for the concealed vehicle, leaving me with the hikers and the polite brunette deputy.

I introduced myself to the hikers, squatting to scratch the dog's ears. Barnabus was fascinated by Darcy's lingering scent on my clothes.

"I'm Matt, and this is Riley," one of the hikers said. He had medium brown hair and a well-maintained beard; he was probably in his mid-twenties. Barnabus's leash was wrapped loosely around the wrist of the hand he shook mine with.

Riley had honey-blond hair tied back in a loose bun that was starting to unravel. "It's kind of exciting," Riley said, also shaking my hand. "We came up here on a whim for a day hike, and we end up discovering both a great trail and a mystery. It really is like stepping right into an episode of *Law and Order*."

"Where did y'all drive up from?" I asked.

Matt stooped to give Barnabus's head a scratch. "We're from Blacksburg."

Riley gave Matt a casual tap with the back of her hand, but she wasn't looking at him. Her gaze was distant as she spoke. "Wouldn't it be something if this had anything to do with that guy who went missing a few weeks ago?" She blinked, focusing on me. "I caught it on the local news, and I've been following clips on TikTok ever since. Did you know there are whole accounts dedicated to open missing persons cases? This guy, his roommate said he left for a meetup one night and never came back. And," she leaned in, raising her eyebrows, "they never found his car."

I thanked them both and moved closer to the scene. The deputy—her name badge read "Wallace"—hovered at my elbow.

A wrecker had arrived while I was talking to Riley and Matt, and all available hands had been hard at work clearing branches and vines from the vehicle, leaving enough of it exposed for the tow to hook safely to the chassis. The sounds of the winch cranking and the branches breaking and creaking, paired with the flashing lights—red and blue from the cruisers and orange from the wrecker—gave the scene a surreal feeling.

Once the car had been dragged free, the sheriff called a halt to the tow truck driver and directed the deputies, who were already pulling on latex gloves, to check the windows. A knot of wide-brimmed hats surrounded the vehicle, peering into windows. The snap of the unyielding handles being tugged reverberated off the trees.

"Doors are locked, sir," a lanky deputy called.

"No sign of human remains," a stocky one reported.

I didn't turn to check, but I could almost feel Riley's disappointed sigh behind me.

The sheriff moved toward the vehicle as one of the deputies jogged to his cruiser to return with the tools needed to force the trunk open. As they waited, chatting, I caught a glimpse of the license plate and stopped cold.

I'd seen this car, not four hours ago, driving out of the parking lot of Valentino's Lounge on the security camera tape.

I pulled out my phone and snapped a photo of the plate, opening a text to Kyle.

I found Mervin Rosser's car.

28

I had barely turned back toward my car before I dialed Aaron. I could feel the eyes of the hikers and a few of the deputies on me as I rushed away from the scene. He answered within five steps.

"I'm on my way out," he said. "Meeting an old friend for drinks. Can this wait?"

"I'm standing twenty-five feet from Mervin Rosser's car—the car he was getting into when he was last seen alive, at least as of right now," I said. "Though I would appreciate it if you kept that to yourself since it's not RPD-derived intel."

I climbed into my car and started the engine, fanning myself even in the air conditioning. The call switched to Bluetooth, and I set my phone in its cradle on my dashboard.

"No problem," Aaron said. "And also, how the hell did you manage that?"

"I don't think the *how* is as important as the *what* here. I know you said Landers would have this on the back burner, so I wanted to let you know the car is near Winchester in Frederick County."

"This gets weirder by the minute. Why is the car out there when Mervin was dead in the woods here?" I heard his chair creak as he sat back down and hoped his friend wouldn't be too mad when he was late.

"I was hoping you might have a theory," I said.

"Not without more information, I'm afraid."

I sighed.

I don't care for sharing stories that aren't fully built out yet—especially not with someone Charlie talks to three times a day.

But I trusted Aaron. And I needed someone the sheriff would talk to, which wasn't me.

"This goes no further. You swear?"

"I won't even tell my wife. Hell, I won't even tell Landers if you say so, and it's his case."

"The last day anyone reported seeing this guy, he left a gay bar just before eleven at night with an unidentified person, both of them in this vehicle. I'm sure you'd like to know who that person is as much as I would—"

"And you think there are prints in the car, but the sheriff doesn't like you," Aaron interrupted.

"Yep. That's about where I am."

"Don't take it personally. He doesn't like anyone."

"Please follow that with an 'except me.'"

Aaron laughed. "Of course except me. What's not to love?"

"I'm pretty fond of you right now, I have to say."

"How does their handling of the scene look to you?" Aaron asked. "Are there going to be prints left to find?"

"They're wearing gloves and being careful," I said.

"Let me call him real quick. Processing the vehicle and running the prints will take time, but he'll send it to me when they have it."

"Thanks. Have fun with your friend."

"Just a quick drink to catch up, nothing fancy. We're getting too old to stay out much past dark."

I laughed, my whirling thoughts stopping on Riley's comment about the missing persons case in Blacksburg. "Say, do you happen to know anyone at the Blacksburg PD?"

"Why?"

"I'm not entirely sure. Something that stuck in my head and a hunch. You feel like tacking an extra visit onto your evening? I'll be back in Richmond in maybe..." I checked the clock. The post office here had been closed for forty minutes already, and every on-duty peace officer was occupied. "An hour and a half, with traffic."

"Sure, he'll be gone by then. We're going to Tobacco Company. That work for you?"

My stomach growled at the thought of their fried green tomatoes. "Perfect."

I hung up and pulled the car back onto the road, using voice control to call Kyle. He listened to the whole story without interrupting.

"Any theories as to why the car was dumped so far away from the body?" I asked.

"Police jurisdictions," he said immediately. "Could be an accident, of course, but every once in a while someone is smart enough to dump the body in one place and the car in another because they know how local law enforcement works. A lot of small departments don't have the time or the manpower to look through shared information, so connections that might be made in the city aren't necessarily noticed out there. The Manson family and the Golden State Killer come to mind from case studies we did at the academy."

"The Manson family. Sure. Because that's who I want to be chasing around the woods after."

"Just an illustration. Let me see what I can find out."

"Aaron is calling the sheriff to get the forensics report on the car's interior. Hopefully whoever was with Mervin when he left Valentino's left some prints in there."

"I'll let him know I'd like a copy of the report, too. We'll get all this straight."

"Thanks, Kyle."

"I know that tone. What's on your mind, Nicey?"

I sighed. "I'm trying to figure out which connections are real and which are figments of my overactive imagination. Coincidences do happen, but... not this many. At least not that I've ever seen."

"I know how you feel. When I fall into a spiral like that, I find it helpful to make a list and start with the things I know line up, and move out from there." Kyle chuckled. "What am I telling you that for? This ain't your first rodeo."

"Never underestimate the power of a reminder from a smart friend. Thanks."

"Happy to help. You headed home?"

"Yes. I'm good."

"Drive carefully."

Left with only my thoughts and the long stretch of road between Winchester and Richmond, I started on that list. Two lists, actually: the missing LGBTQIA+ kids on one, and the dead white supremacists on the other.

Thoughts of both were shadowed by Troy's comment about Ben: just because he ran away didn't mean he wasn't still in danger.

Aaron was waiting at the first-floor bar when I arrived at Tobacco Company after hitting a last-minute surge of traffic in Richmond proper. I had come to a decision regarding these cases and, as much as it pained me to put all my cards on the table before the game was over, finding the missing boys and making sure they were safe would always be more important to me than an exclusive headline. I sat down across from Aaron, ordered a glass of Moscato and some fried green tomatoes, and laid out everything I had: the list of missing boys, links to resources for LGBTQIA+ youth, the GoFundMe that Chad found, and the social media pages. If the police could find these boys, and hopefully make sure they weren't in the danger that Troy so feared, I'd be able to sleep at night, no matter who got the headline first.

Aaron asked a few questions and took some notes, but mostly he stared into his beer and nodded solemnly. "I hate to think what one of my daughters would do if she ever thought me or her mother didn't accept her, all of her. If we ever gave her any reason to doubt that our love for her was bigger than anything else that could possibly come between us." He swallowed hard. "But I know not every parent feels that way, even if they think they do." He tapped his mug on the bar. "Some cases just feel more personal.

This isn't about me or my family, but it could be. And I don't know if that's a selfish thought or an empathetic one."

"Who says it can't be both?" I replied softly. "You want to protect your girls, even if you had to protect them from yourself."

He gestured at the notes he'd taken. "But these boys don't have that. Maybe they did once, but they don't anymore."

"Where do you go when there is nowhere to go?" I asked.

"All too often, you go to the morgue."

Oh, Jesus, I hoped not.

Aaron shook off the dark mood and stood up, glass empty and notes in his hand. "I'll keep all this to myself for as long as I can, Nichelle. And I mean all of it." He rested a warm, heavy hand on my shoulder. "I'll call you if I find anything."

The door rattled shut behind him, and I sat alone with my thoughts, an empty plate, and a half-empty glass of wine amid the rowdy after-work crowd.

29

Grant Parker paced back and forth on my front porch, talking animatedly on his cell phone.

I watched from my car for a minute, blinking more than once to make sure I wasn't just flat-out hallucinating thanks to this crazy week.

I walked to the porch and turned a palm up with a shrug in a silent "What're you doing here?"

Parker answered with a wave and a finger pointing at the door.

I slipped inside.

And found Mel, very pregnant, very obviously uncomfortable, and very much on my sofa, playing fetch with Darcy and chatting with Joey. Pulling my shoes off, I hung back in the foyer and watched for a minute, reluctant to interrupt their fun with my dark mood.

Mel laughed at my energetic little dog as Darcy returned with the squirrel and refused to hand it over.

My eyes—and ears—focused on Joey, though. He peppered Mel with questions about pregnancy minutiae that I wouldn't have even considered asking: vitamin regimens, prep classes, what stretches she was doing to alleviate back pain, what foods she craved and which ones made her sick. My eyebrows ticked a little closer to my hairline with every single one.

"Hey, guys," I said, maybe a little too loud, when he got to the pros and cons of home births.

He stood and reached for my hand, dropping a kiss on my knuckles when I gave it to him. "Mel and Grant swung by to talk baby shower planning. I figured you'd be home soon, so we've just been chatting."

"I heard." I directed a wide-eyed stare at him before I dropped my bag next to the coffee table and bent to hug Mel's shoulders. "Hey, you. How are you holding up?"

"Oh, you know." Mel forced a smile. "Trying to grow a healthy human and not have a nervous breakdown."

I patted her back. Her pre-baby anxiety had Parker anxious, too, though I hadn't understood how stressed she really was until right then.

"Is there a specific thing you're worried about?" I asked, wondering if maybe she'd talk to me about things that she didn't want to say to her husband.

Joey touched my shoulder and slipped out to the kitchen, giving us the room.

"How is a thing the size of a watermelon going to come out of there?" Mel's eyes popped wide, her cheeks red as I took a seat next to her. "And why is Grant insisting on seeing it happen no matter how many ways I try to dissuade him?"

Aha. Putting myself in her sensible pregnant lady pumps, I understood so well my stomach did a slow flip.

"My friend Jenna kept her husband in this region." I waved to my head and shoulders.

Mel pointed. "Exactly! I want him there with me, but there are some things he just shouldn't see."

I nodded, thinking about Joey and his special What-to-Expect edition of twenty questions. "Agreed. I'll talk to him."

Her eyes welled and she blinked hard, sighing and swiping at them with the back of her hand. "Damned hormones. I cried the other day when the mayor told me they were opening an employee daycare at city hall. He was so flustered I think he might have agreed to name it after me."

I laughed, handing her a tissue. "I'm sure he gets it. He has four kids."

"Yeah, that's what he said while I was tripping over myself apologizing." She wiped her eyes and squeezed my hand. "Thanks, Nicey."

"Happy to help."

"I am too, you know. Is there anything I can help you with for the baby shower?"

Thanks to Jenna's party-planning magic, there really wasn't.

"I have it all in hand, Mel, don't you worry. This baby is going to have a beautiful welcome."

Joey poked his head back in, looking between Mel and me.

"All clear?" he asked.

"We're good," I said as Mel nodded.

He took the chair on the other side of the coffee table just as the front door opened. Parker propped himself against the arm of the couch next to Melanie and twined their hands together.

"What was all that?" I asked him, waving in the general direction of the porch. "You looked pretty serious out there."

Parker huffed out a laugh. "Hardly. It was just Tony. We're thinking we want a co-ed baby shower, so I had to make sure there was some sports theming included." He turned to Mel. "Ashton got her health department approval."

"For what?" I asked. Ashton was Tony's wife, and theirs was the kind of lifelong love story I had always thought only lived in fairy tales.

"Did I not tell you she's opening a bakery out on Gwynn's Island?"

I could totally see it—she was driven and organized and brilliant in the kitchen. "If I've ever met anyone who can make a bakery a raging success, it's Ashton Okerson."

"And she volunteered to bake our cake for the shower," Mel said with a grin.

I made a mental note to tell Jenna that we didn't need a cake—and that Parker wanted some baseball stuff scattered about, too. "How are things with the Okersons? Everything going okay out there?" I asked.

I felt more than saw Joey excuse himself to the kitchen. That was twice in ten minutes. I hoped there was food coming because the tomatoes hadn't made up for another day of skipped meals.

"Yeah, they're doing well. I actually called to talk to Tony about Holden

Peters. I sent him your story earlier and wanted to get his take on the whole situation. He said he wants to help in any way he can." Parker ran one hand through his artfully messy hair. "He told me that back in his NFL days, he had a gay teammate who had to keep it to himself until after he retired. Tony says—and I agree—that it's way past time for kids like Holden to feel comfortable in the sport they love."

I nodded, unsurprised.

"He's starting tomorrow, setting up meetings. He'll probably be a staple at Holden's games for the rest of the season—cheering Holden on and making sure no one forgets what that coach put him through."

Joey returned—with food, because he's amazing—and we moved to the backyard since the temperature had dropped sufficiently since sunset. Darcy barreled through the forest of legs to be first outside, courtesy of her dog door. I was the last one out the door, watching Parker's supporting hand on the small of Mel's back as she waddled down the steps.

I ate my weight in toasted ravioli and bruschetta, trying to settle into casual conversation. But the memory of Mervin's car being extricated from the pile of detritus played through my mind any time I wasn't speaking. That was always the hardest part about being in the middle of a sticky story: until the perpetrators were caught and the details ironed out, the clues nagged at me, puzzle pieces waiting to be neatly fit together.

Mel's eyelids drooped after about an hour, and Parker patted her hand. "You tired, baby?"

"I wake up tired these days. At least once the baby comes I can sleep on my stomach again," she said.

As he helped her to her feet and we walked them out, I realized I hadn't been present for more than half the evening. Joey touched my elbow as we walked back into the house.

"What's eating you?" he asked, bumping his shoulder against mine in the narrow foyer.

I leaned against the wall behind me. "It's this story."

"Which one?"

I laughed; it sounded two clicks shy of manic. "Ain't that the question of the week?" I moved through the space, trying to organize my thoughts the way I was organizing the accoutrements of company: the empty bruschetta platter was Mervin's car turning up in the town where I originally went to ask about a charity's PO box; the toasted raviolis left in the bottom of the bowl that needed to be covered up and put in the fridge was the connection my brain kept trying to force between Aryk and Mervin; and the crooked couch cushions were Holden's and Troy's words about danger and self-preservation for LGBTQIA+ youth on the run.

Joey followed me through the house, silent but patient. Darcy yipped at us from outside the bedroom door, wondering why we weren't asleep yet, which broke the spell of contemplation.

Changing my clothes, I told Joey about Mervin's car. "I called you on my way out there just to keep you in the loop, but I didn't even go out there thinking about Mervin Rosser. I was looking for something totally different, and it was more than a little shocking to see my murder victim's car there."

Joey's expression shuttered, eyes and mouth hard, brow lowered. "Did you talk to Kyle about it?" I blinked at his reaction. He and Kyle were friends now, so the attitude made no sense.

"I called him on my way back from the scene." I sat on the edge of the bed, running a brush through my hair.

"What did he say?"

I filled Joey in on the police jurisdiction conversation Kyle and I had, and he nodded, mouth pinched. Hell, he might know more about that than even Kyle did.

"You look worried. The kind of worried I haven't seen you look in months. Do you think someone you know might be behind this?"

His fingers scraped against the stubble on his jaw as he rubbed a hand over his mouth. "I'm trying really hard to not think that. But between this and the single gunshot wound to the head, it practically screams 'professional hit' to me. Which makes me wonder what's going on in Richmond that I don't know about." He reached down to cup my cheek in his palm. "Don't get me wrong, I wouldn't trade our life for the world, but..." He sighed and settled down next to me, leaning his shoulder against mine. "It's a little unsettling, after having my thumb on the criminal pulse for the entire region for so many years, to be just as ignorant of it as any ordinary citizen."

I leaned into him, slotting my head into the crook between his neck and shoulder, and he wrapped an arm around me. I hadn't asked him much about his feelings about civilian life—mostly because his schism from the mafia was sudden, violent, and deeply personal. It hadn't occurred to me that by not asking about it, I wasn't opening up the avenue he may have needed to talk about it. I closed my eyes and just breathed in his scent.

What if I were suddenly at a desk job instead of in the newsroom, rushing out the door at the barest hint of anything interesting? How would that feel?

It would feel like the energy of my world was suddenly turned down, dampened.

Plus, my hypothetical scenario didn't carry the same component of danger as Joey's reality. A desk job would bore the ever-loving hell out of me, but I'd be safe. Someone from Joey's old life could turn up any minute, and the reunion could well be short and bloody. At least as Don Mario's consigliere, Joey had protection. But now? Some hungry young mafioso might see taking Joey out as a way to send their own star rising.

And that didn't even count the tangled mess of crooked federal agents who might be after Joey. The Caccione family had eyes and fingers everywhere.

Everywhere.

Could white supremacists be informants? White supremacists like Mervin or Aryk? And if so, could they have been onto something before they died?

30

I woke to Joey grinding coffee and pulled my computer into my lap to check for local coverage of the missing guy from Blacksburg. Carrying two steaming mugs of coffee, Joey came in wearing pressed shorts and a blue Polo that looked so sexy against his tan I stared long enough to make him flex a bicep and grin. "See something you like?"

"Always." I sipped my coffee, nodding to the computer. "The hikers who found the car yesterday mentioned a missing man from Blacksburg. And I'm getting an idea." I'd found a YouTube video recapping the case. I clicked play.

A reporter with a very impressive Somber Voice introduced me to Tristan Bowen. Tristan was barely eighteen at the time of his disappearance, a high school senior, member of the school's award-winning marching band—and, reportedly, the target of bullies both at school and online. Over photos from the high school yearbook and interviews with teachers, the reporter told the story of a genial kid who got good grades and loved the saxophone but descended into depression thanks to classmates tormenting him—about what wasn't clear. Both the school district and his parents declined to comment on the bullying allegations—or anything else. Weird.

Joey settled next to me in the bed and opened the *Wall Street Journal*, and I went back to Google. Maybe this story ran too early in the timeline for the parents to understand the gravity of the situation. But increasingly recent reports, both print and broadcast, were still riddled with "Tristan's parents declined to comment."

I slapped my laptop shut and jumped to my feet, startling Joey and Darcy both but managing to avoid spilling anyone's coffee.

"You okay, love?" Joey sipped his, eyes closing. The first coffee of the day was like a ritual for him, and he preferred to savor it. It was part of the reason he got up so early every day.

"How do you feel about a road trip?" I ducked into my closet.

Joey peered at me over the lip of his cup. "I'm sorry, I'm not caffeinated enough yet. Sounded like you said something about a road trip?"

"I did." I slipped my favorite tan Manolo sandals onto my feet. "Not that you have to come with me if you don't want to."

He took another sip. "Where are you going and why?"

"Blacksburg, because I've covered missing kids before. No parent of a missing child refuses to talk to the press. I have sat with these people, Joey. They open their homes, they tell stories about their children, they feed reporters so nobody leaves. They cry. And they beg us to find their babies." I tucked my tank top into my shorts. "Something is weird here, and my gut says we're going to go out there and find out that this boy is also gay. If he disappeared only a few weeks ago, maybe we'll pick up a lead that will help with the other missing boys."

"You still think they're all connected." Joey stood, taking what was left of his coffee and my hardly touched mug from my nightstand to the kitchen to transfer them into travel mugs. "Should I change?" he called from the kitchen.

"Depends on whether you want to look like a sexy bodyguard or like you're late for your tee time."

"I can be late for tee time and guard your body just fine." His voice was suddenly a purr at my ear. "Blacksburg, you said?"

"I did."

"Some nice breweries out that way." He waggled his head back and forth in indecision. "But, knowing you, there won't be a lot of downtime." He winked. "Comfortable it is. Ready when you are, love."

It was a long drive, but a gorgeous one this time of year: up and down rolling hills, the looming shadows of the Blue Ridge Mountains on the horizon, the highways lined with gray rock slopes giving way to a sudden intrusion of farmland on the horizon.

Joey's Lincoln ate up the miles, and a lack of road noise combined with leather seats soft enough to sleep in made for a cozy atmosphere. For people who weren't driving or frantically Googling missing persons cases, anyway.

"How could someone keep quiet about their missing kid?" Joey asked. "I saw Grant last night. He'd tear the whole damn state apart looking for his child if something happened to it. Could it really be that different as they get older?"

"It certainly doesn't get this different: Tristan was reported missing by the school band teacher." I looked up from my notes to catch the green-and-blue vista below just as the car crested a rise and started to descend. "In more than ninety percent of juvenile cases, the report is made by a parent. I'm assuming at this point that the parents talked to the police, but the press hasn't been able to get a statement. Not even the TV stations— and most people jump at the chance to be on TV."

"Especially if it means more exposure when their kid is missing." Joey shook his head, easing the car around a truck that was driving five under the limit. "What makes you think it's related to the boy Troy knows? Ben, right?"

"That's why I want to talk to the parents. If it turns out Tristan fits the profile of all these other boys I'm trying to find, it means there's a chance his case, both being so recent and happening in a smaller city, will lead me to the rest of them."

"So we're assuming they're all together?"

"I know it's a big assumption. Maybe *hoping* is a more accurate word."

Joey reached over and laid his warm right hand on my knee. "I've learned to trust your gut after all this time."

"But someone has to keep me grounded when I'm reaching." I sank back in the seat and laced my fingers with his. "If I can get even a thin thread that links all these cases together, Aaron and Kyle and I can blow it all wide open."

"And where does that leave you on the hate groups?" He squeezed my hand. "I don't dislike the idea of you pressing pause there."

The fingers of my free hand curled into a fist of their own volition. I knew why he felt that way. And I couldn't prove what I was thinking, anyway. Talk about a reach. But ever since Mervin's car had turned up in Winchester, I'd had a persistent drive to link the two wildly different stories I'd been chasing all week. I had gone to Winchester searching for information about the missing boys and found Mervin's car. It wasn't a real connection, but it was just weird enough for me to wonder if I might find one eventually.

"I don't know. The timing of these two might just be messing with my head, but..."

But the car. But Valentino's, where Mervin spent what may well have been his last evening. At a gay bar.

Not definitive.

"Did the Caccione family ever have informants?" I asked.

Joey chuckled. "Tons. You already know that they compromised the local ATF branch."

"What about hate groups or other...sort of underground...organizations?"

Joey's fingers twitched. "There was some of that, but I stayed mostly away from it, to tell you the truth. Not my scene."

My phone rang.

"Hey, Aaron." I let the call route through the Lincoln's Bluetooth so Joey could listen in.

"Hey, Nichelle, listen." Aaron paused, the sound of muffled speaking and rustling papers came through; he must have covered the receiver to talk to someone. "I've spent the last fifteen hours, minus about four of sleep, digging through the information you gave me last night. I couldn't stop thinking about those kids."

"You're my hero."

"Takes one to know one," Aaron said. "I called every law enforcement agency I could think of that might have had any dealings with any of these kids and their cases."

This could be it. I tightened my grip on Joey's hand.

"Problem is, I'm coming up empty. No one wants the city cops telling them how to do their jobs—even if they have no leads and the cases are two years cold."

Kyle's and Joey's comments about jurisdiction from the night before came back to me. A killer capitalizing on petty politics to get away with murder. Boys going missing and falling into the cracks that run along county lines.

"Thanks for trying, Aaron."

"I wish I could've been more helpful. I'll keep thinking on it. Let me know if there's anything else I can do to help."

As soon as the call ended and Joey and I were dropped back into the near-silence of the road passing beneath us, I pulled up the notes I'd shared with Aaron the day before. Names, schools, addresses—and family members' names.

"What now?" Joey asked.

"If the cops won't talk to Aaron, they won't talk to me. So we'll ask the families." I was already dropping pins on Google Maps for each missing boy's house, adding stops. I noticed a new pattern, too: not much was out of the way. We were already going to pass most of these on our way to Tristan's house and back, anyway. We'd hit those today, and then I would keep going. However long it took, however many drives out of the city, I would find those boys. I just hoped I would find them alive.

31

Julian Powers's family lived on a small farm—well outside the nearest town, their home was on several acres of weed-speckled land set behind a dilapidated split-rail fence, with a handful of cows clumped together on a hill. The equipment looked well used, dotting the horizon like crooked gravestones in a field. Joey's Lincoln kicked up dirt on the drive but it didn't seem to stick, giving the car an otherworldly shine amid the mud and rust.

We rumbled to a stop and I got out, gesturing to Joey to stay put. He raised his eyebrows but did as I asked. I climbed the sagging wooden porch and knocked on the door. As I stepped back, my heel caught on a splinter the size of my thumb and almost sent me sprawling. I caught myself just in time to see the door open a crack.

"Help you?" The voice emanated from the slash of darkness between the door and jamb. All I could see was a narrowed blue eye.

I ran through the quick-and-dirty spiel and then flashed my press credentials. "I was wondering if I could talk to you about Julian Powers."

The owner of that blue eye was silent for long enough to make it uncomfortable, but I couldn't speak first. I'd never get in the front door if I did. "I have nothing to say to you," the reply finally came.

"Please." I leaned in, studying every visible detail. The owner of said eye was young, with unlined pale cheeks and a slight sheen to unblemished skin where someone older would have bags or shadows. "I'm trying to find him."

The door opened just slightly wider, revealing a skinny girl of no more than twelve in an oversized T-shirt sporting a hole on one shoulder seam. "You can't come in. Pa's sleeping."

"I don't need to," I said. "We can talk right here if that's okay." I dipped a hand into my bag for a notebook and pen.

Abigail Powers shuffled her feet and chewed on hair that could use a good shampooing as she told me all about her big brother. She hedged about his relationship with their father, twirling a crucifix between her fingers whenever she talked about her Pa. I got more than enough to write a story about Julian. The problem was that she didn't have any deep details about his disappearance. It was a school day for them, but Julian had skipped. No, he didn't have a car, but his bike was missing.

I noted every word she said. "Thank you for sharing your brother with me, Abigail."

She nodded, her blue eyes wide and sad. "I hope he found his true love. I hope he gets his happy ever after."

I couldn't catch my breath for a second. "Do you think Julian was looking for love?"

"He was always in the library at school. Messaging someone."

I scribbled that down. Of course, school was closed today.

I thanked her again, then retreated to the car for the next leg of the journey.

At the house of the second boy, Thomas Green, a middle-aged man with a thick beard slammed the door in my face before I could even finish introducing myself. Thomas had been missing longer than the others on my list. I wondered if they had just given up hope and didn't like reminders. With no way to know, believing that at least brought me a measure of peace.

The next boy, Isaac Fletcher, lived in an apartment, but when I knocked, no one answered. A small, stooped woman going into another apartment on the same floor glanced over at me. "Them's gone, miss."

"Gone?"

"Terrible shame," the woman said, shaking her head sadly. "Oldest boy done run away, and the family followed after."

Another miss.

The fourth boy was Tristan. The Bowens' house was in a middle-class neighborhood in a suburb outside of Blacksburg. The lawn was well cared for, and the flowerbeds, while not quite professionally landscaped, were designed and grown with an eye for aesthetics. The gray siding on the house was clean and even, and a basketball hoop towered over the driveway outside the garage. The car parked outside had a Silverfield High School Marching Band bumper sticker.

Joey got out with me that time. He hadn't seen Ben's house, but to me, this felt almost like déjà vu.

Ringing the bell, I took comfort in Joey's solid presence at my back. He stood at the foot of the porch steps, in sight, but not too close to the door. Most people see women as less threatening when a stranger rings their doorbell.

A woman with dark hair and pearl earrings answered the door. She had to look up at me, but that didn't make her seem small. The arch of her brow told me she was trying to make me shrink for her comfort.

"Hello," she said slowly, looking me up and down. "Can I help you?"

"My name is Nichelle Clarke; I'm a reporter for *RVA Week* up in Richmond. I was hoping to talk to you about Tristan."

Before I could blink, she disappeared. One second, I was meeting her almost-defiant gaze, the next there was a closed door between us. It wasn't even the first time that day I'd had a door closed in my face, but this one stung more than the others. I hadn't really realized how much hope I'd been harboring that I could get these people to open up to me when they had rejected everyone else.

When I turned around, Joey was directly behind me, his hand out. I took it.

"I have never met a parent so unwilling to try to help their own kid." I shook my head. "Sorry for wasting your day off."

"A day with you, superhero cape and all, is not a wasted day."

As we walked hand-in-hand back to the car, I spotted a neighbor. The elderly woman was watering the plants in her garden, which spread lush and colorful along the entire front of her home, even more luxurious than the Bowens' garden. I gave Joey's hand a squeeze and jerked my head toward the neighbor.

Joey pointed to himself and then to the car. I shrugged, letting go of his hand before I turned toward the gardener next door.

"Excuse me," I said, giving her a friendly wave. "Did you know the boy next door, Tristan?"

"Are you another one of those sleuths trying to find him?" She took off her pink gardening gloves, tucking them under one arm.

I smiled. "Something like that. I'm a reporter. Nichelle Clarke." I offered her my hand to shake. "I stumbled on Tristan's story while working on a similar case up in Richmond."

The woman, who introduced herself as Eleanor, leaned close to whisper. "I hate to say it, but I wasn't surprised when he took off."

"Took off? You think he ran away?"

"He fought a lot with his parents. Loud enough that I could hear it from right here among the roses." She gestured at the blooms she was tending. "When I was a girl, we learned that Jesus loved everyone and it wasn't on us to judge." She slid her hands back into the gloves, leaving a smear of dirt behind on her shirt. "Nowadays people are too quick to forget that."

Some people, anyway. I glanced at the house next door.

"Do you have any idea where Tristan might have gone?" I asked.

"The police detective told his parents just yesterday that his bank card was used in Winchester the day after he disappeared, and not again after that." She smiled. "I hear more than people think, caring for my garden."

Winchester again. The quaint town sat at the outer edge of acceptable commuting distance from DC—if one were willing to drive more than an hour each way in bumper-to-bumper traffic or take the VRE commuter train. A more rural contrast to the closer and more populous DC suburbs, the surrounding county was known for small-batch vineyards.

I ticked off common threads: Mervin's car was found near Winchester. The LGBTQ GoFundMe PO box was in Winchester. And now, Tristan Bowen's bank card was used after he disappeared—from Blacksburg almost three hours' drive away—in Winchester.

I thanked Eleanor and complimented her roses, hotfooting it back to Joey.

"Home?" he asked.

I nodded, relaying the facts as he drove. He's good at a whole lot of things, not the least of which is being my sounding board.

"Could it be coincidental?" Joey asked as he merged onto the highway. "I know that area isn't very population dense, but still."

"It has to be. What could dead white supremacists and missing gay boys possibly have in common?"

My phone started ringing, co-opting the car's speakers in a blast that made us both jump. We exchanged sheepish grins. It was Aaron again.

"Ben's been spotted," he said without preamble.

"Where?" If he didn't say Winchester, I'd eat my favorite pair of Louboutins.

"He's been to the same diner in Winchester four days in a row, but the owner only just saw the missing persons post on Facebook. I got a message through the RPD Facebook page."

Jackpot. Something was definitely going on out there.

Aaron wasn't done. "I'm telling you because you've gotten to know his sister. The guy says the kid is quiet, but no one is obviously holding him against his will. You think she might want to try going out there and speaking with him before I send the local sheriff notice to pick him up? I told the owner of the diner not to indicate that he'd recognized him."

"I bet she will," I said. "I definitely think it's worth asking her. You want me to do it?"

"I'll call her, thanks. It's not every day I get to close a missing persons case with the news that the individual is alive and doesn't seem to be in danger."

"It's nice when it works out that way," I agreed. "Thanks, Aaron."

"Winchester," Joey said on a sigh when I ended the call.

"Starting to come together."

Finally.

32

Ben wasn't dead. He didn't even seem to be in trouble. It was fabulous news —I just couldn't find a way to fit this newest piece into the growing, shifting puzzle in my head.

"But how did he get all the way out there?" I mused aloud, alerting Joey to my train of thought.

"Didn't you say there was one last outgoing message from his Instagram account?" Joey asked.

"Come get me," I recited.

Joey tapped his fingers against the steering wheel. "It sounds like whoever was on the other end of that message might know something about how Ben got to Winchester."

"And then there's Mervin, the dead Nazi whose car was found in the woods right near there." I looked at my map of missing boys again, with all the pins in place. Switching pin colors, I added pins for Mervin and Aryk: where their bodies were found, where they lived, and where Mervin's car was located. Other than the little clump around Winchester, there were no obvious patterns.

"Objectively," Joey said, "the video of the Nazi in the gay bar plus a slew of missing gay teenagers would suggest to me that the Nazis were following these boys home and killing them."

"Except the boys—at least Ben and maybe Tristan—are alive and the Nazis are not," I said.

Joey pursed his lips. "Yeah, that's what's throwing me for a loop, too."

My phone buzzed with a text from Troy. *Evie just got an update from the PD. We want to see if we can find him at that diner. Want to come?*

"They want to go to the diner themselves," I said. "And I think they're going to need better backup than an investigative reporter with a penchant for finding herself on the business end of a gun."

"But you're going anyway," he said. "And I have meetings all day tomorrow and only one dinky little .22 to my name at the moment."

"I need backup too." I texted Troy back and filled Joey in as a plan began taking shape. "The kind with a badge is probably handy here."

I called Kyle, because having him on board meant we had resources if we needed interference to save Ben. A federal agent holds more sway than a reporter in a dangerous situation eleven times out of ten.

By the time Joey and I got home, the sun was dipping beyond the western horizon. A simple dinner, a game of fetch with Darcy, and we practically collapsed into bed. I was leaving before dawn to stake out a diner in Winchester.

Coffee and co-conspirators on board, we raced the sun northwest. The mood in the car was subdued, partially because it was very early and partially because anxiety was rolling off Evie in smothering waves. Troy sat with her in the back seat, their shoulders pressed together.

We pulled into the diner's lot at 6:30 and poured ourselves out of the car in search of more coffee and a good old-fashioned diner breakfast. We picked an unobtrusive booth near the back where we were out of sight, but Troy and Evie had an almost unobstructed view of the door. Even at this hour, they both snuck glances over my shoulder every time the door opened.

The waitress brought a pot of coffee and three mugs, filling them and introducing herself as Rosie. "Y'all need more time to look at the menus?"

We did not.

Evie ordered an omelet with whole grain toast, Troy opted for the Grandpa's kitchen sink platter with pancakes, sausage, bacon, eggs, and hashbrowns, and I asked for a stack of pancakes. I was more interested in the coffee right then, but we were in this for the long haul, so food was a must. Evie looked like the last thing she could possibly want was food, but since she couldn't just order her brother off the menu, she needed something to do with her hands.

The door swung open every few minutes to an almost constant stream of long-haul truckers getting a hearty breakfast off of I-81. They all greeted Rosie by name, and many of them had a "usual." The place did a roaring business.

We finished our breakfasts, with Troy coaxing Evie to eat more than just the pitifully few bites she managed at first. Meanwhile, I was on my third cup of coffee by the time Rosie elected to just leave the pot on our table. As soon as the plates were out of the way, Evie clung to her mug like a wardrobe door that would keep her out of the water the Titanic just sank into. She hardly ever lifted it, but she never took her hands off of it.

"What are you going to do if you see him?" Troy asked, bumping Evie's shoulder with his.

"I'm going to hug him." Evie's voice was small, her fear for her brother sapping the energy she'd been running on since Troy first called her home. "I just want to make sure he's okay and that he knows that I love him and will support him however I can. I don't want him to think that I didn't care or notice that he was gone." She stared right at me with red-rimmed eyes. "I want him to be safe and happy and know that I will always have a place for him."

We waited. And waited. And waited some more. We drank so much coffee I was pretty sure one more cup would have me seeing noises, and I checked my email no less than six dozen times. Evie tapped her phone to check the time about every five minutes. Troy's leg bounced under the table as he read something on his phone and took notes on a napkin—it looked like math, which brought back terrible memories for me.

The door opened less often after the breakfast rush, but Troy and Evie jumped to attention each time the little bell chimed. Evie's face brightened with hope that she couldn't quash over and over.

Four hours in, the bell tinkled for the hundred and seventy sixth time, and Evie launched herself from the booth. Troy reached for her but didn't move to follow, and I turned to watch. On the other side of the restaurant, a young man in baggy camo with a ball cap pulled low over his face was lugging a very large to-go order—large enough that he was having a bit of trouble juggling it with only two hands. He slipped out the door before Evie got to him, and she barely stopped in time to avoid getting smacked with the door.

Troy braced against the booth, ready to follow.

"Give her a minute," I said. "She'll get a lot more out of him than we will, and she needs this."

"It's a little hard to tell with that outfit, but he looks...fitter." Troy fiddled with a sugar packet. "Like he's filled out some. He used to be a pretty scrawny kid."

"He hasn't been gone that long."

Troy shrugged and changed the subject. "Weren't you working on another story? Something about hate groups?" When I nodded, he asked, "How's that one going?" He spun the sugar packet on the table, then started batting it between his fingers. He needed distraction. That, I could help with.

"I'm still trying to fit all the pieces together. The weirdest thing in a lot of weird things is that Mervin Rosser's missing car was found not all that far from here." Maybe Troy could connect those dots. He was a smart guy. "He's one of the—"

I didn't get "victims" out before Troy's eyes flicked to something behind me, and he got up and slid into my side of the booth unprompted. I looked up just in time to see Evie and Ben settle in across from us. Evie's eyes were teary, and Ben looked stoic. For the first time all day, I wished I was facing the restaurant instead of the wall; I couldn't tell if anyone was watching us closely.

"Hey, man," Troy said quietly in greeting. "We've been worried about you."

Ben's eyes, blue like his sister's, flicked between Troy and me, but he didn't meet our gazes. Instead, he looked at our hands on the table, Troy's restless, mine steady. "Thanks for worrying. For, you know, caring about me." His voice was low but sonorous, the kind that would probably lend itself well to theater or singing. "I hope you're taking care of the others. Sorry for bailing after I promised to help you."

"Do you need help, Ben?" I asked, dipping my head slightly and trying to catch his eyes. "Because we can help you."

His head jerked up. "I don't need anything. I have a new family now, one I chose, who chose me." The intensity in his gaze fizzled, and he shrugged, looking down again. "It would be better if you all just forgot I ever existed. That's all the help I need from you."

He stood and walked out without a backward glance, long strides eating the distance between our corner spot and the door. Evie, Troy, and I stared at each other in shocked silence. I watched a few stray tears trickle down Evie's cheeks before she wiped them away.

On the drive home, Troy said what I was thinking: "What did he mean by a 'new family'? Is he talking about those other boys? Boys like Skylar whose family said he died, who mourned him, who let us all mourn him too?"

Skylar was the boy from the memorial post Troy had sent me. But maybe, for these boys, dead to their families didn't mean dead in a grave—hell, maybe the boys had flipped the negative and decided their families were dead to them. Ben had said as much.

Evie's tear-streaked face in my rearview tugged at my heart. She'd gotten what she went there for: her brother was alive, he at least claimed to be happy...and he wanted nothing more to do with her.

33

Ben's hunched posture, his baggy clothes, his lack of eye contact: all that tracked with having been a victim of bullying, trying to hide and make himself small.

I stared at the notes I was typing out on my computer screen, tapping a finger on the edge of the case. There was something here I wasn't seeing. There had to be.

Ben's dismissal of his sister didn't fit with the story Evie had told me of a kid who was starved for love and acceptance—she'd said over and over again that the two of them were close, she obviously loved him—and he'd dismissed her as no more significant than a passerby on the street.

Why?

I dove back into my notes. So many young men missing, whose only common thread was their sexuality. They were from all over the state, with multiple socioeconomic backgrounds, different races, different interests. Why didn't anyone but a reporter see a pattern here? I checked my pin-drop map again. Was something hiding there?

The pins ran from Richmond to the mountains.

There was space between them.

A decent run of space. I turned back to the laptop, searching for a map of Virginia counties and holding my phone next to the screen.

"I'll be damned to saddle shoes forever," I muttered, looking at the lines. "Jurisdiction."

Every missing boy lived in a different county.

I wrote it down and clicked back to my notes on oddities around these cases.

The sheer number of people who didn't want to talk was weird, too. Two doors were shut in my face during my road trip with Joey on Sunday, and one family had moved away. Not to mention the hoops Aaron had to jump through just to get Ben and Evie's parents to come clean about the fact that Ben was missing.

Covering cops will teach the most idealistic young reporter that humans can in fact be horrible to one another. Sitting there looking at my notes and lists, I was more shocked and saddened than I'd been by a story in a long while. Growing up is hard enough, and the idea that kids were trying to navigate it without the love and acceptance of their families, that they were disappearing, right here in Virginia, by the literal dozen with minimal fanfare, that TV newscasters were looking harder for them than their own parents—it was the saddest thing I'd seen in years.

Even Holden had said that he waited until college to come out because it felt disrespectful to his parents. His brain was probably the closest to Ben's or Tristan's or Julian's or Isaac's that I could pick.

I texted him. *Do you have a minute to talk?*

My phone rang almost immediately.

"Thanks for calling so quickly," I said. "Do you mind if I ask you a personal question? Off the record, I just want to get a sense of something."

"Sure, go ahead. I just got out of class, and I'm on my way to the gym; it'll take me a few minutes to walk to that side of campus."

"When you were still in high school, playing football and living at home and not dating, what was the thing you wanted most in the world?"

"To feel like I really belonged somewhere. Anywhere. I mean, isn't that kind of the overarching goal for most teenagers? Being gay just adds a thick layer of extra anxiety around it."

I scribbled the word "belonging" in the margins of my notes. Holden probably had ten times the confidence of the average young gay man who grew up in an environment that didn't accept him. To come out amid national scrutiny, to face negative consequence head on, and to fight back against the injustice of it rather than backing down—the kid had a hell of a lot of courage.

"Holden, have you ever hated anyone?"

I only knew he was still on the line because I could hear his even breathing and the soft hush of wind blowing across the speaker as he walked. "I suppose I've never really considered that quite so directly, but every time I see a news story about a queer person who has been attacked or killed just for living their truth and being who they are, I hate the person behind that."

That. His words crystallized the nebulous thing that had been zinging in my brain for the past several days. "Thank you. That's exactly what I needed to hear. Have a good workout." I hung up.

Mervin going to the gay bar was not enough of a correlation between these two stories to warrant a second thought. Logically, I knew that; it was why I had been working the two stories as separately as I could, with the backbeat of "Winchester, Winchester, Winchester" ringing in my head. There was no evidence that any of the missing boys met with foul play, at least not yet, and Ben Winter wasn't old enough to get into a bar—even a very good fake ID wouldn't have gotten Ben past the bouncers I met at Valentino's.

Looking through my notes, I came across my conversation with Vida. Most hate groups were just a place to talk, she'd said. Violence took an extreme amount of escalation.

Her words were fresh in my head when I called Holden, and he'd just knocked the connecting nail straight home: he hated people who committed hate crimes against people like him, people who yelled, who assaulted, who murdered people like him. Because of course he did: not many people wouldn't.

But what would happen if someone decided to act on that hatred? Maybe a handful of someones?

I went back to the information I'd gathered on Mervin and Aryk. Both had gun licenses before their first felony offenses.

Among the missing boys, four were now of legal age to have handgun licenses in Virginia.

I dialed Kyle. "Hey, can you check some records for me?" I listed the names. "I want to see if any of these guys have gun licenses."

"Hello to you too," Kyle said jovially. "What's got you checking gun licenses?"

"Just a hunch for now. Humor me?"

"Fine. Keep your secrets."

I could hear the tapping of his keyboard in the background. Then Kyle gave a low whistle. "There really is something to those hunches of yours."

"Which one has a license?" I was eager for new direction, and with this lead, I could look for arrest records or warrants or...things I hadn't even thought to look for yet. I just needed a green light.

"All of them."

Oh shit. My brain played it on repeat such that I almost missed what Kyle said next. "Did you see Charlie Lewis's teaser for the evening news?"

"No, but your tone tells me I ought to YouTube it."

"I can give you the highlights. She's teasing a connection between Mervin Rosser, Aryk Larsen, and another victim she found a lead on in Charles City."

"Damn, damn, damn." I smacked one palm flat on my desk. "Someone really did bring her A game, and it wasn't me."

"Sorry, Nicey."

"Thanks for your help, Kyle."

"Always."

I hung up and turned to my computer, bringing up the Channel 4 site. They didn't have a name for the third vic in Charlie's story yet. I double-checked my files, but I knew I hadn't found anything in Charles City. I clicked to their police department site, hoping for online reports.

Their public records only went back twelve months, and there was only one remains discovery during that time: in December, a man was found in a shallow grave in the woods after animal activity unearthed part of one leg. No identifying marks or clothing was noted. The report said decomposition was advanced. The victim was identified as Billy Wayne Jessup, thirty-four, a lifelong resident of the county and short-haul truck driver.

Another truck driver, which put me at three for three.

I might be reaching, but I was damned sure there was something there to grab.

I just needed to figure out what before Charlie did.

34

Billy Wayne Jessup's mother lived in a postwar tract house with a neat but sparse yard, a clothesline hung with peachy-pink sheets blowing in the wind, and a wreath of bright silk sunflowers on the front door. A small woman with steely gray hair, her torso encased in a large and complicated back brace, greeted me from behind the screen door when I rang the bell.

When I introduced myself, she invited me in. I took a seat on a dated sofa in a close but tidy living room. I offered condolences for the loss of her son, however late they might have been at this point, and that was all it took for her to spill her life story.

Mrs. Jessup was lonely.

"I raised two boys on my own in this very house. My oldest is a lawyer at a big firm in DC, and I buried my youngest the day after Christmas." Her head drooped slightly, marking the emotional impact with minimal spine movement. "I worked, sometimes double shifts, at a defense factory running a tube bender for almost thirty years." She gestured to the brace. "The job was: push a heavy machine, pull it back, bend over to pick up the part. Over and over all day. But it paid decent, and my kids had good insurance. Fucked up my back, though."

She described Billy Wayne as a good boy and a decent student, not like his brother but still passing. "He never got too interested in college," she said, "only went to class for a year, fell in with a bad crowd, and dropped out."

"Can you tell me a bit more about this 'bad crowd'?"

"Just a bad influence all around. Drinking, smoking, getting tattoos." She waved one hand. "Whole passel of boys who didn't seem to get that the Confederacy fell a long time ago."

I sucked in a long, slow breath and kept my face blank. Mervin had a Confederate flag, too, just not as prominently displayed as the swastika.

Mrs. Jessup was still talking. "I never taught my boys anything except that the Good Book says Jesus loved the people rich society hated, and that man ought judge not lest he be judged, and that nobody was better than them, and they weren't better than nobody else, either. But Billy Wayne... my boy floundered. Patrick was in law school and headed for a big career, and I think..." She caught her breath, fidgeting in the brace, and let a tear fall without regarding it. "I think Billy needed to believe he was better than someone, because the whole world thought his brother was better than him." She dropped her chin again. "He hadn't spoken to me or his brother in nearly two years before the sheriff called saying they'd found his body."

"Thank you so much for speaking with me, Mrs. Jessup," I said, standing. "And, again, I am so very sorry for your loss."

"We lost him a long time before he died, and then lost him a third time when they gave up looking for who killed him." She looked me in the eyes with a fire I hadn't yet seen from her. "My boy was misguided, sure, but he didn't deserve to go like that. No one deserves to go like that."

Back in my car, I Googled Patrick Jessup's office and left a message with the receptionist.

I walked back into the office just in time to catch Charlie's segment. Mervin, Aryk, and Billy Wayne were immortalized in the minds of Channel 4 viewers with their mug shots and the eerily identical circumstances of their deaths. Charlie avoided using the phrase "serial killer" when she talked about the connection between the three victims, but the insinuation was there. What wasn't was anything about who might have been responsible for their deaths.

"Getting it first is not always getting it better," I reminded myself.

Even after a year at the weekly, it was hard not to begrudge Charlie her faster timeline—especially knowing that she was a good match for me head-to-head.

She was right about Mark: he was a performer, not a competitor. I would bet the contents of my closet that tomorrow's follow-up in the *Telegraph* would be mostly mug shots, peppered with a cherry-picked, sensationalized rewording of Charlie's report.

I, however, was a competitor. When my story went out, it would blow Charlie's fast reporting out of the water.

It had to.

35

Patrick Jessup kept closer tabs on his younger brother than even his mother knew.

"I have always had political aspirations and..." Patrick cleared his throat. "Billy Wayne's interests, his associations, and his personality were the kind of things that would...come back to haunt me during a campaign."

Lorretta Jessup was sympathetic to her younger son, viewing his beliefs as a straying from the moral path she'd set both her boys on. She didn't see Billy Wayne as an embarrassment or a black sheep.

Patrick, on the other hand, seemed to view Billy Wayne through the same lens that Billy Wayne had seen himself—at least according to Lorretta: Billy Wayne was only worth whatever he reflected back on Patrick. Lorretta's words made so much more sense after listening to just a few sentences from Patrick's mouth.

"Look, Miss Clarke," Patrick said. "I want to help you however I can, but..."

He was going to ask me to keep his name out of the story. Men like him always do.

"I'll give you everything I have on my brother's dealings before his death." A phone rang in the background, but Patrick spoke over it. "In exchange, please keep my name out of whatever you end up printing."

Every time. Politicians are the easiest people in the world to read. I didn't give one damn about printing his name—which was not nearly as important as he seemed to want to think. All I wanted was more information on Billy Wayne, but when the guy on the other end of the call has an ego as big as Texas, saying that out loud is ill-advised.

"You have my word, Mr. Jessup."

"What's your contact info? I'll put you in touch with someone in my employ who can get you what you need."

Someone in his employ? What was this, a spy movie?

Sure enough, shortly after we hung up, I got a call from a Richmond-based private investigator who described himself as "employed by Mr. Patrick Jessup" to keep tabs on "Mr. Billy Wayne Jessup's activities," as if Billy Wayne were a cheating boyfriend rather than a white supremacist. But my ears perked up when this guy said he'd been following Billy Wayne for three years before his death.

"Thank you so much for getting back to me so quickly," I said.

"It's what Mr. Jessup pays me for," the PI said gruffly. "I sent you an email with some of the photos I took of Mr. Jessup's brother, but I have much more information on paper than I have on the computer—I'm sure you understand."

I murmured something that probably passed for "sure," opening up my email to see what he'd sent. I flipped through dozens of image files named "BWJessup" and a date. They showed years of regular meetings with large gatherings of white men in remote places over the course of about three years before Billy Wayne's death. In the background, I spotted Confederate flags, Nazi flags, and American flags among the various crowds. By itself, personally abhorrent but not particularly damning—or particularly useful to me. But a guy like this would've amassed hundreds of pages of notes in three years of surveillance. If he could link Billy Wayne with Mervin and Aryk—or, God forbid, the missing boys—even the possibility was worth my time.

"Are you able to meet with me sometime today to go over some of this in more detail?"

We agreed to meet at Capital Ale at seven.

"I'll tell you, I wasn't surprised to hear he died. Billy Wayne was into some pretty gnarly supremacy organizations," he said. "And not just one. He was attending meetings up to three times a week at one point. These groups were the hardcore kind where anyone who isn't a straight white man is subhuman and deserves to be hated. I never saw him in a white hood myself, but it wouldn't have shocked me if he had one in his closet."

～

Private Investigator Ryan Dietrich was three minutes early and brought a file folder more than three inches thick. It landed on the table in front of me with a heavy *smack*.

"Thank you for meeting with me, Mr. Dietrich. I really appreciate it."

"I've heard of you, you know," he said. "You'd make a good PI, if you ever wanted to get your license."

"Shockingly, you are the first person who's ever said that to me—usually I get cop." I pulled the folder closer and, at his nod, started flipping through pages.

"Similar jobs, but when you're a PI, you write your own schedule." He grinned. "There's a similar sense of freedom with being a short-haul truck driver like Billy Wayne. From the sheer number of meetings I followed him to over the years, he didn't have a set schedule from week to week, which allowed him to go to these...gatherings wherever and whenever they might be."

I kept scanning pages. Many of the pictures were similar to the ones Dietrich had sent me earlier: Billy Wayne going to or coming from a large gathering. But then I saw some news articles that gave me pause.

He'd collected extensive coverage of a sort of Woodstock for hatred, where several groups mobilized hundreds of members from as far away as four states over to gather for three days of demonstrating what they deemed their racial and genetic superiority with marches and chants and plenty of large firearms. Protesters rallied as well, and by the last day the scene turned violent.

"How many people died here again?" I asked, scanning a second clipping.

Dietrich leaned forward to see what I was reading. "Three."

I tapped the headline. "Was Billy Wayne there?"

"There are pictures of him—torch and all."

I fanned through pages until I found the pictures. Billy Wayne, clearly identified with a big red circle, marched in line with a group of white men in black shirts, carrying torches and yelling, their faces immortalized in a paroxysm of hatred.

"Did you take these?"

"No, but I knew he was there, and I combed through thousands of photos from journalists until I found them. Patrick was damned lucky Billy Wayne wasn't doxxed on Twitter in the aftermath. So many were, and I caught him in the background of a few of those photos as well."

I kept my eyes on the contents in front of me, trying to keep it casual. "It looks like you knew Billy Wayne better than his own family the past several years. Do you have any idea who killed him?"

Dietrich pinched the bridge of his nose between two fingers. "Patrick is a good man, a good employer, and I think he would make a good politician." He lowered his hand and looked at me. "But Billy Wayne was not. Billy Wayne was full of hate and impotent rage, hating the world and everyone in it because he felt inadequate."

"He was shot in the head, buried in the woods, and left to rot." I shook my head. "Does anyone deserve that?"

Dietrich spread his hands palm up on the table and shrugged, his voice even and devoid of emotion. "His death was quick. I feel pretty confident saying if he had been the one dealing out vigilante justice, it wouldn't have been so merciful."

"You didn't like him." It was a statement, not a question.

"I also didn't kill him, just to be clear," he said. "But let's just say that if I'd been there when Billy Wayne was killed, I probably wouldn't have done anything to stop it." He paused to take a long draught of his beer. "To answer your question, though, no—I wasn't there, and I don't have any idea who finally did what many people might have wanted to."

"Do you have copies of all this?" I asked, laying one hand on the folder I was less than halfway through.

He waved a hand. "It's yours—everything Patrick needs, he already has."

I thanked him and headed home, more than ready to curl up with a glass of wine and let Joey help me forget this nightmare for a little while.

36

Joey wasn't home.

I checked my phone for a text or voicemail letting me know he was running late, but there was nothing. I sent him a "Where are you?" text and took an impatient Darcy out to the backyard for a short game of fetch.

As I threw the squirrel, I looked up at the sky—still light enough that one might think it was only early evening when my tired eyes told me it had to be getting close to bedtime. It was still humid enough to make even my hair curl, though the heat was fading slightly. Soon it would be cool enough for scarves and long sleeves, and I was ready. Fall in Virginia is my favorite time of year.

When Darcy tired out, we went inside and I checked my phone again. Still radio silence from Joey. Usually, he was timely with texts, shooting a quick reply almost no matter what the situation. Probably just a meeting that ran late. I couldn't help but worry a little, but keeping my hands busy would help alleviate it. I put my phone down and focused on food.

My chef skills were nothing compared to Joey's, but I'd lived on my own much longer than I'd lived with him, so I wasn't totally helpless. Rummaging through the fridge, I discovered leftover roasted chicken, a few tomatoes, and a block of cheese.

"Tacos it is," I said to Darcy as she settled in front of the stove where she'd be sure to catch anything I might drop.

As I shredded the chicken and heated up a pan, I let my mind wander back to Ryan Dietrich. It wasn't until I started stirring cumin and chili powder into the chicken that I figured out what I'd missed on the first pass.

Dietrich had said that the groups targeted "anyone who isn't a straight white man." My experience with white supremacists until this point had been focused on the "white man" part of that statement, but the other word, "straight," was no less important.

Leaving the chicken to simmer, I went back to the burgeoning file on Billy Wayne, flipping through a few more photos. Ten pages in, I stopped and picked up the picture, turning it and squinting at the low-slung building and surrounding parking lot.

Holy Manolos.

The parking lot was Valentino's, where Mervin Rosser was last seen alive.

And Billy Wayne's blue-and-orange truck was parked right outside the front door. There were far too many coincidences piling up here for them to be plain old coincidences.

I pulled out a piece of paper to start brainstorming ways that Valentino's could be a connection between the white supremacists and the missing gay boys. The obvious answer would be that Mervin, Aryk, and Billy Wayne (still no confirmed sighting of Aryk there, but I wasn't ready to discount the possibility) were there scoping out someone to beat up. All three of them had prior convictions for assault, so it was no stretch that they might continue on that path.

But...the most obvious answer is not always the right one. What if they'd gone there looking for hookups instead? Billy Wayne's entire introduction to white supremacy came from a place of self-loathing and feelings of inadequacy when compared to his brother. What if he loathed his own sexuality and desires as much as his lack of financial and academic success?

Following that train of thought just led to more questions: How could going in for hookups end with them dead? What went wrong?

I flipped back to my notes from my conversation with the hot bartender in his Victorian-themed getup. I had to have missed something. But not according to my notes, I hadn't.

The front door opened, and I dropped the photo and dashed back to check on dinner, which was ready to serve. I turned off the stove and pulled out the tortillas, sour cream, and lettuce; chopping it and the tomatoes took long enough for Joey to change. Or it should have, anyway. I sliced half an avocado, shredded cheese, and got out plates, finally turning for the hallway as he stepped into the kitchen.

I had to fight to keep a gasp in check. He looked positively haggard, which wasn't a look I'd ever seen on him before. Drawn, worried, furious, sure—but not this. I rose to my tiptoes to kiss him hello, and he turned his cheek to my lips and stared through me.

Okay.

"I made chicken tacos. They're ready when you are."

"Thanks," he mumbled.

"Everything okay, baby?" I touched his arm lightly, half expecting him to pull away.

"Everything's fine." He didn't flinch, but he didn't look at me, either.

Everything was most certainly not fine.

"Would you like some wine with dinner? I didn't open a red in time, but we have some white in the fridge."

"Water's fine." He was already moving to fill a glass with ice and water from the tap.

I felt too large in my own kitchen, like every move I made put me on a collision path with him. We usually coexisted in the space like we had a preternatural understanding of each other's movements, but our rhythm was off.

I watched Joey assemble tacos on his plate. His movements were steady, but he hadn't met my eyes or smiled at me since he got home. That was so far past weird for him, it couldn't even see weird in the rearview. "How was your day?"

"It was fine, nothing special." The tightness in his jaw said he was either lying or fighting not to be irritated with me. I wasn't sure which made the two bites of food I'd taken roll into a brick in my middle, but I didn't like the idea of either.

Journalism even before the age of the internet 101: silence is effective. Knowing when to back off and be quiet is essential for getting all the necessary details without offending, stifling, or annoying the interviewee.

We finished dinner in silence, my thoughts a scattered mess of Joey, the missing boys, and white supremacists. As we were getting ready for bed, I offered yet another olive branch. Maybe Joey wouldn't talk about his day, but he could help me with mine.

"Can you think of any reason all four of the missing boys who are eligible have gun permits?"

"Self-defense," he answered immediately, though his back was to me. "How many more men out there are like the guys in these hate groups you've been chasing?"

The last thought I had before sleep was Ben's comment about having found a "new family." The rhetoric of a found family was common to queer stories, according to my online research. It was also common in cults and hate groups.

Maybe there was more of a reason to link these two stories than I ever could have guessed.

37

Morning brought sunshine and clarity: Joey's words about self-defense the night before and Holden's profession of hatred for people who hurt others for being different crashed together to give me a theory: Could my three dead guys have been the kind of people even Holden hated? Maybe trying to terrorize the wrong people and they ended up dead because of it?

I needed to see Mervin's, Aryk's, and Billy Wayne's arrest records. The state system showed only charges for all three men because each took a plea deal in every case. I wanted to know what they got arrested for, with the kind of detail only an officer's narrative could provide. The problem was, that took time: I had to track down the jurisdiction of each crime and possibly make a formal Freedom of Information request for each report. Which a department could in theory tie up in red tape for three months. Which meant sweet-talking some officers was probably on my to-do list.

A note on the kitchen counter said Joey had an early meeting and would call me later. The "Love you, J" scrawled across the bottom helped soothe my frazzled nerves.

My phone rang as I filled Darcy's food bowl.

"What's got you up early?" I asked Kyle when I picked up.

"It's seven thirty on Tuesday," he said. "I have a job. And I have some interesting news for you."

"What's that?" I asked.

"You said the kid you were looking for was at a diner in Winchester the other day, and that's where you found Mervin Rosser's car," he said.

"Right." I dragged the word out, reaching for a pen.

"Guess where Aryk Larsen lived for the last six months before he was murdered?"

"He did not!" I dropped my pen. "I have an address for him, it's in Henrico."

"It's one of those PO box places that looks like an apartment on paper. One of my guys caught it yesterday because they're popular with crooks of all stripes. I dug in this morning and found that he was sharing a trailer with two other guys up in Winchester."

"This could not get any weirder, Kyle."

"Don't say that out loud. I assure you it can."

"I should know better by now," I agreed. "Thanks, Kyle."

"Sure thing. Just do me a favor and call me if you're going to take off out there, okay?"

"Consider yourself called," I said. "And I know—I'm careful."

I hung up, opening my email to a message from Vida, who had compiled a comprehensive list of hate groups that used the Yggdrasil symbol. She had even ordered it by proximity: the Richmond area, the rest of Virginia, the mid-Atlantic region, the East Coast, the United States as a whole, and even one group in Canada. It was much more detailed than I had been expecting.

Between Mervin's Facebook profile and the patch on the guy I'd spotted at Valentino's, the symbol was fresh in my mind and achingly relevant, demanding to be investigated further. I turned my attention to Stop Hate Virginia's notes on each group. For the most part, each group's goals and focus were a little different, but each one specifically called out a hatred for the LGBTQIA+ community.

I brewed my coffee—with the Keurig, none of Joey's fancy stuff—right into my travel mug, grabbed my laptop, notes, and files, and loaded the car. From the driveway, I texted Bob. *The key to this whole damn thing is in Winchester County. I'm going to see if I can find it.*

Janis Joplin on the radio to keep me company, I pointed the car northwest.

~

I made it to the Winchester sheriff's department just as the senior deputy clocked in for the morning. This time, I actually set foot inside the building, since the quiet town was actually quiet.

"You look familiar." The deputy narrowed his eyes at me.

I smiled sweetly at him. "My name is Nichelle Clarke. I was at the scene of that car extraction in the woods the other day."

His eyes damn near disappeared into slits. "The department has no further comment on that at this time."

I waved away his suspicion. "I understand. I was actually hoping I could ask you about a cold case." I held up the box of pastries I'd grabbed from Can Can on my way out of Richmond. "If you have a minute to chat. I understand if you're busy."

His gaze riveted on the pastry box, he invited me back to his office. He led the way through a narrow maze of empty desks—some scattered with papers but most markedly empty and covered in a thin layer of dust. His office was small but cozy, everything from papers and files to personal effects neat and organized.

I set the pastry box on a bare corner of the desk and turned it in his direction. "Please, help yourself." I waited until he pulled out a Danish before I threw out a casual question. "I was wondering if I could see the department's arrest record for Aryk Lee Larsen."

The deputy grimaced around his first bite. "It's usually frowned upon to speak ill of the dead—especially in a small town like this." He wiped his mouth with a napkin. "To them, it doesn't matter what bad he might have done while he was alive if he ain't alive to do any more." He took another bite.

It was highly likely that this guy didn't know every resident of the county by name. Which meant Aryk had made an impression on local authorities in just a handful of months here.

Pretty much exactly what I'd been hoping for.

"I understand that." I leaned forward in my seat, flashing my most earnest smile. "There's just something that's been bugging me about this story I'm working on, and I think it might be this guy, you know? I'd just like to peek at it. Five minutes and I'll be out of your way."

He took another bite of the Danish, chewing for a minute before he spoke again.

"Sometimes people disappear out here, and it's not always anything mysterious. Maybe these boys came across a bear while they were hunting, who knows...why, just Thanksgiving before last, the preacher reported the church pianist missing because she'd not been to choir practice or service in months, and it turned out the lady was just holed up in her place, keeping to herself, probably tired of the local church drama—I wouldn't go either if my wife didn't drag me."

I nodded understanding. I knew a thing or two about church drama. "It's only a hunch right now, but if I'm right about this arrest record, it could save a life." I paused. "Maybe even more than one."

That was a whole lot dramatic, and maybe even a little bit of a lie. But from the look on his face, he didn't know that.

He rumbled out a sigh and put the pastry on his desk blotter, his fingers moving to his keyboard. "I know you have to sell papers, but..."

The printer whirred to life and spat out a handful of pages.

The deputy looked them over before passing them across the desk. "Miss, please be mindful what you say about people's dead kin."

I thanked him and left, leaving the box of pastries perched on his desk. A half-dozen Danishes was a small price to pay for the prize in my hand. I jogged the last few steps to my car and dove into the seat to read.

Larsen's first count of aggravated assault was up first, the victim a young man, described in the officer's narrative as skinny, white, and in his early twenties, wearing tight jeans, a white T-shirt, and bright green eye shadow. The victim's friends, who reported the crime, described Aryk as vicious. Aryk allegedly took the victim down with two punches to the face and then proceeded to kick him as soon as he was down on the ground, shouting slurs. The victim's injuries included two broken ribs, a cracked tooth, and several bruises to the face and abdomen.

The second arrest was for a bar fight. Aryk was the aggressor, dragging a young man out of his seat and throwing him to the floor. He pulled a gun on the prone man who had, just before being thrown to the ground, been holding his boyfriend's hand under the table. The police were called, and Aryk was escorted off of the premises before any more harm could be done.

Both arrests were for targeted attacks on men Aryk assumed to be gay. If that wasn't the Golden Gate Bridge of all connections between the white supremacists and our missing boys, I didn't know what could possibly be.

38

My next stop was the diner where Troy, Evie, and I had talked to Ben. In small towns, the local greasy spoon is second only to the church ladies' auxiliary as a hotspot for gossip. Often, an hour at the diner will yield more information than any ten detectives could dig up in a week.

And after talking to the deputy and reading the reports, I wondered if the good old-fashioned grapevine wasn't just what I needed.

The waitress from before, Rosie, gave me a big smile and a mug of coffee at the counter when she saw me. "All by your lonesome this time, huh?" she asked.

"Just have a couple questions for the owner." I jerked my chin at the man behind the register. "I can wait until he's less busy." I raised the mug in salute. "Just keep the coffee coming."

Rosie laughed, showing all her teeth. "Sure, darlin'. Flag me down if you want some more of Herschel's pancakes." She nodded before she walked away, expertly weaving between tables with her coffeepot in one hand and notepad in the other.

I sat on a tall stool at the counter, nursing the best diner coffee I'd ever had and waiting for a lull. When the owner stepped back from the register for a minute, I hopped down and strolled over, introducing myself.

"You helped a boy the other day with a really big order." I held a hand at chin level. "He was about this tall, wearing camo, with a ball cap pulled down low." I dropped my hand. "He was reported missing in Richmond."

The man nodded. "I saw that on Facebook. I reported it to the police, just like I oughta, and they said not to do anything." He shook his head. "He comes in to pick up those big orders regular."

"Do you know why they're so big?"

"No clue." He pulled the rag from over his shoulder and twisted it between his hands. Rag out of the way, I could see his name tag: Francis.

"What about who they're for? Where do they go when they leave the diner?"

He frowned. "We don't do delivery or nothing, so it ain't like I've been taking down an address. He calls to order the food, he comes in and picks it up, he pays in cash, and he leaves." He started wiping down the counter between us with the rag, his eyes roving, keeping track of Rosie and gauging the customers' satisfaction. "It's always a big order, so I figure he's feeding a lot of people."

"But no one recognizes him from a local business? He's not taking the food in for a crowd at work or something?"

He shrugged again. "I take the orders and fill them. I recognized the kid in the picture I saw on the internet, so I called the number. That's all I know about it."

I found it odd that he didn't know his regular customers better. Rosie seemed to have a name for every face that walked in the door and a mental database of everyone's regular orders.

As I thanked Francis for his time, I noticed a wiry man in an olive green ball cap and dungarees a few seats down the counter, eyeing us over his sausage-and-egg sandwich. I took a seat next to him.

The second my butt was on a stool, Rosie appeared across from me. I ordered an iced tea, and almost before I could blink it was on the counter and she was gone again. I took my time, fiddling with Splenda packets— and kept the man and his sandwich in my periphery.

Just like with Joey the night before, sometimes it's in a journalist's best interest to stay quiet, to invite conversation rather than to seek it. There are times when letting someone talk is much more valuable—especially when they look like they have something to say.

I could hear him chewing a bite, followed by the rustle of a napkin as he wiped his hands. He laid it on the counter and cleared his throat. "You looking for one of those kids that's in and out of the Taubin place all the time?" he asked.

I stirred a tiny mountain of Splenda into my tea, ice cubes clinking against glass as I turned to him.

"I might very well be," I said. "If I knew where that was."

"It's out off Route 746," he said.

My hand paused, seemingly of its own accord, as the road number bopped around my head. It was familiar. Too familiar. My memory threw up an image of the number on a road sign. Right next to where I parked along the road where they found Mervin's car.

I swallowed hard. "You said 'one of those kids'—do these folks have a lot?"

The guy shook his head. "Norma had one son, Ricky, and after her husband died, she ran that farm as best she could and raised the kid on her own. I went to school with him. Queer as the day is long."

His use of the word didn't sound as natural or kind as it did coming from Holden or Troy, but it also didn't feel like a slur. There was a matter-of-fact air that said he didn't believe queerness was a bad thing. More like an unfortunate thing. Which was probably pretty true around here in some ways.

"Ricky didn't fit in around here," he continued. "Got himself jumped one night leaving the library and beat damn near to death. His poor momma prayed over him nonstop for months before she turned him out for not repenting. He disappeared, she quit leaving her house, and a couple years back, she started collecting boys. My daddy thought they were doing work on the old place for a while, but best we can tell, they just live there. More show up every now and again."

Norma Taubin. The people I'd spoken to at the shelters in Richmond talked about a woman named Nora. Could it be a pseudonym? Or had they misheard?

Collecting boys. I jotted it on a napkin, like there could ever be a danger that I'd forget it. Such an odd turn of phrase. Collecting them for what?

"Can you give me an address for this farm?" I asked.

He did so, adding, "Big ole sign says 'Taubin' on it; can't miss it," as he handed me the napkin he'd scribbled on. He turned fully to face me for the first time. "You said you're a reporter. That mean if she's doing some sort of weirdo shit out there, you're going to let everyone know?"

I nodded. "Some sort of weirdo shit" was my specialty, after all. I handed him a business card. "Keep an eye on the *RVA Week* website for the next few weeks."

~

Back in my car in the parking lot, I opened the map with the multicolored pins for both stories and added a red one for the Taubin farm—it wasn't even a mile from where Mervin's car was found. Interesting.

I touched the directions button. Seventeen miles was kind of far to go for lunch on the daily, but the restaurant button confirmed that the diner was the closest restaurant to Norma's place.

I navigated to the county property records, the slow cell service and long load time trying my patience. The county listed the parcel as 53.4 acres, and Google's satellite view showed three main buildings and a large open area surrounded by densely packed woods.

I only saw one way in and out—for cars, anyway.

I didn't have nearly enough to warrant a call to the sheriff, but my gut said the key to at least one story—and maybe both—was seventeen miles away, tucked between a stream and a stretch of thick woods.

I sent Joey and Kyle a text with the address.

Going to ask a few questions. If I don't call you in a couple of hours, this is where I'm headed.

I put the phone in its cradle and started the car.

39

Diner guy wasn't kidding about the sign—it was half the size of a small billboard, set just on the edge of the trees, *Taubin Farm* in letters as tall as a car, with smaller type underneath: *tomatoes, peaches, jams, crafts, and bakery.* I wondered why Norma didn't take it down if she didn't open the place to the public anymore as I turned into a gravel drive that meandered a half mile through crepe myrtles still in full pink and magnolia trees heavy with blooms.

The trees opened up to reveal a farmhouse that looked much bigger than the roofline I'd seen on the satellite image. I was tempted to check my location, but that sign was pretty specific, and there were no other driveways for miles in either direction.

The sound of my car door closing behind me ricocheted off the trees and into the open fields. The house boasted a wide wraparound porch with two swinging benches and at least a dozen chairs, some Adirondack and some rockers, all in good condition. Board games, cards, puzzles, and a few books lay scattered about on tables. My heels clonked on the steps as I climbed them to the front door.

I rang the bell and waited. Two minutes. Three. I rang it again. No answer—and not so much as a floorboard squeak from inside.

I stepped off the porch. Orderly rows of hay bales to the right of the house caught my eye. They were well spaced out and stacked to about head height. It wasn't tall enough to be a maze, but it had to be something, and I didn't see any livestock. Walking over, I found high-tension crossbows, plastic garden urns full of arrows, and stacks of paper targets. A private archery range.

From there, I spotted an in-ground pool behind the house, surrounded by a wide concrete patio. Also not in the satellite image. At one end of the pool was a volleyball net, a stray ball batting against the filter as the motion of the water tried to drag it inside.

Beyond the pool was what could only be described as an obstacle course: chain link and slatted privacy fences for climbing, a wooden wall with a rope, a mud crawl topped with a zigzag of barbed wire, and balance beams of varying heights.

I walked on, toward the far end of the field, stopping and pulling my phone out to snap a few photos of a homegrown gun range housed in an old lean-to that looked like it was once a farmer's market. Beside it stood a metal barn with a green roof, which was definitely not in the satellite view. Was Norma Taubin running some kind of camp program? Evie's words about her brother mingled in my head with Diner Guy's assertion that Norma's son was gay, and I wondered for a moment if this was where the Winters sent Ben last Christmas.

But why would he run away to come back?

Evie said he'd been distant. If I was standing in the middle of a conversion camp, what the hell had happened to Ben here?

Rounding the corner of the barn, I caught sight of the truck Ben had driven off in when we cornered him at the diner. I hadn't gotten the plate but remembered the rust stain on the tailgate in the shape of a lopsided heart.

I took a picture of the pickup, making sure to get a good shot of the license plate, before stepping into the gun range. Standard targets shaped like human torsos with crosshairs marking fatal wounds were lined up at increasing distances. Each had clusters of neat round holes in the head and chest, the mid-distance targets showing a remarkable head-shot and center-mass accuracy.

To the west, I saw an honest-to-God corn husk maze, thick rows of stalks stretching at least twelve feet into the sky on either side of a path just wide enough for two people if neither was particularly large. The maze walls were mostly obscured by huge, hand-painted burlap banners depicting city buildings.

I have rarely been more curious about something I stumbled across chasing a story, but I wasn't about to risk getting lost in there. Not when I still hadn't seen a soul.

I turned back, my eyes stopping on the barn. Shiny metal unmarred by weather or rust meant it was relatively new no matter how old the satellite images Google had for the property were.

Looking around outside, I had to see what was inside.

The door was heavy but almost soundless as it slid on its tracks.

It took a moment for my eyes to adjust to the dimness when I stepped inside, but when they did, they settled on a woman, tall and lean, wearing a plaid button-down, jeans that fit like her legs had been shrink-wrapped in denim, and scuffed black leather boots. Probably in her fifties, given that her face showed evidence of some hard years, she stared, unblinking, a long-barrel rifle in her hands leveled at me. I noted the laser sight. While I didn't have a mirror, her post atop two hay bales and steady hands plus the targets I'd seen outside equaled a pretty good chance the little green dot was dead in the middle of my forehead.

"Norma?" The lack of tremor in my voice even surprised me.

"Shut the door." Her voice was high but hard. "We don't take kindly to trespassers around here."

40

My heart hammered in my chest as I slid the door closed behind me. "I went to the door and rang the bell, but no one answered," I blurted, trying to find the middle ground between quick and calm. Panic is rarely wise, especially not when the person holding a gun on you is rock steady. "I drove out hoping to talk to Norma Taubin."

Norma narrowed her eyes at me, but she dropped the butt of the gun so the barrel tipped up, the laser dot dancing on the ceiling in time with her breath. "Why?"

I'd take talking over shooting.

"My name is Nichelle Clarke. I'm a reporter for *RVA Week* down in Richmond, and I'm working on a story about a missing boy, Benjamin Winter. His sister is beside herself with worry and asked for my help." I jerked my head to the right where, on the other side of the barn wall, the truck we'd seen Ben drive was parked. "A boy matching his description was spotted driving that truck in town. I tracked him here and was hoping to speak with him. If that's okay with you." Investigative journalism and general life skills 101: always ask politely when they have a gun and you don't.

Norma's eyes flashed, her mouth settling into a hard line. "My boys are happy and healthy and doing the Lord's work."

Her boys? I kept my face set in an understanding expression, nodding. "I'm glad to hear that."

She tipped her head to one side like she wasn't sure what to make of me.

"Do you help the boys see the error in their ways?" I kept my voice gentle and nonjudgmental, looking only for a sense of what I was dealing with.

A laugh lurched out of her chest, her hand tightening on the gun. "They help me atone for mine, missy." Norma dropped her chin to her chest, while I turned the words over in my head.

Not the kind of camp I'd been thinking, then? What the hell was this place?

"It took tragedy in my own life to see the error in my judgment." Norma raised her head, shifting the rifle to the other hand. "My son came out to me after he was attacked and beaten outside the library—right here in this town. A town his blood kin built, served through the council and the church. His home." She shook her head, her voice hitching the barest bit on the last word. "And the people here nearly killed him for being different. Ricky came to me as he was healing, for love, for acceptance. I turned him away, shut him out of my heart, told him he was an abomination in the eyes of the God I had raised him to serve." Her voice broke on the word *abomination*. "I was ignorant. I didn't understand that God is love, and a loving God could never hate a child He created. But my son vanished long before I realized the error of my own ways."

I held so still I was afraid to blink, letting her talk. Maybe it was because I said Evie missed her brother. Maybe it was because I told Norma I was a reporter. Maybe it was just because I was another woman who was finally there for her to talk to—but Norma had a story. And it poured out of her like she needed to tell it more than she needed her next breath.

"It's been ten years, and I've never found so much as a whisper of my son. I've spent my husband's family fortune on private detectives, reported Ricky missing to the police, done everything I could think of. I'm afraid someone killed him long, long ago, and I'll never know for certain."

I wanted to ask if she'd thought about people like Evie, who loved and worried themselves sick over her boys, but I didn't dare interrupt. There'd be time for questions later. Assuming she kept the gun pointed at the ceiling.

"When I lost my boy, I turned first to my faith and my Bible, but I didn't find what I thought I was looking for. It turned out I didn't know the Good Book as well as I thought I did." She talked about Paul's Letters to the Corinthians and 1 Timothy and how for years she believed in her heart that the Bible plain-out said homosexuality was a sin. Bought it so much that she turned her back on her only child. Norma paused and looked me straight in the eye. "Did you know that the first time homosexuality was even mentioned in the Bible wasn't until the 1940s?"

Not until last week. Working the youth group story in the shadow of Mervin Rosser and the hate groups, I'd wondered why so many folks believed judging gay people was a Christian thing to do. I grew up in a Baptist church in Texas and never once heard our pastor say gay people were unloved by Jesus—our congregation fully embraced *Love thy neighbor*, and no qualifications applied. A research rabbit hole had led me to dozens of relatively recent articles by pastors and theologians centered on a mistranslation of two Greek words—two words in a volume of more than three-quarters of a million—by a committee of Christian scholars tasked with approving a new translation of the Bible. By the time a seminary student pointed out that their choice of "homosexual" (Holden, Troy, and Farrelly's gay uncle) instead of the more accurate "pervert" (child molesters and rapists) could have grave consequences for Christians everywhere—and they agreed it was a mistake and changed it—the New International Version of the Bible (and a few others) had been taken from their original document. Within a generation, something many people of faith saw in the past as a character trait they maybe didn't understand now became an abomination. And had Norma here convinced that God wanted her to throw her teenage son out of her house.

But I didn't think she was really looking for a deep theological discussion, so I just nodded. Norma returned the gesture and kept talking.

"But once I ran out of money trying to find Ricky, the very next day, the Lord sent me a sign: a young Black trans woman was found dead in the woods a few miles away. She'd been dragged behind a car, beaten, and strung from a tree naked." She sniffled and scrubbed at her nose with the back of one hand. "If that's not a lynching, I don't know what is. Nobody was ever arrested, even though half the town knew who did it." She shook her head, her knuckles turning white as her grip on the gun tightened. "The same town that allowed my Ricky to be beaten half to death right outside the library. The boys that did that never faced a single consequence either."

"I'm so sorry." I was trying to be quiet, but I couldn't stand there and not say something to that.

"In that young woman's senseless death, I found my calling: to teach young people like my son to stand up for themselves and fight back." She squared her shoulders. "We don't live in a world where football players stuff little gay boys in lockers and high-five their friends. We live in a world where bigots murder them and walk free."

I wanted to tell her that we lived in a world where some football players were little gay boys themselves, but listening to her story, it seemed she and Holden lived in worlds that were at least different enough to allow him to be open about his sexuality when her son couldn't even live in the closet. I was getting good at nodding, though.

"My Ricky would have come home by now if he was still alive; I know he would have. So I live every day trying to make him proud as he looks down from Heaven." She waved a hand to encompass the barn, or maybe even the farm as a whole. "I've created a nice home for my boys—they are safe and loved here when they weren't at their old homes, and they're learning how to stand up for themselves when they go out on their own."

I thought about the phrase "violence only begets more violence."

"I know my Ricky must have been born gay because I sure didn't teach him to be," she said. "But I damn sure wish I'd taught him how to fight back."

My eyes locked on the weapon in her hands.

She had a gun range outside, and she was teaching her boys to fight back.

Jesus, were Norma and her boys using real live bigots for target practice?

"I'm sure your son would be proud of you." I kept my tone light. "How many boys have you helped now?"

My eyebrows lifted of their own accord when she told me her boys numbered forty-two, between the ages of fourteen and twenty-one. I couldn't help wondering if all of the twenty-one-year-olds had handgun licenses. Probably better to ask that one when there wasn't a gun that could easily be pointed my way again—or maybe even leave it to the sheriff.

"These boys come to me lost and broken, abandoned by their own families. They just needed love and acceptance, and I offer it to them, in the same way I would have wanted someone else to offer it to my Ricky when I failed to."

"I really think I have enough information for my story to help people understand," I said.

Her spine stiffened as she hefted the rifle.

Was it something I said?

"I can't have this getting into the paper. The police will send so many of my boys back to the homes they left. No one is here against their will. I didn't do enough to protect my son, but I learned from that, and I'll do anything," she hit the word hard, "to protect my boys and keep them safe here with me until they're ready to be out in the world on their own."

Damn. Me and my big mouth.

She had a gun, and I had no cell service and a sneaking suspicion she could beat me in a foot race to my car—if she didn't shoot me first. If Norma was as good a shot as those targets suggested, it was time to beg.

"I don't have to put anything about you or your boys in my story if it makes you—" I didn't get "uncomfortable" out before the door opened behind me.

And Ben Winter strolled in, confusion plain on his face.

His gaze tracked from Norma to the gun, then to me, and back to the gun.

"You know my sister," he said slowly. "What's going on here?" The last was directed at Norma. Ben looked taller when he wasn't hiding beneath the baseball cap, and Norma's face lit up at the sight of him. She waved him closer and handed him the loaded rifle, which he handled with care and confidence.

Norma turned away briefly, then turned back with a handgun that she fetched from a workbench against the wall.

Lord, please let Kyle and Joey be on their way out here by now. I didn't dare check the time to see if two hours had passed since I left the diner. It felt like five minutes and six days all at once. But surely two hours was a realistic medium there.

I took a deep breath, facing them and squaring my shoulders. "I didn't come here to hurt anyone."

Norma pursed her lips, looking from Ben's increasingly uncertain face to mine.

"I cannot promise you that none of my boys will use their training to make you sorry if you break your word, miss," she said, pointing the handgun at the ground.

"Thank you," I whispered to the ceiling, nodding as I looked back at Norma and Ben. "I understand." I kept nodding like a novelty bobble head, my only remaining goal to get the fuck out of there immediately. "I gave you my word that I'd kill the story, and I'm good for it. I wouldn't be a good journalist if I didn't keep promises." I took a few steps backward, watching to see if Norma would raise the gun again, but her hand didn't so much as twitch. I turned to go, grabbing the heavy sliding door.

"I'm glad you understand," Ben said suddenly. "About the dead bigots."

I froze, both hands still poised on the door. I didn't have to be looking at her to know that Norma had her gun trained on me again. I heard the round chamber for good measure.

Norma's voice was tight. "Explain, Benjamin," she said.

Ben answered before I could puzzle through how he could've possibly known I knew anything about dead bigots. "She was at the diner with my sister, and I heard her say something about Mervin. It's such an unusual name and, well, she was talking about the car being found."

"You." Norma's voice could've sliced clean through a diamond. "Turn around."

I held my hands up, turning until I faced them again. Norma leveled the gun at me, feet apart and both hands wrapping the butt. Ben looked stricken, his grip on the rifle slack. I took a step back toward the open door, every cell in my body screaming *run*.

"A safe haven for gay boys is one thing," Norma said coldly. "But you cannot leave my property with murders in your back pocket."

"Momma, no!" Ben's shout rattled the rafters, echoing along the metal walls. The meek and quiet boy from Instagram and even the diner was gone. His voice boomed, commanding—demanding to be heard. "She is not our target."

Norma didn't fire, but she also didn't lower her weapon. "This woman has to die for the good of the mission. One word from her could jeopardize everything we've worked for."

"You've lost sight of the mission if you think killing an innocent person is ever necessary—especially when she's only here because she wanted to help my sister and me." He sucked in a deep breath and laid a hand on Norma's arm. "She's a good person. I trust Evie and Troy."

Norma swung on him, gun still aimed and tight in her grip. Ben's hands flew up, putting the rifle between them. A scuffle. A scream. And a deafening shot.

Blood bloomed on Norma's torso, and as she fell, she laughed.

"There's the instant defense reaction we've been working on," she coughed out from the ground. "Don't think, just strike."

41

The cavalry arrived maybe ninety seconds after the shot fired.

When Kyle led a tactical team through the door, I guessed my two hours were indeed long past, but his team immediately turned on Ben, whose grip on the rifle was slack as he gaped at Norma.

The ATF agents shouted: "Put the gun down!"

I screamed over them: "Don't shoot, don't shoot!"

Ben let the rifle fall to the dirt floor, stumbling back several steps. He was almost immediately cuffed by one of the agents as both the rifle and Norma's handgun were wrapped in evidence bags.

Kyle stopped in front of me, resting his hands on my shoulders and blocking Ben from view. I tried to crane my neck, to keep track of the boy I had come here to...what? I wasn't here to save him, not exactly. I wanted to peel the layers of the story that led him here, to give Evie and Troy something to hold onto, to be able to point at and say, "Here, this is why Ben left."

"Nichelle, are you hurt?"

"I'm fine. I just want to make sure Ben is okay—can I talk to him?"

Kyle glanced back over his shoulder. Already, Ben was seated in a chair against the wall with a burly agent hemming him in, reciting Miranda rights. Meanwhile, a knot of three agents tended to Norma, one holding pressure on her wound and two barking quick orders into radios.

"Let Markham handle the talking for now, but you can hang out over there with him." Kyle raked his hands through his hair, shaking his head. "Jesus, Nicey, you really gotta stop getting yourself into shit like this."

"Gotta keep you on your toes." I gave him a playful punch on the arm, but when he didn't break into a smile, I softened. "Thank you for being my knight in shining armor."

He squeezed my hand and smiled as I left him to run the scene while I checked on Ben.

"We were training to be stronger, tougher, to stand up for ourselves. The goal was to fight back against people who would try to hurt us just for who we are," Ben told the agent taking his statement before he slumped against the wall, hands awkwardly pinned behind his back. "You can't just beat the queerness out of somebody. All hatred from others does is make us hate ourselves."

Agent Markham's mouth twitched at that, his posture loosening.

Ben strained for a glimpse of Norma, who was being loaded onto a stretcher by local paramedics. "She's a good mom—maybe a little fanatical about the Bible, but you have to find meaning in something, right? And I've learned a lot of stuff about Jesus I never knew. We have Bible study every night after supper. Did you know Jesus hung out with, like, beggars and prostitutes because they were nicer people than the rich people who tried to be his friends? Norma says Jesus saw the real person inside, he wasn't fooled by people pretending to be better than others." Ben sighed. "Jesus was a good friend. And I found that here. I found my meaning in this brotherhood. I belong. I deserve to be happy. I deserve to feel safe. I deserve to be able to stand up for myself." He recited it like a well-used mantra. "I deserve to not have to fight, but we're not there yet, so I will stand up, I will fight, and I will welcome others who have been beaten down."

Dammit, my favorite sapphire Louboutins for a notebook. I patted my pockets until I came up with my phone, swallowing a triumphant cry as I opened the voice recorder and waved it at Ben with an eyebrow up. He nodded, and I clicked it on.

Ben turned back to the agent. "A friend of one of the older guys was assaulted outside a bar near Richmond, this lounge called Valentino's—must have been, like, two years back. From then on, the older boys have been keeping tabs on the place, going often. One of them even got a job there."

I wondered who it was, and if I'd met him. Was Norma ready with the gun earlier because she knew I was asking questions?

"Were they looking to harm the assailants?" Agent Markham asked.

Ben shook his head. "They wanted to make sure no one else got hurt."

"And what was your role with this bar in Richmond? That's pretty far from here."

Ben hunched over. "I never killed anybody." Tears sparkled in his eyes, dripping out onto his green pants when he rested his head on his knees. He pinched his mouth shut tight, shoulders curling up around his ears. A sob escaped his lips. "Me and the other boys, we just helped hide the bodies." The last was a whisper: "Until today."

"I'm going to need you to clarify that," Markham said. "Until today?"

"I'd never shot anybody until today. I didn't even mean to."

Markham softened his tone. "Walk me through it."

Ben told the story of how Norma got shot, Markham's eyes going to mine for confirmation when he finished. I nodded. "That's what happened. He stopped her from shooting me."

"Who else got shot, Ben?" Markham asked. "Can you tell me what you were just talking about?"

"It started with Skylar."

Skylar was Troy and Evie's school friend with the Instagram memorial.

"They lost him—one of us, a brother—over a year ago." Ben chomped down on his lip. "This outsider, Billy Wayne, saw Skylar in town, followed him here, and shot him. Right out there by the pool. No reason, except he thought Skylar looked queer." He shook his head. "Momma flew into a rage. She grabbed a rifle and ran out, and she shot that Billy Wayne asshole dead right up by the road, before he got off our property."

Markham flinched when Kyle came up behind him.

"Skylar's grave is out there." Ben jerked his chin at the south wall. "Beside the barn, there's a white cross marking his grave. Billy whatever wasn't so lucky."

It seemed Ryan Dietrich was right about what kind of person Billy Wayne Jessup was.

"Then it turned out we weren't the only ones casing Valentino's. Some gang with creepy tattoos, they started going in there, waiting to see if they got a come-on from someone, looking for an excuse to hurt someone. Someone like me." He looked up at us. "Was it so wrong to want to strike first?"

I blinked back tears and even caught Kyle swiping at an eye. "We can lose the cuffs here, Markham. Mrs. Taubin isn't pressing any charges."

Markham removed the cuffs and helped Ben to his feet as Kyle turned to me.

"She going to die?" My eyes stayed on Ben as I spoke.

"Doesn't look like it. And she told me herself that she drew on him first. Clear self-defense."

"Y'all need me for anything?"

"I need you to go home and let Joey keep you out of trouble for a while."

"Done." I pocketed my phone and strode to the door, never so glad to step out into the warm sunshine.

As soon as I was on the freeway and had a signal, I called Evie, and she insisted that I conference Troy in. I told her where to find Ben. "Kyle's not pressing federal charges, and I don't think the sheriff will take him in, but I didn't see him before I left."

Evie said she was on her way. "Fuck my parents," she said. "They don't deserve to see him." She hung up, leaving me and Troy on the call.

"Thanks, Nichelle," Troy said. "You did right by those boys. And the bigots, too," he added, grudgingly.

"Because of you," I said. "You are a fine man, Troy Wright, and I'm damn proud to call you my friend."

42

It seemed almost obscene that the sun was still up as I rolled toward Richmond, that the day wasn't as done as I was. I hadn't ever wanted my dog, my couch, and my boyfriend quite as desperately as I did right then.

I told Siri to call Joey when I hung up with Troy—the sheer volume of missed calls, voicemails, and texts that flooded in when my signal came back told me he was worried.

"Thank God." He let out a long breath when he picked up. "You can't just send messages like that. 'If you don't hear from me in a few hours'? That's like a lifetime. You're seriously taking years off my life."

"Funny, you'd think organized crime would be much more aging than one little old reporter with a penchant for trouble."

Joey was quiet for a beat. "I didn't love the Cacciones like I love you."

"Will you still love me at the end of the longest short drive home in the history of the world?"

"I'll be waiting."

And he was. I wasn't even all the way into my driveway when he bounded out the front door. He yanked my door open, and I threw my arms wide and grinned.

"Not a scratch this time, and we still saved the day. I'm getting better at this."

I may have looked no worse for wear, but the same certainly couldn't be said for Joey. He was downright disheveled. His hair was messy, his shirt partially untucked, his eyes slightly bloodshot. I took his hands in mine. "Something's been bothering you."

"It's nothing," he said gruffly.

"This," I said, pointedly looking him up and down, "is not nothing."

He licked his lips. "Would it be better to say I'm not ready to tell you?"

I ducked my head to catch his eye, squeezing his hands at the same time. "Are you in danger? Because I'm not stupid, I know there are plenty of scary people bopping around out there who don't like one or both of us. We can handle danger, but I need to know to be ready for it."

He cupped my face between his large hands, dark eyes meeting mine. "It's not that. I promise."

My phone rang from its place on the dash before I could ask anything else.

"Hey, kiddo," Bob said. "Mel's in labor—get your ass to the hospital."

I groaned. "But the shower is tomorrow!"

Joey dove behind the wheel of his Lincoln, engine roaring to life. We sped to the hospital, where we found Bob, Grant's and Melanie's parents, Troy, and the Okersons—in town for the shower Ashton had spent hours on a cake for—in the Labor and Delivery waiting area.

We chatted and laughed as we waited, the stress of the week ebbing with each passing minute until I felt happier and more hopeful than I had in a while.

We swarmed when Parker emerged from the double doors, the bundle cradled in his arms almost as big as his smile. Already wrapped in an oversized softball-style onesie with "Parker 00" stitched on the front, she looked around with wide gray-green eyes, her tiny lips pursed in a bow.

"Congratulations, Parker." I beamed. "She's gorgeous."

Joey, standing at my elbow and looking down into the baby's sweet face, melted, the harsh lines of his expression over the last few days easing into a warm smile.

"Beautiful," he said. "And so small."

The Okersons took their turn with Parker, and Bob tapped Troy's arm.

"Son, I know you worked closely with Parker not too long ago on that internship at the *Telegraph*."

"Yes, sir," Troy said, casting a glance my way. I shrugged. No idea.

"Parker's got a lot on his plate right now." Bob nodded to the baby. "I'm wondering if you'd be able to fill in for us while he's on leave. I think you'd be a real asset for the *Week*, and you might even learn something."

Troy's face lit up. "Yes, sir, Mr. Jeffers."

The sports column was in good hands, even if Troy Wright had insisted he would never work in print. Maybe we could convert him one baby step at a time.

The moon set and the sun rose outside my kitchen window as I wordsmithed dozens of pages of notes—on white supremacy and hate groups, on LGBTQIA+ youth issues and the unique vulnerability of the community, on love and a missing son and the surrogate sons raised in his stead—into a story Bob and I could be proud of.

I closed my laptop just as Joey shuffled around the corner, sexy and rumpled in boxers and bedhead.

"How'd it go?" he asked.

"It is probably the longest and most complicated story I will ever write." I yawned. "And I'm proud of it."

"Coffee or sleep?" he asked.

"Sleep. I'm so far beyond exhausted there's not a word for this except maybe dying."

He grinned and held up one finger. "Give me two minutes."

I ambled to the bathroom with a furrowed brow, my brain too melted to puzzle out another single thing.

Waiting outside the bedroom door, Joey had combed his hair and shaved his face. But he hadn't found a shirt.

He was always sexy, but I wasn't kidding about the "possibly dying" thing.

He led me into a bedroom dancing in candlelight. I was so startled I froze in the doorway.

He turned, tugging my fingers. "Grant and Mel's baby girl threw a cute little pink wrench in in my plans."

Was he nervous?

He sucked in a deep breath, his hands opening and closing at his sides.

"I want to meet your mom." The words rushed out like he was afraid they'd bite him if he didn't say them.

The only boyfriend who'd ever met my mother was Kyle, a long, long time ago.

My mom was my everything. But now, so was Joey.

"Why?" I blurted. It wasn't the smartest question I've ever asked.

Joey reached for my hand, swallowing hard but more calm than I'd seen him in a while.

"I have a question I'd like to ask her."

I scrunched my brow, the exhaustion dragging at my brain, making his words difficult to process.

He smiled and led me to the bed, turning my blankets back without another word.

"Oh. Oh!" I clung to his arm, collapsing on the sheets when my knees went to water. "That question?" Tears welled and started falling before I could blink.

"I will be forever thankful to Lila Clarke for raising the woman I love, and, at the very least, I owe her the respect of speaking to her before I say anything more." He sank onto the bed next to me and laced his fingers with mine. "Family is important—whether it's blood or one you've chosen for yourself. Just ask anyone you stayed up all night writing about."

"Are we really ready for this?" I whispered, searching his face for any sign of insecurity or doubt.

He flashed a rakish grin and stole a soft kiss as he pulled me back onto the bed like I was the most precious thing in his world, tucking my head into its spot near his shoulder and resting his chin on my hair.

"I have zero doubt, love."

∽

Mel positively glowed, every hint of anxiety gone as she cooed at her tiny daughter. She and Parker were enraptured by the tiny human they'd made, from her wide eyes to her thumb-sized, wrinkled feet. Everyone who stopped by was immediately pulled into the trio's orbit.

Even Kyle popped by to offer his congratulations. He clapped Parker on the shoulder and gave Mel a gentle hug, letting the baby tug on his finger. He also stood at my shoulder to whisper some case updates in my ear while everyone around us fawned over the baby.

Norma would recover in the hospital for another couple of days before being transferred to jail to await trial—she faced at least five counts of murder, plus two counts of assault with a deadly weapon, for Ben and me.

Kyle was working with the halfway house Holden had tipped me to in DC and the shelter in Nashville, connecting the boys who weren't welcome in their homes or who were adamantly opposed to returning with resources that would keep them off the streets and provide job and life skills. I squeezed his hand.

"Thank you."

"I'm not done yet." He grinned.

I raised an eyebrow.

"We found Norma's son."

My hand clapped over my mouth. "He's alive?"

"He lives out in Oregon. Married, two kids. I have his phone number."

I dragged Kyle to the hallway. I had a story to tell Ricky Taubin. But did he want to hear it?

Only one way to find out. I put the call on speaker so Kyle could listen in.

"Hello?" The voice on the other end of the line was wary. He probably saw my Virginia area code and assumed the worst.

"Is this Ricky Taubin?" I asked.

I wondered in the deep pause that followed if he would hang up.

"Not in a very long time. Who's asking?"

"My name's Nichelle Clarke," I said. "I'm a journalist who very recently met your mother."

"Does a mother turn her only child out of his home for being different?" Ricky's voice caught, and he cleared his throat. "I'm sure you mean well, Miss Clarke, but I haven't had a mother in more than ten years."

I couldn't blame him. "She's in jail," I said. "I wanted to let you know. And you should know she didn't ask me to call you. She doesn't even know —" I stopped. There wasn't a polite way to say she thought he was dead.

He laughed. "Jail? Norma Taubin is the straightest, rule-following-est, most upstanding citizen in Virginia. Questionable moral choices aside, what do they think she did?"

He's a lawyer, Kyle mouthed.

"She murdered five people," I said flatly.

A clatter said he'd dropped his phone. I gave him a minute. "Are you still there? What kind of evidence does the sheriff have?"

"May I have your email address, Ricky? I'd like to send you a story."

He reeled it off, and I pulled the article I'd finished overnight for Tuesday's paper from the cloud and sent it to him.

I heard the clicking of a keyboard in the background. "Got it."

Kyle and I leaned back against the wall while he read.

"I have some questions," Ricky said, his voice hoarse.

He asked about the boys, about the farm, about the town he left behind. He asked about his mother's faith and how they chose the men they killed. He asked about hypocrisy. He asked about love.

I answered everything I could based on my research and the one conversation I'd had with Norma, but I knew it couldn't possibly be enough.

"I just can't believe she cared this much. Not only did she look for me, but she found people like me and took them in, protected them, mothered them."

"I do have someone else here who might be able to get you some more answers."

"Momma?" I almost didn't hear his whisper.

"Not quite," Kyle said. "I'm Special Agent Kyle Miller with the Bureau of Alcohol, Tobacco, and Firearms. I was the arresting officer."

"Can I visit her?" Ricky blurted.

Kyle gave him visitation details, and Ricky thanked us both and hung up, already looking at plane tickets. He wouldn't bring his husband right away, but he hoped that Norma would be able to meet his family someday, he'd said. Even if they had to visit her in jail to do it.

Kyle left, and I went back into Mel's room. Joey waited on the little sofa, watching Mel and Parker hover over their baby girl. I settled in beside him, feeling the warm and reassuring weight of his arm around my shoulders.

Grant laid the baby in my arms, and I stared into her sweet, pink, perfect face and considered how lucky bitsy Abigail Marie Parker was, with a lifetime of unconditional love ahead of her.

FEAR NO TRUTH: Faith McClellan #1

"Just when you think you know what's going to happen, she plunges you down another dark and deliciously creepy path." —Lisa Regan, USA Today bestselling author of *Her Silent Cry*

As the rebellious daughter of a Texas political dynasty that groomed her to be a trophy wife, freshly-minted Texas Ranger Faith McClellan is determined to carve her own path. She's grinding away each day, hoping to land one of the coveted assignments on the cold case unit.

But when a young woman is murdered in one of Texas' most affluent communities, Faith uncovers a series of shocking connections.

Secrets that could destroy the carefully curated reputations of those in power.

And they will do anything to stop her.

From AMAZON CHARTS bestselling author LynDee Walker, FEAR NO TRUTH is the first book in the heart-pounding Faith McClellan mystery series.

Get your copy today at
severnriverbooks.com/series/faith-mcclellan

ACKNOWLEDGMENTS

First and foremost I must thank LynDee, who has been a fount of wisdom, experience, and mentorship throughout this process. I couldn't have asked for a better role model. Thank you for choosing me to go on this journey with you and trusting me with Nichelle, who lives so close to your heart. It would have been far too easy to leave me as an island, and I'm so glad you didn't.

Thank you also to my agent, John, and the team at Severn River for giving me a chance with only the barest of writing samples.

I wouldn't be writing this without Art Taylor, whose first introduction to my writing was a short story with way too many dialogue tags. That Power-Point slide still haunts my nightmares, but you didn't give up on the loud-mouth engineer in your fiction writing class. Thank you for not letting me give up on my dreams.

Thank you to my day-to-day support system: my parents, my book club, the friends I would text in the middle of the night because I wasn't sure I was going to finish on time, the baristas at the Peet's Coffee where I would sit every Saturday writing for 6-8 hours during a pandemic (masked and vaxxed, of course). And to the team of bookstagrammers (and friends) who helped me launch into the author world: @TheReadingChemist, @KimBookwyrm, @CristineTheBookQueen, @GrayscaleBooks, @ForeverInAStory, @JLM.Bookstagram, @TaylorCatherineMaReads, and @Risas_Reads.

And, of course, thank you, dear reader, for coming with me and LynDee —and Nichelle, Joey, Kyle, Troy, Holden, and Ben—on this journey.

—Laura Muse

∿

My foremost thanks this time to the readers who love Nichelle enough to have kept her story going for nearly 10 years now—I have been so blessed in the past decade to get to meet so many of you, and to get kind notes and messages from so many more, and I treasure every single one. I never imagined, years ago looking at the words "the end" on my screen for the first time, that my characters would find a home in so many of your hearts, but I am eternally grateful that they have. This book truly wouldn't exist right now without your requests for it, and I hope you enjoy catching up with Nichelle and the gang as much as I did.

Next, my thanks to Laura Muse, who loved the characters and bravely jumped in to help make the ninth book in the series a reality, which was a taller order than I knew when I invited her on board. I so appreciate you lending your considerable talent to Nichelle, and am so proud of this book we created together.

As always, thanks to my editor, Randall Klein, for making the story shine and pushing me to rethink the parts that didn't fit; to Kate Schomaker for lending your super-human eagle eyes to the manuscript and making Laura and me look so much smarter to our readers with every mistake you rooted out and corrected; to my agent, John Talbot, and to Andrew, Amber, Mo, Keris, and the entire team at Severn River Publishing for making this crazy idea I had that I wanted to write fiction a lovely and rewarding career.

This story had some complex pieces I didn't entirely trust myself to handle given my lack of life experience with them, and I'm so thankful to my friends Shunta Summers and Jay Roecker for lending their own experiences and opinions to make the story better.

Last but always most, thanks to Justin and the littles for their unfailing support and faith in me, even when deadlines make me difficult to live with. I love you all right up to the moon...and back.

As always, any mistakes you find are mine alone.

—LynDee Walker

ABOUT THE AUTHORS

LynDee Walker is the national bestselling author of two crime fiction series featuring strong heroines and "twisty, absorbing" mysteries. Her first Nichelle Clarke crime thriller, FRONT PAGE FATALITY, was nominated for the Agatha Award for best first novel and is an Amazon Charts Bestseller. In 2018, she introduced readers to Texas Ranger Faith McClellan in FEAR NO TRUTH. Reviews have praised her work as "well-crafted, compelling, and fast-paced," and "an edge-of-your-seat ride" with "a spider web of twists and turns that will keep you reading until the end."

Before she started writing fiction, LynDee was an award-winning journalist who covered everything from ribbon cuttings to high level police corruption, and worked closely with the various law enforcement agencies that she reported on. Her work has appeared in newspapers and magazines across the U.S.

Aside from books, LynDee loves her family, her readers, travel, and coffee. She lives in Richmond, Virginia, where she is working on her next novel when she's not juggling laundry and children's sports schedules.

Sign up for LynDee Walker's reader list at
severnriverbooks.com/authors/lyndee-walker

lyndee@severnriverbooks.com

∽

Laura Muse is a software engineer. She spends her free time reading books, reviewing books, photographing books, and promoting books on social media. Thanks to her past life as a competitive barista and barista trainer, she has developed a refined palette for both coffee and wine and spends weekends visiting small vineyards throughout Virginia with her family. She lives by a river in northern Virginia with her diabetic cat, Hero. DANGEROUS INTENT is her first published work.

Printed in the United States
by Baker & Taylor Publisher Services